Saving Grace

A novel by Christine Zolendz

This is a work of fiction. Names, characters, places, and incidents are the products of the author's imagination or are used fictitiously. Any resemblance to actual events, locales, or persons, living or dead, is entirely coincidental.

Book Cover Design by okaycreations.net

Editor - http://frankiesfreelanceediting.blogspot.com

Dedication and Thanks

This book is completely and utterly dedicated from the bottom of my heart to…

Samantha Baer Taylor and the awesome reviewgasm she gave me. To the Blog Queens, without them I would not know what the hell to read! Maryse at http://www.maryse.net, Lori at http://lorisbookblog.blogspot.com and Minha (Brazilian Girl) for all her support!

Life is about living every single moment like it's your last. If you treat each goodbye, each hello, each hug, each day, and each kiss like it was your last... how amazing would each moment of your life be?

Thank you all for waiting so patiently for Saving Grace (and some of you not so patiently, I loved your daily messages!) And thank you all for taking a chance on an Indie author, who can't write a lick of words, but loves to tell stories…

PROLOGUE

There's a very old story that was found written on an ancient scroll hidden on the northwest shore of the Dead Sea. There were many stories written on many scrolls, but the one in particular that I am talking about is called the Book of Enoch. You may have heard of it, or maybe not, but I feel I must tell it. The story is about the Grigori, a band of angels that were dispatched to the earth to watch over the humans because they were fragile and precious and needed protecting. *Blah, blah, blah.* And of course without complaint, the angels did as they were told, nicknaming themselves the Watchers.

Now, as time passed, the Watchers began to notice how beautiful the human women were (of course), and took for themselves human wives. The offspring from these unions were called the Nephilim, who grew into mighty savage giants that pillaged the earth and endangered all of humanity with their chaos.

To rid the earth of its poison, the

humans and Nephilim were destroyed in a continuous raging storm, and the angels were thrown into a dark abyss in the middle of the earth for eternity.

But what the book doesn't say, was that not all of them shared the same fate. One angel and one human shared but one kiss. The angel of course, because his brothers were of a jealous nature, was treated like the rest of the fallen angels and was imprisoned along with them. The human however, was to live the rest of her eternity as a lost soul in search of the angel that she once loved.

The Book of Enoch was once cherished by many religions throughout the world. However, it later fell into the disfavor of many powerful theologians for the simple opposition of the controversial deeds of the fallen angels. So it was kept hidden, and most of humanity does not know this story to be a true part of its history.

But, I know it's true. Because I'm the freaking lost soul. And just when I finally found my angel, all hell breaks loose to try to keep us apart. *Seriously*.

Chapter 1

I didn't have a clue how long I had been walking. All I was aware of was the sun slowly setting behind me, far in the distance. The fiery orb slowly melted into a horizon littered with sand and rock. A lone asphalt strip traveled through the center of this expanse of land. My feet quietly moved over the gravel and crushed rock that it was made of.

A thin mist settled all around me. As I walked along, it thickened and the raw smell of wet earth filled my senses. Large drops of rain fell against my face, landing on my eyelashes and splattered cool sparks of fire along my cheeks. The rain stung my face and arms. It bit my scalp and shoulders; yet it was a relief from the blasting sun. I raised my head to the sky, but not one cloud could be seen.

I kept walking.

So far, I hadn't seen another soul out *there*. I didn't even know if *there* was real. The only thing I was sure of was that somewhere the beautiful body I had been living in for the last ten years was laying in a coma in a hospital bed. So here I am stumbling through the *freaking desert* trying to find my way back to it, my body and consciousness.

Oh, and let's not forget that there seems to be a gang of idiotic, fallen angels after me. Honestly, they could all kiss my ass. I set my mind on one thing. Okay, two things. First, I was getting that body back. Second, I was going to find Shane and punch him square in the face (maybe, and I mean *MAYBE*, after that, I'd kiss him. May…Be.)

I had a lot of time to think about it on that desert road. The more steps I took, the angrier I became. In all of existence, and yes I mean ALL, I have been wronged more and longer than any other human. *EVER*. I have been punished for…truly, I don't even know the exact number of centuries, for a single kiss. *One freaking kiss*. One earth shattering, heart stopping kiss, *but still, it was just a kiss!*

But the thing that really gets me angry. The thing that really makes my fists clench and my skin tight, is that perfect kiss, that kiss that I saw a glimpse of heaven in, was with someone who ended up to be Shane Maxton. Shane Maxton, New York City's very own personal Man-Whore of the Year.

Shane. I would have never thought it would be him. I mean, yeah in a cheesy romance novel, chick flick kind of way I should have probably guessed it was him all along. My God, for someone who has been around as long as I have, I sure am naive. *Yeah, I know you're agreeing with me, thank you so much for rubbing it in. Like I don't have enough issues right now.*

Shane. The last time I laid my eyes on his perfect face, I could see his heart breaking while I walked away with another man. If I knew who he really was, that he shared the same secret as me, that he was the one I'd been looking for all these centuries, I would have never left his arms. Ever.

But that was before. Before Gabriel showed me how Shane tried to forget my existence, how he tried to erase the memory of me. *And now, I'm just seriously pissed off at him.*

An enormous black bird flew down through the raindrops, screeching its piercing caw right above my head, stopping my thoughts short. *What the hell, is that a vulture?* I jerked to a stop as the bird landed in front of my feet. *Not a vulture, those things are butt-ass ugly.* This was a beautiful sleek feathered raven. Its head tilted up towards me as if to say hello. It had secrets too.

Folding my legs beneath me, I slowly sat down on the road, meeting the birds black gaze.

"What are you doing here? Are you in a bird hospital in a coma too?" I joked.

The damn bird cawed at me

loudly and bird hopped closer.

"Okay, you're a pretty bird and all, but seriously, if you come any closer to me with that sharp-ass beak I'm going to kick you hard," I said.

The bird tilted its little birdy head at me again and flew away in a cloud of soft black feathers, raindrops and wind.

I watched the bird spread its giant wings and soar through the rain toward the direction I was heading. In the distance, I could make out the shadowy shapes of buildings that weren't there before. "Wonderful. Thanks bird. That must be the *Secret Garden* and I must be *Mary freaking Lennox. Fan-freaking-tastic.*"

I stood up, with my hands on my hips, raindrops continued to blast their little electric spikes of heat onto my face. I chewed at my lower lip, wondering if I should just walk in the opposite direction. I hadn't even thought up a plan yet. I had no idea where the hell I was. *Was I dead?* I couldn't be. When I stood completely motionless, I could still hear the sharp beeps and hisses of the life support machines hooked up to my body somewhere. Low somber sounds just a breath above the desert silence.

My head swam with dizzying thoughts. The assault of the rain on my skin sent bursts of sheer adrenaline just underneath the surface. *What am I going to do if the archangel Gabriel was here? How do I fight against him?*

The raven reappeared and circled high above me. My *lives* would be complete if it crapped on me, seriously.

Without thinking more about it, my legs started moving. Long strides over the wet desert sand. I figured I would need to deal with things as they came. One foot in front of the other was a saying I've lived by for centuries. But this nonsense has to end. The let's drag *Selah's* soul through hell campaign stops now. I walked toward the buildings with a mission.

The dusty streets were deserted except for the slow ghostly roll of a few tumbleweeds. The drowning of the sun behind me washed the bricks and mortar of the buildings with graying reflections of color.

The raindrops ceased in their attack against the deserts stillness. I stood at the entrance to the small city of concrete buildings and watched the last of the sun's rays glimmer and fade. A slow, sad death of day. A powerful sense of the unknown, the supernatural, cast itself along the emerging shadows of the buildings. I shuttered thinking about what ethereal creatures lived within its darkness, since I knew the evil of the creatures that lived within its light.

A loud sharp scream erupted from deep inside one of the large edifices. It called my name in a low raspy melody. The hairs on the back of my neck rose as I wondered if that could possibly be the person I so desperately wanted it to be.

My quick strides crunched over the broken gravel to the building where I knew the voice had come from.

I stood before the door as if I was looking at a gateway into some unknown plane, an alternate universe and moving forward through it would bring me to a place from where I would never return.

What was I really up against? A band of fallen angels who were led by Gabriel. Gabriel the Archangel who wanted to create more Nephilim with yours truly, so he could rule the world. Gabriel, who said he's always loved me.

What did I want? Did I want my punishment to end? *Oh, yes.* Did I want *to be* Grace, the body of the person I had lived in for the last ten years? *Oh, hell yes.* I wanted to live the rest of her normal life, whatever that held, for as little time she may have left and then cease to exist. I didn't want to live anymore lives. I didn't want to die even one more time and jump into another empty humans body. I was done being a lost soul. I had found the angel I had been looking for and he turned out to be a piece of shit. Okay, so I was just really angry with him for becoming so human as Shane. Maybe I was acting like a child. A jealous, selfish child. But I didn't deserve any of this and I planned to go down fighting. We were going to play by my rules now. I didn't want to even think about Shane being my angel right now. I was not thinking clearly enough to form a definite answer to how I felt about him, or if that bond of what we shared was gone. The mere mention of his name in my mind caused me to think of his lips, his hands on me and that brokenhearted look on his face when I choose Blake over him.

My heart sunk deep in my chest. It folded in on itself and hardened into a solid granite rock. Unmovable and unbreakable.

Because seriously, *let's think about this, shall we?* I just spent **centuries** saving my heart and soul for someone, while *that someone* had been trying to erase the memory of me through the lacy thong, dirty-ass panties of New York City's most self-loathing, easy, skanky little.... Okay, I'm just really angry. And jealous, *oh my God am I jealous.* What girl in the world likes to learn that they are easily replaceable and forgotten? Not. Me. And then, THEN he tells GRACE that he **loves** *her! Yes, technically I was Grace, but still! He didn't know that!*

Do you see how unfocused and crazed that man makes me?

After taking a deep breath, I yanked the door open and walked in.

Oh crap.

I collapsed to my knees. Straining my eyes to see through the dimness, I tried to take in everything that was around me. All my senses were heightened to a painful capacity, almost snapping me in two. Pure raw bliss enveloped my body, wrapping itself tightly around me, draining me of all my hate and anger.

The smell of the most exquisitely fragrant flowers rushed past my cheeks on the sweetest breeze of air I had ever experienced. As my knees slammed painfully into the cold granite slabs of the floor, I could hear the slow sweet melody of an ancient choir of voices caressing their soft words against my soul. My hands grasped at the coldness of what lay beneath me; I needed an anchor, something to hold on to so I didn't feel like I had been knocked off the face of the earth.

What was laid out above me, I had only seen through a kiss lifetimes ago. Spreading from my raw fingertips to the soft pads of my toes was the warm feeling of coming home. Yet, a shadowy covering encased the edges of what I was seeing as if I was looking at the heavens through a dirty window.

A lone hazy figure gradually emerged from the depths of the shadows, and a desolate humorless laugh broke through my lips. I couldn't let myself believe for a second that this was my entrance to heaven. *What? Was someone going to try to sneak me in the back door?*

The background of the heavens dimmed gently and along with it went the sounds and smells of paradise. I remained slumped on my knees in a small room beautifully lit with the soft glow of dozens of candles.

There was something about the eerie silence of the room that seemed to unravel my nerves. I couldn't help but think there should be some sound of life to be heard, but I supposed everything would seem dead and silent after you've had a glimpse of heaven. My body shook violently in its withdrawal.

The figure I had seen before, now sat in the corner of the room deep in the shadows. The candlelight threw small impressions of light against it but it gave me no clues to who it was. The person, I couldn't tell if it was human or angel, leaned forward in its seat with its head held in his hands. Silky clumps of short dark hair hung over the hands and a tiny nip of a butterfly's wing quivered somewhere deep within me.

I caught a flicker of tight toned muscular arms as hard as stone pillars holding up an achingly beautiful face. The shadows and soft flashes of candlelight danced along the perfectly sculpted arms revealing the dark lines of the sharp beauty of his tattoos. I now understood the story behind them. The beauty of the swirling clouds, the dragon-like serpent devouring their innocence, ending in the broken winged dove. *Shane*?

My windpipe tightened as if invisible hands were crushing it. I was suffocating from his beauty, from my anger and hurt, and from how much I loved this being. My jaw clenched tight as the tears blurred my vision of him.

Shane sat shirtless, his powerful lean muscles flexed with the slow movement of lifting his ancient eyes to mine. The glow of the candles shifted and flickered brighter, allowing me to see into the depths of the blue eyes that were once my hearts captive for centuries. Did they still have a hold on my soul?

"Grace."

The quick streaks of tears burned down my cheeks and I sputtered a small unintentional whimper. I wanted to close my eyes against his beauty, against everything that he stood for and everything he was. Yet, at the same time, I wanted to throw myself at him and never let go. I tightened my fists and waited for him to speak.

In a blur of motion, he knelt on the floor before me; his ancient blue irises echoed his rage and agony.

"I didn't know it was you," he breathed. "Everything is perfect now. We will be together and no one will ever hurt you again."

I cringed with each word. They

didn't sound right. They didn't sound real. It didn't sound like *him. Or, did I just not care anymore?*

I balled my fists tighter, pulled back and punched Shane in the face as hard as I possibly could.

Chapter 2

Shane looked at me deadpan with accusation and hate in his eyes. The expression seemed to cause a riot of butterflies in my belly. Maybe they sensed the danger. I almost apologized to that beautiful face. *Almost.* I swallowed back the apology because I was not the one who should be sorry. If it weren't for any of these fallen angels, humans would still live in Paradise.

Something didn't feel right and it made the hairs on the back of my neck stand at attention. *How could Shane be here with me?* "Thanks. But I think I'll pass on the bullshit," I replied. I stood up. "I'm done. Game over. Pick a new toy to play with." I turned my back on him and walked away.

Shane was in front of me in a flash, his eyes barely an inch away from mine. "Never."

"Never what?" I asked, quickly taking a step away from him.

"I will never let you go." He moved forward with me.

I stepped back against a wall that *wasn't* there a minute ago. Shane leaned in closer. I tried to swallow, but it only got caught in my throat. Suddenly, Shane's face was so close, I couldn't even think straight. His hands moved so fast I didn't even see them coming. He crashed his body against mine, hammering his open hand into my throat and then taking hold.

He hovered his lips above mine. "You are mine. I've waited so long to be with you. *Selah*, I need you." He kept one hand on my throat and reached for the buttons of my shirt with the other. Instead of unbuttoning them though, he tore my shirt open. I heard the scatter of buttons hitting the tiled floor beneath us. He pushed his body harder against mine.

"What was the gift you gave me the last time I saw you Shane...*Shamsiel*?" I whispered.

"I've been trapped in hell for

thousands of years. Remind me." His gaze lowered to my mouth. His body tightened and hummed with an electrical power.

"You wouldn't know the answer to that question, would you, *Gabriel?*" I choked.

I tried to rip his hands from my throat. I should have never let him get this close to me. Dumb mistake.

His body rumbled with deep laughter. His hands tightened around my neck. *Both* hands now. He moved and dragged me with him. My feet slid across the floor as my hands thrashed and clawed at his face. Nothing stopped him.

He lifted me by my throat; my feet dangled freely kicking at him. His strong arms threw me; flinging me like a crumbled piece of paper. A circus of black and white spots clouded my vision and a rusty taste filled my mouth as my blood slowly dripped from where I bit my lip when I landed. A deep roll of laughter barked from his beautiful face, "How do I look as that boy toy of yours? Do you find me attractive?" His deep laughter echoed through the room.

Trying to stand, I searched around the room for something, anything to protect myself with.

"You are so entertaining with your thoughts of surviving against me."

A flush of rage ignited across my cheeks. "So why don't you just kill me, instead of talking about it?"

Shane's image faded. Gabriel's face flashed in front of me placing his tremendous hands on each side of my face and leaned them against the wall. Sharp steel-like feathers spread the width of the room behind him. A raw energy hummed from his entire body. His irises blazed a fiery fury of colors. I could see my reflection in them. My eyes were wide but not with fear. With anger and fury.

"Choose me and we will take

over the heavens together. Choose me or I will break you until you do," he whispered.

I laughed. "Never. I will never choose you. I'll be his until the end."

Then he kissed me. He growled and his mouth was on mine. I slammed my lips shut. Gabriel's hands slid around my neck and squeezed. He withdrew his lips from mine. "Wrong answer."

Chapter 3

My body felt too heavy. I felt as if gravity was sending my broken body right through the center of the earth. Pulling me with a feral hunger.

I couldn't take a breath without feeling a sharpness deep within my chest. My butterflies were dead and gone, leaving me cold, broken and alone. They were all I had left.

I pried my swollen eyes open. An acidic taste covered my tongue and my throat was scorched dry. I couldn't move. Thick metal chains looped tightly around my battered body bound me to a hard wooden chair. I was too weak even to cry.

My muscles felt torn and mangled; my skin ablaze with fire. Somewhere a tormented scream ripped through the darkness. I franticly tried to kick my feet out, but only managed to send my chair crashing against the floor. There were more screams, more voices; agonized, tortured and desperate. They were calling my name.

Jacob's beautiful face emerged from the darkness; my brother Jacob. *Grace's* brother. My heart burst with fear for him if Gabriel found him there. I tried to tell him to run, but the only sound that came from my lips was a muffled cry. I strained to see the brown irises of his eyes. *Would Gabriel pretend to be him too?*

Jake pulled at the chains that held me and my body retched from the feeling of being free from them. It quaked and convulsed with pain.

Just when I thought my soul could take no more, the beautiful image of Shane collapsed to his knees in front of me. His ancient blue eyes looked agonized and stunned. He gently brushed my matted hair from my face and whimpered my name.

My tongue felt too large for the inside of my mouth, but I still tried to talk. There were tears falling down his perfect face. "Shh, baby, I'm here now."

I love you, Shane.

If you are really Shane. I love you.

"What was the gift you gave me?"

"Shh, Baby, it's okay..."

"No...I need to know it's you...if after everything...it's you."

Hovering above us stood the archangel Michael. He glared down at me through his ancient blue eyes. "Shamsiel, are you positive about your decision? Gabriel might still come after the girl."

Shane gently pulled me into his arms and I trembled in the warmth from his body. He softly ran the tips of his fingers along my jaw as grief and pain darkened his features. "Absolutely, Michael, she's worth it."

"So be it."

Shane held me closer, placing his lips against my temple. "No matter what happens from here, know that I have always, I will always love you and I will always protect you."

I could feel the last piece of my heart crush to dust under the weight of his words. My breath came out in rough gasps. "What did you do?" I pleaded.

He inhaled deeply and an eternity seemed to pass between us. His jaw tightened. "If it weren't for me, you'd be where you're supposed to be. So this is my chance to let you start over. It's over, baby. Your punishment is over."

At first, I didn't get what he meant. I just let him hold me in his arms while I stared into the eyes that I've searched thousands of years for. It didn't click until he stood up carrying me and handed me to Michael.

I tore myself away from the angel and landed on my knees; shattered. The screams roared through my lips, "NO! No! It doesn't end this way! You can't leave me!"

My heart broke a thousand times more as I watched my angel turn his back and walk away.

Things became hazy and thick. A dark blackness enveloped around me, tucking me in warm and tight. I heard hushed voices floating from somewhere above me but my eyes were too heavy to open, so I pulled myself in tightly and waited in the shadowy corners of the dark room.

At times, I could distantly feel warm fingers sending trails of heat along my skin and hushed whispers begged me to open my eyes. But I was too broken to comply. I wanted to stay in the darkness, to let it take over and consume me.

Eventually, the darkness of the small room slowly faded into the bright sterile walls of a stark white hospital room. A room drenched in the pungent smells of ammonia and vomit where Grace's body had been healing. *My body*. I was Grace now and no longer a lost soul.

The only physical pain I could feel was the achy stiffness from laying still. *Oh yeah, and the freaking pain of the gaping hole where my heart was ripped from my chest.* No, let's not forget that.

Chapter 4

Crisp white blankets were tucked tightly under my body and my hospital gown lay limply off my shoulders. The way the bones of my shoulders jutted out of my skin was surreal to me. *How long have I been here?*

A small television screen, hanging by a flexible metal arm, played an old black and white movie. Cream-colored curtains stretched across the ceiling blocking my view of the hallway. Curled into a ball on one of the chairs was Lea's sleeping form. My best friend's head leaned awkwardly to the side and through her open lips, low snores could be heard. A *Cosmopolitan* magazine was tented like a hat on the top of her sleeping head. In spite of my situation, I barked out a laugh.

Lea jumped at the sound and the magazine fell, glossy perfumed pages flew everywhere.

"Holy shit! Hoo...leee shit!

You're awake. You're awake, right? Holy shit! Gray, is it really you? Holy, holy...please tell me it's you and not somebody else in there! Holy shit!" She just kept repeating the same thing over and over as tears streamed down her face. "Holy shit! Stay right there! I gotta get the nurse. Don't go anywhere!"

Where in the world did she think I'd be going?

Lea was jumping around like a high school cheerleader on crack when the doctors came in. "Miss, you are going to need to calm yourself down while I give my patient a small examination," the doctor snapped.

Lea's eyes were as wide as our salad plates. "Calm down? Holy shit! Holy shit! She's awake! How am I supposed to calm down?" Lea pointed her hand at me.

"Um, Lea you look like you're about to have a heart attack. Maybe you need this hospital bed more than I do," I croaked.

"Holy shit!" she bawled. *"And she's* freaking cracking her wise-ass jokes!"

Two nurses gently shoved Lea out of the room. At first, she got all snarky and defensive. But one of the nurses was upwards of three hundred pounds and looked like a linebacker. Lea seemed to calculate her chances of tackling her and thought better of it. *See, miracles do exist.*

As the doctors asked me questions and examined me, I could hear Lea in the hallway ranting and screaming that I was finally awake. I pictured her getting a hold of the hospital PA system to alert the entire building. Crap, if given a chance, she'd probably announce it over the National Broadcasting System.

I zoned out as the doctors droned on and on about extensive tests, medical induced coma, brain activity, blood transfusions, life support, memory loss, confused thoughts, *blah, blah, blah.* I wanted Lea to come back in to see what the hell happened when I was gone. *Or, just what happened period.*

She bolted in when the doctors left. "How long have I been here?"

She hesitated for a brief moment and started fumbling with the sleeves of her shirt, "A little over four weeks."

I hung my face in my hands. The IV needle that was in my right hand pulled tightly against my skin as I moved. Nausea wracked my insides and my head was spinning. "What happened?" There were long dark holes in my life where I thought memories should have been. *What the hell?*

She sat still, staring at me. Just stared at me and chewed on her bottom lip. It felt like an hour had passed when she finally whispered, "Gray, you should just rest now and we'll talk about all that stuff when you're one hundred percent better and home. Okay?" She inhaled quickly and let out a long low sigh when she exhaled.

"You also, um, need to talk to the detectives when you are ready. If you remember anything, the doctors say you may not." *Remember anything?*

The only thing I remembered was the back of my angel as he walked away from me, abandoning me in my Hell on earth. It's over, my ass! I'm still here.

My eyes stung and welled with tears. I tried to hold them back. I tried to stop them from falling past the edge of my lashes, but one quickly slipped away. It tumbled down my cheek escaping from the deep sorrow that I was filled with. "Where is Shane?" As his name slipped past my lips, they trembled and the dam that held my tears was broken. Nothing could console me.

Lea's shoulders slumped forward and her lips turned down. "I don't know. He, um, hasn't been here."

He really was gone. If Shamsiel's soul was still in Shane's body, he'd be here with me. *He* really left me here, when all I ever did was count the breaths until I'd see him again. I swear, my soul, my spirit, whatever it is that a human is made of, that part of me just folded up and drowned itself beneath my tears. I didn't have to strain to hear the shattered pieces of what was left of my heart as they scattered across the cold hard hospital floor.

Chapter 5

I leaned heavily against the wall. He slowly slid his body against mine.

"*Shane,*" I breathed.

He rested his forehead against mine, his hands slid over my shoulders and down to my waist; slow and gentle. *Oh, my God, I'm on fire.*

Brushing his lips across my cheek, he buried his face in my hair, "Grace, all I want to do is kiss you right now," he whispered. Softly, he pushed my hair back and grazed his lips along my neck. His lips were warm and soft; I wanted them all over me. *I wanted him.*

"Shane, please," I whispered.

His hands subtly slid to my waist, one finger hooked itself under the lace trim of my panties.

"Oh, my God!" I woke with a start. Sweat drenched my body and a maddening ache pulled between my thighs. Panting, I tossed my damp sheets to the floor and stomped out of bed.

I should have been used to the damn dreams already. The damn *memories*. I've had them every night I've been back home. It's always Shane and I'm always left wanting. But they were the only thoughts in my brain that felt real, everything else was covered in a thick suffocating fog.

Striping out of my sweaty clothes, I rummaged through my draws and threw on the first things I grabbed, an old vintage Hendrix shirt and a pair of ripped yoga pants. I leaned against my dresser and slowly slid my body down the front of it until I was sitting on the floor. The antique metal knobs of the drawer scratched lines through my skin as I traveled down. The burn was only a secondary pain to my broken heart.

The only furniture that occupied my room was the dresser and a mattress that lay right on the floor without a bed frame. If I breathed in deep, I could still smell the bitter odor of burnt wood from the fire from a few weeks before. But honestly, it didn't bother me because I was barely breathing.

On the floor next to my dresser laid a half bottle of Jack Daniels. I wondered how it got there, but only for a brief second before my fingers encased the bottle and I twisted off the cap.

My guitar stood next to the window, I hadn't touched it. Although my fingers ached to play my instrument, I had no energy to pick it up. Even though I was awarded Grace's body, her beautiful precious human life, I felt *lifeless*. My mind was too cloudy, too ragged; as if I was looking out of someone else's eyes. What was the point in living when all that I've been living for was taken away?

The soft red glow of my alarm clock red 9:30.

10:30

12:30

2:30

At 3:00, I found myself at the kitchen table hugging a gallon of ice cream. There was one spoonful left and the bottle of Jack sat empty in front of me. I had no fucking clue how I got there.

"Oh, my God, Grace! What the hell are you doing?" Clad in plaid pajamas, Lea stood at the kitchen door, eyes wide, raking her teeth against her bottom lip over and over. *When had she started that habit?*

I shrugged my shoulders and shoved the last spoonful of ice cream into my mouth. *I couldn't even tell you the flavor if you put a gun to my head.*

"I just bought that ice cream today," she said. Her eyes opened even wider, "You just ate a whole freaking gallon of ice cream and drank a bottle of Jack Daniels?"

"WhatcanIsay?" I slurred.

"Seems like Ben, Jerry and Jack are the only guys that are trustworthy around here. At least I know exactly what I'm getting into when I put my lips to them." I tried to crack a smile, but I realized just then, I was too drunk. And, my tongue was way too thick for my mouth.

She slid her tiny frame into the chair across the kitchen table from me. She pulled her long wavy blonde hair away from the front of her eyes. "Yeah, Grace. One hell of a killer headache and a fat ass, that's what you're gonna end up with." She leaned across the table and grabbed the empty ice cream container and spoon from my hands. "You need to talk to me. You've been hiding in that room for three days. You haven't talked about anything since you woke up. I'm really freaking out about what to do for you and the detectives keep calling to set up a formal interview with you."

She dumped the container in the garbage and tossed the spoon into the sink. It made a sharp metallic sound as it landed against the basin, echoing through my head. She pulled her chair closer to me and sat down grabbing my hands. "Please tell me what's going on. Please?"

"Psf. For centuries I believed I was taking the advice of the beautiful angel that was sitting on my shoulder." I choked out a laugh. "But, the truth was, the freaking devil on my other shoulder was just one hell of a ventriloquist." There was a small drop of the dark bitter liquid left in the bottom of the liquor bottle, and I reached my hand for it. My body craved the numbness.

Lea yanked it away quicker than I could grab it. Her eyebrows pulled together and she offered me a strained smile. "Is that a quote from somewhere? I don't understand." Her big brown eyes pleaded with me for an explanation.

I offered her none.

"Grace! Snap out of it! You almost died! *Again! He* tried to kill you. The doctors said you probably wouldn't make it, but YOU'RE HERE! Okay, so Blake wasn't the person you've been looking for. So what? After all this time, you're going to give up? That's not the Grace I know." She slammed her palms against the tabletop. "I don't even know the person who is sitting in front of me right now, and Grace, really, I'm the only person who knows who you really are!"

My vision of her blurred. When I stood up it became worse. Then there were three to four Leas floating and circling past my eyes. I didn't know which one to focus on, so I just walked past her and held onto the door frame of the kitchen. "Nope. You're right, wasn't Blake. Turns out my angel is gone, he chose something else, something much better than me. But at least my punishment is over. This will be my last life. He gets to go back to heaven, and I get all this," I waved my arms in the air franticly almost making myself fall over. "I hope they staple his fucking wings back on."

I tried to stumble my way back towards my bedroom, but I passed out somewhere along the way.

Chapter 6

Somebody who was about to get a smack in the face, was shaking me awake. "Hey, Grace, come on, you have to get up and return to the land of the living," Lea's voice whispered. She pulled me forward, "Come on, Gray, I have a cup of mint tea for you here."

My mattress spun under me. Sharp painful throbs pulsed in my temples and my stomach muscles convulsed. I forced my eyes to open, fully expecting to see my liver crying in agony on the pillow next to me. Nope, just Lea sitting next to me with a cup of something that smelled a hell of a lot stronger than mint tea.

I slowly pulled myself up and groaned.

"Grace, we need to talk. You can't keep this up," she said handing me the cup.

Carefully I took the cup from her, placed it to my lips, and sipped. *Oh, holy horror, the woman spiked it with Jack Daniels!* I cringed and swallowed. "Ugh, that's nasty."

She smiled and offered me a water bottle. "They say you have to give yourself a little alcohol when you wake up with a hangover, it's supposed to make it better. You know the hair of the dog that bit you?"

"Lea, just let me rot in here for a while. Please?"

Pinching the tip of her nose, she scolded me. "You certainly smell like you're rotting in here. And no, I'm not letting you do that, so shut the hell up about it."

I placed the cup of mint poison on the floor next to my mattress and pulled myself up more to lean against the wall where the headboard of my bed *used* to be. I ran my hands through my hair, well at least I tried, but tangles of knots stopped me.

"Listen to me," she begged, nudging my knee softy. "I have no idea what happened with that angel of yours, but if he chose something else over you, he doesn't know what he'll be missing and he sure as hell isn't worth all the time you spent searching for him. But, Grace, you are here and from what I can piece together, he isn't. So my advice to you is pull yourself together and start living your life. Forget about him."

I exhaled a long breath. "Yeah. Just forget him."

Something sparked in her big brown eyes. "You've heard the saying that I live by, right?"

"Hmm. Which one is that? The one that Mae West said? *A hard man is good to find.*"

"Oh, yeah that's a good one. No. *The best way to get over one man is to get under another one!* I don't know the first girl who said it, but those are words to live by!"

I actually cracked a smile. But it was short lived. I thought about the first pair of lips that had ever touched mine. How my soul had never quite recovered from the absence of them.

"By the way, I um, I kind of told Shane some things about your past when he was in the hospital with me, before, um, everything. Hopefully, he'll just think I was having a moment of insanity and forget everything I said," Lea whispered. Her hands twisted at the cuffs of her sleeves again, and tears brimmed her eyes. "This is all so screwed up; it's majorly fucked on so many levels."

I was surprised my eyes stayed dry after hearing his name again. "No worries. Trust me, Shane isn't the same person he was when I was in the hospital. He probably doesn't even remember the conversation."

She tilted her head and gave me a questioning stare. She opened her mouth, about to say something else, but I interrupted her before she could speak.

"Look, forget about it. I'll go take a shower now and maybe I'll go for a walk or a run or something." I didn't want to think about Shane Maxton anymore or what soul lived in his body now. I could barely manage to figure out how to step one foot in front of the other, let alone how I was going to deal with Shane.

I eyed my sneakers in the corner. "Yeah, I think I'm going to try to go for a run. That always makes me feel better." I picked them up and ran into the hallway, leaving Lea sitting alone on my mattress in my empty room.

"Wait!" Lea yelled after me. "You should really clean yourself up first! You look like crap! And what about the detectives?" She screamed some more profanities at me, but I was already halfway down the block.

Without even stretching, which I completely acknowledged I would be kicking myself in the ass for later, I ran full speed towards Fifth Avenue. I crossed Fifth and ran straight into Central Park, pounding my heels against the pavement. It had been over a month since I ran and I felt the shallow breath in my lungs immediately, but I didn't stop.

It was a warm day for New York City even though it was the middle of March. *That was the month now, March.* I missed the rest of February, completely missed Valentine's Day and now it was *March. The end of March.*

In the last five and a half weeks of Grace's life, my life, it had completely turned upside down. Five and a half weeks ago, I was the hot rock goddess of the popular band Mad World, staring at an intense, um, sexual relationship with the most exquisite man on earth and now, well, right now I felt like hurling myself into one of the lakes in Central Park. How the hell am I supposed to get through this? Just like always, pretend that everything is great? Everything is normal? How the hell am I going to look at Shane Maxton again? Not that he's been around at all. He's the only one that hadn't visited me since I woke up.

I pushed forward. I focused my eyes on an invisible spot on an invisible horizon and just ran. I didn't feel it when my sides began to ache, or when my shins and knees protested against my movements, but when my endorphins kicked in, I felt the rush. I felt the rush of life through my veins. It spiked with a blinding white heat across every part of my body. I stumbled to a park bench and sat down heavily against the wood planks.

I inhaled the crisp cool air and closed my eyes. The foggy thoughts that had been hanging heavy in my mind seemed to clear a fraction. Yeah, maybe Lea was right. Maybe I should just start living this life.

Chapter 7

He slid his warm hands under my shirt and slowly traced his fingertips along the small of my back and up my spine. His touch was killing me, killing my soul; just leaving me wanting and needing.

I slid my hands up the front of his shirt, telling myself it was for the warmth, but I was never a good liar. His body was soft and deliciously warm, and the restraint was torturous.

A low moan escaped from his lips. He pushed himself up against me and gently pulled me into a sitting position, my legs straddling him. This is too dangerous, too toxic; too beautiful.

He ran feathery fingers through my hair and around to the nape of my neck. I trembled under his touch. I was a complete dripping, hot disaster; falling into pieces, wanting him to fill me and put me back together.

"Do you have any idea what you do to me, Grace?" His voice was low and husky, and he gazed at me, ice blue eyes concentrating hard. It took my breath away. "Just one kiss, Grace..."

His slow deliberate hands moved over my skin, fingers trembling. It unleashed an inferno that coursed through my body. Every move he made was so freaking erotic.

"Just one," I whispered. Then his lips touched mine. It was barely a kiss; his lips hovered over mine, taking the briefest of moments to savor the intensity.

"Grace," he sighed and his lips devoured mine. I fell completely apart in his arms, his touch unraveled me, and his kiss brought me back together, complete. I wanted all of him; *I was completely in love with this man.*

"Grace! Wake up! Hurry up!" Lea was banging on my bedroom door. She threw it open and it bashed itself against the wall, knocking down my guitar case. "Crap! Sorry." She bent down and fumbled with the case, leaned it back against the wall, and looked at me for the first time. "Are you okay? You look like you have a fever or something."

"Uh," was all I could get out of my mouth. My lips still felt raw from my dream and I desperately wanted her to get the fuck out of my room so I could finish it.

"Get dressed and come into the living room, the detectives are here to interview you about what you remember. Since you haven't gone to them, they're here, so let's go. Ethan and Conner are on their way for moral support and all." She gave me a strained smile as her eyes flitted around my room. *What the hell?*

Lea sighed, opened my dresser draws, and pulled out a black bra and a pair of red underwear. She held them up, "Where are your matching sets?" Tears slid down her cheeks and her shoulders trembled as she stood there waiting for my answer.

"What the hell kind of interview

should I be expecting? The fuck I care if my bra and panties match." I was still breathless from the dream and I could still feel his fingers trail along my skin. Hot streaks of lava. *Crap*.

"This is important, Grace. You have no idea what this has done to everyone! Snap out of your shitty funk and get the heck up and get dressed!" She was sobbing uncontrollably.

What has this done to everyone? What the? The last time I checked, I was the only person who got stabbed by some psycho fallen angel and spent four weeks in a medically induced coma. A place where, I might add, allowed the psycho fallen angel to torture me. Oh, and let's not forget that I watched the love of my existence walk the hell away from me and leave me here to rot on earth! And the fact that I can't make a clear freaking thought in my head because I feel like it's stuffed full of cotton!

Some sort of enraged expression must have crossed my face, because she covered her eyes with her hands and sobbed harder. "I'm sorry, Grace. This is just hard for me. You almost died, and it's all so messed up."

I felt my features soften. My fists that had my sheets tightly clenched in them relaxed, and I gradually made myself stand up. "Everything is okay, Lea. Look, I'm fine. I'll get dressed and come out in a minute. Go make some coffee for the detectives or something. I'll be right there."

Changing into the unmatched underwear, I watched myself in the full-length mirror on the inside of my closet door. The scar along the left side of my body ran from the top of my ribcage all the way to my left hip. It was a thin pink jagged line, raised a bit over the rest of my ivory white skin. *Frankenbelly.*

I understood why Lea was a mess. She just went through the loss of my brother Jacob, who was like a brother to her and me almost dying on her. I needed to remember how sensitive she was, but yet, I couldn't help feeling selfish and not care as much as I should. I wanted to stay in bed, wear the same old ratty clothes, and drink myself stupid until my once vibrant world faded into the soft hues of gray. Into nothingness. I wanted the loss of *him* to consume me until I was no more. For the first time in my existence, I didn't want to care about anybody else but me, and how to stop my heartache.

The doorbell rang and I could hear Lea introducing Conner and Ethan to whoever the officers were. Exhaling a deep breath, I felt relieved that Conner was there for Lea. He always made her feel better. Safer.

I slipped on a pair of old jeans and a plain white tee shirt. I twisted my waist length jet-black hair into a messy bun. Wavy tendrils of hair spiked out all over the top of my head; I reminded myself of Medusa. Slipping my fluffy teddy bear slippers on, I walked out of my bedroom and down the hallway.

Two plain-clothes detectives were standing in the living room. Before I could catch my breath, Ethan and Conner were standing next to me. Ethan grabbed me in his arms, "I can't believe this is all happening. We're right here if you need us," he whispered his hot breath into my ear.

I gawked at him. I wondered if I lost some important body part in the hospital that no one told me about yet. "Yeah, um, okay…thanks, Ethan."

The male detective held out his hand to me. "Miss Taylor? Good morning. I'm Detective Steve Fanning and this is Detective Vicki Sorens. We're here to formally interview you about your incident; I hope you're feeling better."

His handshake was firm and strong. Detective Soren's, not so much. She kind of eyed me like I was her favorite dessert and gave me a tight smile painted blood red. I pictured her pulling out a riding crop and lunging for me.

I shook the thoughts away. "Hello, detectives, would you like to sit?"

Detective Fanning sat on one of our side chairs and offered me thanks. His eyes were kind and he kept a friendly, fatherly sort of smile on his face. "Sorry, we don't mean to interrupt. We realized that it was proving to be difficult for you to get down to the station house for our interview. I hope you don't mind us paying you a visit like this. I know you've been through a very traumatic experience, and we understand that you've recently awakened from a medically induced coma, so you may not remember many answers, but I'd like you to answer the best you can, okay? Just the facts and circumstances as you remember them."

I nodded. I lost track of where the other detective was, she seemed to fade into the background along with my friends and got lost in the fog that seemed to occupy my thoughts daily. I sat down on the couch and pulled my feet underneath myself, crushing the faces of the cute teddy bears on my slippers. For a split second, I became horrified that the poor things were hurt. I wished I could crawl back in bed.

"Can you tell me your full name?" Detective Fanning asked.

"Grace Avery Taylor," I replied.

"Miss Taylor, can you tell me your birthday?"

I hesitated. I looked around the room a little then answered, "December 21." I started to freak out a little bit. *That should have been an easy question, right?*

"Do you recall what high school you went to?" he continued.

Tears welled in my eyes and I sucked my cheeks in. It took me a minute to visualize the front doors and the name written there. *Why were these questions important? Did they want to see how long it would take me to snap? Because I was getting really tight around my neck and I squirmed uncomfortably on the couch.* "Brant Point High," I seethed.

"That's good, Miss Taylor. You're doing great. Brant Point High, that's one of the most prestigious schools in New York City. They have a great football team, eh?"

When I made no sound to answer, he continued with his questioning, "Okay, Miss Taylor, what's your mother's maiden name?"

My hands balled into fists. "It *was* Evelyn Canton, but she passed away about ten years ago. My father's name *was* Carlson Taylor, but he passed away the same time as my mother. My brother's name *was* Jacob Taylor, and he passed away about six weeks ago. Would you like to know about my pets as a child?"

"Miss Taylor," Detective Blood Red Lips snapped, "We appreciate the extent of your loss and the traumatizing effects of being a victim of such a violent assault. Our job is to make sure we get all the facts. We're still trying to understand what happened, so the perpetrator can be prosecuted to the highest degree." As she spoke, she placed her hand on the crook of my arm. It wasn't gentle.

I waited for the riding crop. It didn't come out, but I knew she wanted it to.

"Do you remember what happened to you?" Detective Fanning asked. I could hear Lea whimper.

"I was…um…stabbed. Along the left side of my body," I whispered.

"Do you know why?"

Yeah, jackass. A fucking fallen angel busted out of hell and had his sights set on me and taking over the heavens. "No. I don't know."

"Do you remember how it happened?"

"I was running away from him. There had been a blizzard and I tried to run through the snow, but I didn't get very far. He hit me with something," I explained hesitantly. The more I talked, the more the haziness that blurred my thoughts cleared. "He um, kneeled over me and pinned me down. I remember the knife by my face while he talked to me, and I could see the snowflakes falling. Then he cut me. And dragged the knife down."

"And what did Mr. Maxton say when he talked to you before he allegedly stabbed you?"

"Wh…who?" I stammered.

Detective Fanning offered me another one of his kind smiles. Immediately I wanted to rip it off his face. "Your attacker, Miss Taylor."

"You said Mr. Maxton, Detective. Are you talking about Shane Maxton?" I asked, voice cracking. A strange heat spread across my chest and shoulders. My heart pounded against my chest.

"Yes, Miss Taylor. Shane

Maxton is being held on an Assault 1, it's a Class B felony."

"Excuse me? What the fuck did you just say?" Hot tears poured from my eyes.

Ethan and Lea rushed over to me as I stood up. They each grabbed a side of me. Lea was crying and Ethan looked as if he was about to.

"Miss Taylor," Detective Fanning interrupted. "Shane had your blood all over him. He was saying it was all his fault. At first, it looked to be a clear-cut case. A love triangle. Shane the jealous lover."

I looked both detectives in their eyes. It was like I had just woken up that very minute from my coma. "I don't have a *lover,* Detective, let alone a triangle of them! Shane Maxton did not attack me! Blake was there, ask Blake!"

Detective Fanning's kind smile disappeared, his deep brown eyes looked surprised and he turned to my friends with an accusatory stare. "We tried to take Blake Bevli's statement at the hospital, but he was incoherent."

"So ask him again! Shane Maxton did not hurt me physically in any way!"

Unprofessionally, Detective Sorens barked out a laugh, her red lips curled back like she was a demon, "Yeah, well we can ask him now can we? Dead people don't usually talk."

"WHAT?" I yelled. Waves of nausea rolled through my stomach, crashing themselves against my insides. I clutched at my stomach and looked around the room at the people who were surrounding me. Lea was cradled in Conner's arms sniffling, and Ethan hung his head down low. *How could no one have told me this? Or had they, and I was too heartbroken and drunk to remember?*

Detective Fanning gently took hold of my hand and he gave Lea, Conner, and Ethan, one last disappointed glare. "I'm sorry to have had to be the one to tell you," he said in a soft voice. "I'm truly sorry. What was your relationship with Blake Belvi?"

My mind whirled and spun out of my control. *I should have realized Blake would be dead.* He had to have been dead if a fallen angel took over his body. It was the only way they could be human; as human as they could be for a while anyway. Blake was dead before I even met him the day before the snowstorm.

"Uh, how...what?" I couldn't form a complete sentence. I grasped through the fog in my head to try to find the answers they needed to hear. If I couldn't, Shane would be gone for a long time and he didn't deserve that.

"He overdosed." The statement floored me. I wondered if that's what really happened to him when that damn angel had taken over.

Detective Fanning's soft voice continued probing, "What *was* your relationship with Mr. Belvi, Grace, you haven't answered that question yet."

I focused my eyes on the detective's. "I did not have a relationship with Blake. I had only known him for a day, Detective. He was Tucker's cousin. Tucker and the rest of my friends thought it would be safest for me to stay at the Belvi's winter house, because someone tried to kill me by starting a fire in my apartment." I took a deep breath, "A fire that I only survived because Shane Maxton crawled through flames and carried me out!" I started pacing the floor.

"That's the reason we need your statement about the events of the night, Miss Taylor. Things just don't add up, there are many holes in the story and we'd like you to fill them in," Detective Sorens explained.

I swallowed down the bile that was threatening to explode from my insides. My head throbbed and I clutched at my stomach, wishing that this were all a bad dream. I feverishly rubbed at my temples trying to clear my brain from the cobwebs it had collected over the last month. *They had holes in their story and needed my statement, needed me to fill them in on what had happened.* They had been under the impression that Shane had been the one who tried to kill me. *Shane.* The Shane that begged me to kiss him. The Shane that wanted to know why I had a pair of broken angel wings tattooed on my shoulder and what he could do to become the man good enough that I could love. My heart beat faster.

Both detectives watched me; both weighing my silence against my body language. My friends waited, breaths held, to hear the truth in my words. What would I say about Blake? Do I tell everyone the truth? That Blake was the one that held the knife that introduced my warm blood to the cold snow. But it wasn't Blake. It was Psycho Angel. Shane and Blake were both innocent. At least in the case of who tried to kill me.

I tried to stand up as straight as I possibly could. "Detectives, Shane Maxton did not attack me. Blake and I stumbled into an intruder when we returned to the Belvi's winter residence. Blake had just gone back to the house with me to ah, get my guitar. We were all at the resort bar singing karaoke and everyone wanted me to play." *I was not about to tell them I mistook Blake for my long lost angel and was taking him back to the house to continue the kiss he gave me so long along.*

Think. Think. Think. Shane's heartbroken expression when I walked away with Blake to the bedroom. The loud crash and shatter of glass breaking. "The intruder wore a black ski mask and was dressed all in black. He was holding one of the Belvi's antique glass vases when we came inside. We must have startled him, because he dropped it when he saw us."

I watched Detective Sorens give a slight glance to her partner, acknowledging the fact that I had just explained part of the crime scene. *Think. Grace think. What happened next? Oh, my God, was Shane in jail this whole time?*

The bedroom. Blake, who really wasn't Blake, I hit him in the head with a snow globe. "We ran into one of the back rooms and the guy with the ski mask ran after us. He smashed Blake over the head a few times with a snow globe and I tried to run away, but he caught me. He pulled his ski mask off to try to kiss me. He had blue eyes and blond hair. He had no facial hair." I gave a detailed description of Gabriel, six foot four inches, bronze skin, muscular, between 180-200 pounds, wasn't it really the truth? Wasn't it Gabriel who tried to kill me while I was in a coma? I just didn't tell them he had wings.

"No way in hell was it Shane, and Blake was passed out cold. When I finally got away, I ran into the snow and he came after me. He hit me, I think with the same snow globe he used on Blake. That's when he cut me. I think Shane was the one who found me. I think he was the one who saved me." I looked over to Lea who stood with her hands covering her mouth. "I remember thinking he was my angel that came to save me. *And he was.*"

The interview went on and on. They asked me a million questions, many of the same questions but asked differently. I didn't crack. I didn't falter. I knew how to keep secrets. I had so many of my own.

When the detectives were satisfied with my statement, they immediately called the District Attorney's office. I was then driven downtown to the Manhattan D.A.'s office on Centre Street to repeat the same answers to the exact same questions in front of the District Attorney. *Great times, seriously.* I suffered through four metal detectors, had a wand run over me (and that's always fun since I have a ton of metal pins in my body from the car accident when my parents died) and a slew of personal questions that left me feeling more violated than I'd ever felt in all of my existence. But it was worth it to get an innocent guy out of jail. The District Attorney ended up withdrawing charges against Shane and sent an order for his release from Riker's Island.

And, that's where Shane had been for the five weeks since his arrest, Riker's Island. Now, that must be a fun place to be for someone as pretty as Shane Maxton. *Crap, is he really going to hate me now.*

Chapter 8

After spending the entire day with them, the detectives dropped me off at the curb in front of my apartment. It was five o'clock in the afternoon. I stomped straight up the front steps and kicked the door open with a loud thud. I could hear voices coming from the kitchen. I stormed in and slammed the front door as hard as I could. I didn't give a damn if it ended up falling off its hinges.

When I walked into the kitchen, I was met by three of the guiltiest faces I had ever seen. Lea, Conner, and Ethan sat around the table; their voices cut short. Slapping my palms down on the cold tabletop, I stared into each face one at a time.

Lea, as always, was the first one to speak. She folded her arms across her chest defiantly. "It's about time you woke up from wherever the hell you've been. I've tried to talk to you for days."

My tense outstretched arms

softened a bit and I collapsed onto a chair. She was right and I had no right to be angry with any of them. I'd been keeping myself shut in my own darkness, mourning the loss of something I never had the right to have.

It was time to surrender to this life. *He* was gone, the one I loved for so long and so intensely. He left me here. I needed to get over it. Get over him.

"I feel horrible that Shane has been in jail this whole time. And Blake? I just can't..."

Ethan grimaced, but then the beginning of a smile crooked his lips. "Please, Grace, it's not the first time Shane's been locked up. He has one hell of a past, it's only in the last few months or so that he's changed his ways. And Blake. Blake always used drugs and that's why we never hung around him. I'm not saying he deserved to die or anything, but when you mess with that heavy stuff, it's bound to happen."

"I just..."

"Need to take a shower? Brush the knots out of that hair? Slap some make-up on that face? Get the fuck outta the house? Talk to us? To me?" Lea snapped.

"But..."

Ethan cleared his throat, "That's some really awesome advice from Lea right there." He took my hand and pulled me to my feet, "Come on. Go clean yourself up; we're taking you to Boozer's for a drink, some music, and laughs."

"What about Shane?"

Ethan pulled me through the hallway and gently pushed me into the bathroom. He raised his enormous arms over his head and leaned them on the top of the doorframe. "Tucker and his father are getting Shane. Don't worry about him. Just put yourself together, Grace, you've completely unraveled and we need you back together again." He closed the door quietly and slipped back down the hallway.

A few moments or hours later, I had no idea which, I found myself hugging my knees under the icy cold stream of my shower. My clothes were still on. I tugged and yanked the cold wet material from my body, and for the first time in days, washed myself.

When I was finished with trying to scrub my sorrow away, I stood in front of the misty mirror and wiped it clean until Grace's reflection stared back at me. *My reflection.* I held my stare for a long time.

I was strong enough to get through this. I was strong enough to move on. Millions of people have lost someone they've loved. Millions have had someone walk out on them. This was no different. I've lost everything and everyone worth anything to me so many times over, I could probably write one hell of a book about it. *It might not be good, but I could write one.*

Life goes on. So will I.

I dried and brushed my hair. The amount of strands left on my brush from the war with knots I waged was staggering.

Walking back through the hallway, I could hear the murmurs of my friends in the living room. *Emotional wreck. Lost. Depressed. Withdrawn.* And of course, Lea's, *'she just needs to get laid.'* In time, I knew I would tell her the truth about Shane once being my angel. I wondered how he pulled it off, not allowing Shane's body to die with his soul. Was the old Shane Maxton back or some other new, poor soul? Whoever it was, I had deep sympathy for, Shane was a hard act to follow.

I dressed in a simple pair of jeans that were so old they had tears ripped in both knees, the bottom cuffs and to my surprise, where the curves of my ass were. I didn't care, they were comfortable and they really didn't show too much. I showed more flesh doing one of Mad World's gigs. I dug through my drawers in search of my favorite tee shirt. I smiled when I finally found it, a tight black tee shirt with the words, *All I Need are Shoes, Booze and Bad boys with Tattoos*.

"At least slap some heels and lipstick on," Lea said from the doorway. "Come on, Gray, it's time for you to be human." *I just wished I knew how.*

I slipped my feet into a pair of black stilettos and smudged a bit of creamy red wine colored gloss on. I dragged my leather jacket over my shoulders, dragged my butt into the living room, and followed my friends to Boozer's Bar.

Boozer's was literally right around the corner from our apartment, which made it very convenient when wearing freaking pinpoints for heels. A bright, pulsing, neon light screamed its name and usually music and laughter spilled out its front doors, though tonight it seemed quiet. Antique lanterns hung on each side of the doors and reflections of their dancing lights flickered against the large glass window. It felt good to be back.

The bar was practically empty, save for a rowdy bunch of frat-looking college boys surrounding a table full of empty beer bottles. It looked like they were building something with them. They drunkenly whistled at Lea and I as we passed, and Ethan protectively put his arm around my shoulder and flipped them off.

We walked straight to the bar and when Ryan the bartender saw me, he hopped over the bar like a gymnast and grabbed me in his arms. "Damn girl, it's good to see you out of that hospital bed." He held me at arm's length and looked me up and down as if he didn't believe it was really me. "How you holding up? Grace, I swear, if I ever lay eyes on that son of a bitch Shane again, I'll kill him." His pale green eyes were serious, frightening.

I grabbed Ryan's arms. "No, no, Ryan. Shane did not do that to me. We were attacked, Blake and I. Shane was the one who saved me. I gave my statement today. He'll be released soon. He's innocent." *My God, everyone thinks that Shane tried to kill me. How much is this man going to hate me if he sees me again?* "Ry, I need to get drunk. Think you could help me with that?"

His face softened and I knew he was relieved to hear about Shane. "Came to the right place. What's your poison tonight, Sweetheart?"

"A bottle of Jack."

He cocked his head seductively and with a huge grin emerging across his lips, he vaulted back over the bar.

"And Ry? Not in a glass. The whole bottle. Whole. Bottle."

His eyes stared into mine and he winked at me as he walked backwards toward the wall of liquor bottles. "Yeah. Sure, Grace. Whatever you need tonight, anything you want, it's on me." *Wow, awesome customer service, does that come with a massage?*

I jerked my gaze off him only to find Conner, Lea, and Ethan gapping at me with open mouths. I rolled my eyes. "Only God can judge me, I don't need a three person jury right now," I snapped.

Ryan placed four shot glasses in front of them and the bottle in front of me. He leveled his line of sight with mine and gave me a little smirk. *Holy hot bartenders, he was flirting with me!* I felt my face heat up.

"Want a straw with that too?" Lea asked in a shaky voice.

I turned my gaze right to her eyes and gave her a disgusted smile. "Wanna meet me in the bathroom in a minute?"

"Yeah. Why don't we go now?"

Grabbing the bottle, I poured

each of us a shot. I nodded to the glasses. "Shots first." I put the hot liquid to my lips and waited for them to follow. I wished I could have erased the looks on their faces, but I couldn't. And I was burning, dying on the inside. I wished they would understand. They hadn't picked up their shots yet, so I growled at them. Yes, I *growled*.

They each took a hold of their glasses. That was the affect I was looking for.

"Cheers," I whispered and gulped the fire down.

Four more shots, and Ethan brought his hand to my knee, gently tugging the material of my jeans. His eyes pleaded with me. But all I wanted was to get his hands off my body. I didn't want anyone else's skin to touch mine. I was nowhere near being drunk enough.

Lea yanked me off the barstool. "Let's go! Now!" She pulled me across the empty dance floor and passed the front of the quiet empty stage, it made my stomach drop. I followed her, remembering the first time I tried to follow her to the bathroom in a crowd of dancing people, the same exact path I took now. The first night I saw Shane, heard Shane; smelled Shane; felt Shane. *Oh God. I actually missed him!*

We barely made it all the way into the bathroom before Lea flipped around and got in my face. "You are scaring the hell out of me, Grace! I've never seen you like this. Not after your accident. Not after your parents died. Not after Jacob died. Tell me what's going on! Is it what happened? Tell me what to do for you! Tell me how to get my best friend back!" Tears streaked down her face and she wrapped her arms around herself. *Oh, Lea.*

I closed my eyes tight and took a long, deep, breath. I opened them blinking back tears and exhaled slowly. "Shane," I whispered his name because I could barely stand to hear it pass my lips.

Her eyebrows drew themselves together, her eyes red and swollen still spitting out tears. "You're mad at me because you didn't know he got locked up? You haven't talked to me. We had no idea what happened, we thought maybe he got jealous..." She looked down at her hands and twisted her sleeves between her fingers. "Please tell me what happened," she said sobbing.

I leaned my back against the cold tiles of the bathroom wall and slid down, my hands falling limply to my feet. I stared past her. "Shane was an angel, Lea. *My* angel." Cool tears rolled down my cheeks. I could feel them hang off the curve of my chin and fall to the floor. "This has nothing to do with being stabbed or by who." I looked at her then. My eyes went wide and I stammered and spit, "It was Shane all along. He tried to forget me with every girl he took home. Then he, he...left me." Lea didn't need to know more. She didn't need to know fallen angels were around and prayers don't get answered anymore. She didn't need to know that humans were play things, easily broken and replaceable. She just didn't need to know.

She wiped at her tears, huddled next to me and held me. "Gray, I'm so sorry. Shane, wow, well that explains the deep intensity between the both of you. What are you going to do?"

"Lea, maybe just give me some time, okay? Just let me...hurt, let me grieve. This stinks. It hurts, Lea, it hurts so damn much." I closed my eyes. "I searched for him for over 2000 years Lea. That kind of love and devotion should've been enough to conquer anything. It should've gotten me more than, *remember I always loved you, oh, look at those pretty new wings!*"

"But, Gray, what about you and Shane now? Maybe you guys can make something out of this...you could..."

"Stop, Lea. I don't get happily-ever-afters. Those are just for fairytales and porn." I tried to give her a smile.

"I'll be fine. Please just let me deal with it my own way."

Lea nodded her head. "Yeah, well I still think you do really need to get laid though." And that's why Lea was my best friend, because she puts everything in perspective for me.

I nodded my head at her. "I know, Lea, I'll start living it up with you, but you've got to let me be sad about this and grieve first."

A soft knock on the door interrupted our discussion. Conner's head peeked in, his face twisted with concern, "Hey, you two okay in here?" he asked softy. Ethan's head popped in over Conner's with a matching worried expression.

I yanked on Lea's hand and hauled her up off the floor. "Come on, Lea. Help me get to oblivion, it's the only freaking place I feel comfortable in this skin right now," I whispered.

She swung her arm across the back of my shoulder and kissed my forehead. "Whatever you need me to do to help you get my best friend back to me. Please hurry though, because I miss her and I need to have someone to go shopping with," she whispered into my ear.

More people were sitting in the bar when we finally walked out of the bathroom. The frat boys were still there; the leader of the group stared at me hard as I walked past. I met his gaze until *he* looked away. I could have easily had him take me into oblivion, but the thought was cut short by the memory of Shane's lips on mine. I looked to the front doors of the bar and wished I could just see him walk through them.

I sat down on the bar stool next to Ethan while Lea and Conner talked in whispers between themselves. I looked past Ethan at them. Conner stood with his arms wrapped around her and she laid her head on his chest while they spoke. He looked down at her with such love in his eyes. Watching them and the way he looked at her, it made me think for a split second that maybe the world wasn't such a shitty place. Just for a second though; *a split one.*

Ethan nudged me with his elbow. "Shot for shot Grace, after each one you tell me what's in that pretty little head of yours." His face was set in a serious smile, his brown eyes waited patiently. He poured us both a shot and slid my glass and his stool closer to me. Our arms touched as we both leaned on the bar.

I picked up my glass and clinked it up against his. "Shot for shot. Tale for tale. Drink up buddy." We both lifted the glasses to our lips and watched each other over the rim.

I gulped mine down first. "Remember that night you walked me home and I told you I was in love with someone?" I watched him nod. "Let's just say I guess I didn't know him like I thought I did and he destroyed my heart. But he didn't just destroy a small piece of my heart, he desecrated the whole thing. I was the idiot who just handed it to him. Because for so long, I really, really believed...I had faith in him, but I was wrong. Your turn."

He swallowed his drink. "I knocked out my best friend and held him down while the cops cuffed him because I thought he hurt you. I wanted to kill him Grace." He studied my gaze waiting for my reaction.

I poured us another shot. I grabbed my glass, slammed it back fast, and slid my glass on the bar until it clunked into the bottle of liquor. I placed both my wrists on the bar and showed him my scars. "I've come close to death so many times. I'm more afraid of being here than I am being there."

Ethan's eyes widened when he saw the scars on my wrists and the tattoos that covered them. He raised his eyes to mine. We sat there staring at each other. Picking up another shot, he drank it back and cleared his throat, "I was in love only once in my life. She got pregnant, but when she was only five months along, she went into labor, and my daughter was stillborn. I visit her grave every weekend and lay down a single white rose on her headstone. The girl left me right after."

I entwined his fingers into mine. "Ethan, I'm so sorry."

He shook his head and stopped me from saying anything else. "Just don't say anything. Only Shane knows."

"Same here. Only Shane and Lea know," I whispered back.

He studied my face. A ton of emotions appeared across his features. "How close did you and Shane get? I know it's none of my business, but Grace, I gotta know."

I tilted my head closer to him. "Why?"

His eyes drifted to our hands. "Because, Grace, I don't want to do anything else that will ever hurt

Shane."

I shook my head and pulled my hands away from his, shrugging my shoulders. "You're going to have to ask him that, Ethan. The last time I saw him he said some pretty amazing stuff to me, but I don't think he still feels that way now."

"How do you feel about him now?"

If there ever was a time when my old friend Jack Daniels shuts off my brain to mouth filter, this was it. "Don't call me one of his stupid girls. I never slept with him, but Ethan, I could lick that boy from head to toe like a big old lollipop. He was the only one who ever made me forget who I was trying to hold on to."

"Hey," Lea cut in. "What the eff are you two alcoholics talking about? You're all hovering over each other like you're plotting to take over the world." She put her arms around both of us, "You know you can't do any of that fun stuff without me."

"Psf. I'm not an alcoholic. An alcoholic needs a drink. Look here," I explained raising my next shot to her. "I already have one. So therefore, I do not need one. Which makes me not an alcoholic."

"Yeah, okay. Whatever you say. Listen, Ethan can you make sure she gets home okay; we have to get out of here. I have work tomorrow. Oh, and don't let her go anywhere near any ice cream."

Ethan nodded to her and we all said our goodbyes. I wasn't going anywhere because I could still feel the heartbreak, and the bottle of Jack was still not empty.

"Hey, Grace, let's go back to my place and drink the rest of this."

I smirked at him.

He put his hands up in the air. "I promise I won't lay a finger on you."

I don't even remember how we got there, all I remember is thinking maybe I could lay down just for a minute in Shane's room, just to remember how nice it was to sleep in his bed.

I never made it to Shane's room.

Chapter 9

It was four o'clock in the morning when I woke up on the floor in Ethan's room with a pillow under my head and an itchy blue blanket over me. Ethan was asleep on his bed, his breath even and slow. A faint stream of light spread across his body, lit by his bedside table lamp.

Oh, God, please no. Please, please, no. No, no, no. My heart pounded hard against my rib cage when I tried to remember what happened to make me end up in Ethan's bedroom. *We just talked.* The intense rhythm of my heart slowed down gradually when I remembered the last of the conversation we had and what a complete gentlemen he was. Even though nothing happened between us, it didn't stop the tears from coming when I thought about how out of control I'd become. *Thank God, I was with Ethan. Imagine if I had drunk with Tucker. He would have slept with me, married me and forced me to eat sushi all in one night without me even knowing it.*

Although the situation was completely innocent, I felt a sudden pang of panic to get out of the room. I overstayed my welcome. I came here under the guise of hoping to see Shane again. Even though I was angry and hurt about the whole situation, I wasn't going to lie to myself anymore. I couldn't get him out of my head. The last time we were together we almost, and I almost…My God, he *was* the only person I had met in the last two thousand years that could make me forget about my angel.

Without making a sound, I folded up the blanket and placed it with the pillow at the end of Ethan's bed. The gentle giant did not stir.

With my shoes in my hand, I quietly pushed the door open and idiotically stumbled into the hallway, falling over my own feet. My stilettos went flying and I slapped my hands over my mouth to stifle my giggles. *Damn, I was still drunk.*

The air in the hallway felt

different; heavier; thicker, damp. A sweet, minty, smell drifted through it making my thoughts turn to Shane again and remembering how it felt to wake up wrapped in sheets with him. My inner thoughts were like a category 5 hurricane; blasting through my brain at two hundred miles per hour. I had no clue what thoughts to hold on to now that I had no angel to vow my love to. I was lost in a violent storm, drowning in the harsh currents of despair. I heard a small whimper escape through my lips and realized I was crying. Yet again.

"What the hell?" The low raspy voice slid right through me, rocking me back on the already unsteady heels of my feet. I had to sink my teeth into my bottom lip to gather the nerve to look at man that the voice belonged to.

Oh my God.

Perfection. He was utterly the most breathtaking, painfully beautiful man I had ever laid my eyes on. A stampede of frantic butterflies tore through my insides and I gulped down a deep breath of air, because I had somehow stopped breathing.

His dark hair was longer than I remembered and lay wet and disheveled across his forehead. Drops of water glistened on his shoulders, his face, *and his bare chest. Bare chest!* They shimmered along the dark contours of his tattoos making the story of our forbidden love dance with reflections of light. A soft white towel that hung low on his hips was a stark contrast to the hard toned muscles that tensed under the beautiful sun-kissed skin of his stomach and chest.

Hard, steely, gunmetal blue eyes coldly stared down at me. *Through me.* They shined dangerously against the soft light that spilled itself across the hallway from the bathroom.

So fiercely breathtaking, with the swirl of the mist from the shower and his beauty, I would have said he looked like an angel. But I knew better.

"What. The. Hell?" The heat of

his voice took my whirling thoughts to places that they had no right to go, *but damn did I want to. Scrumdillifuckingemious. I just wanted to wrap my legs around his face.* "Did you just *come out* of *Ethan's fucking bedroom*?" His voice was thick with venom and the air in the hallway became so much denser I struggled to catch my breath.

Oh crap.

Sickening warmth spread across my cheeks and bolted down my spine. "Yeah, but nothing..."

"Save it. It doesn't matter." Cold. Callus. Completely indifferent, he walked past me. "Don't worry about locking the door behind you, we have easy ass like you coming in and out of here all the time."

Oh crap. My world shifted off its axis and spun out of control, it left me leaning up against the wall fighting against gravity. I was still too drunk to talk straight. "We were talking..."

A deep laughter rumbled in his chest, "Right, was that before or after you fucked him? Save it, why the hell would I care? I don't want to listen to the blow by blow of your night."

I tried to take a steady breath, but the rage boiled in my chest spiraling up my throat and my fists clenched against the hardness of the wall that helped to support me. "Fuck you, Shane!"

Before I could take my next breath, Shane's body slammed painfully into mine. He leveled his right shoulder into my stomach hard, swung me up in his arms and over his shoulder. He grabbed the back of my thighs and carried me through the hallway toward the *Bone Room*. I didn't have enough air in my lungs to scream.

He opened the door to their communal *poke-a-skank* room and dropped me right in front of it. I dropped straight to the floor. "Fuck me? *Fuck me?* You want to go in the

Bone Room with me?" He stood over me screaming with those intense ruthless eyes. He crouched down to my level and slammed both his palms against the wall on either side of my face. "Because I could really get off on some head right now, since I've been in *fucking jail* for over a month." He slid his hands down the wall slowly, never breaking his icy stare. "I usually don't like my girls still wet from Ethan, but hey, if you're game...but if not, get the *fuck* out of my hallway."

I was too stunned to speak. So I slapped him. Hard enough to turn his whole face away from me, I slapped him. "Don't you ever lay your hands on me again Shane." I slid myself up along the wall never leaving his steely gaze. "Get the hell out of my way," I whispered.

He stood up slowly, eyes still locked on mine.

Slamming my shoulder against his, I walked past him and down the hallway. I picked up my shoes and headed for the front door to his apartment without looking back. "*Sweet* fucking pants, I bet Ethan really enjoyed that hot little ass of yours. Sure you don't want to change your mind about the Bone Room?" I flipped him the bird without turning my head.

I heard his door slam as I quietly opened the front door and let myself out.

I walked into the front lobby on trembling legs. I opened the lobby doors to the icy cold March winds and the sounds of an early New York City. I stood in front of his building looking at the street that lay before me. My breath faltered and came out shallow and uneven.

Barefoot, I walked down the street toward my apartment. I eyed my Jeep parked on the corner of my block and walked towards it, the filthy concrete of the streets scraping against the tender soles of my bare feet.

I searched through my jacket,

found my car keys and beeped the unlock button. Yanking the door open, I climbed in. *I should leave. Leave and start over. Lea would need to understand.* I jammed the key into the ignition and turned on the engine. The heater blasted on and my audio system erupted into *Exit Wounds* by *The Script*. I could picture the angels laughing down at me all dressed in their Sunday best.

Assholes. *Motherangelfucking* assholes. Pieces of Higher than Thou good for nothing, life sucking, seven deadly sinning shit stains! I gripped my steering wheel so tight my fingers ached and was disgusted with myself when the tears pooled in my eyes. I pressed the heels of my trembling hands to my eyes to stop the tears from falling. I was not going to allow myself any more grief. I had lost myself somewhere along the way *and then I lost my way*. I waited forever to find my heart and start my life. Forever is over. I'm not spending one more minute on it.

When the song ended, I turned off my ignition and yanked out my keys. On the passenger seat next to me was my cell phone with the drained battery that had been left in my Jeep since who knows when. I grabbed it, jumped out of my truck, and found my way home. It wasn't in my nature to drive this drunk anyway.

The apartment was silent when I walked through to my bedroom. I locked my door behind me when I got inside, plugged my phone in and fell asleep somewhere between the phone charger and the bed.

Chapter 10

Something was buzzing and it wouldn't stop. I begged it too, in my head at least I did. I didn't want to open my eyes and find out what it was. But, it wouldn't stop taunting me.

It took me at least twenty minutes to pull myself up and fully open my eyes. The sun blasted through my window, assaulting me with all its head splitting brightness. I looked around my room to find the source of the ear bleeding noise. *Ugh. My cell phone. Shitfuckphone.*

I crawled across the mattress, *and across the floor*, because I could barely stand to move. I grabbed the phone and crawled back to my pathetic excuse for a bed. I poked the phone repeatedly until it stopped its screeching and promptly feel back asleep.

The next time my eyes opened, night had settled outside my window. I vaguely wondered if it was the same day, at least my headache was gone.

And I kind of felt better.

Still in my hand, sat my cell phone and I poked the side button to turn on its screen. I slid the lock off to see three voice messages. Hmm. I pressed the icon and cradled the phone to my ear.

"Monday, February 13th. First new message," the recording announced. *Two days after the angel pretending to be Blake attacked me.*

"Grace, it's me, Shane. You've just got out of surgery," his voice was shaking. "It's been eighteen hours and we don't know if you're going to make it. I just, I um, just, damn it. Grace, if you get to hear this, fuck I hope you do, I'm going to do everything I can to save you. Lea told me everything; I can't believe you've been here the whole time. I never knew. I'll find Gabriel, or Michael, or any of them. I'm going to do anything to help you. I love you Grace."

"Monday, February 13th. Second new message," the recording

announced again.

"I can't leave your room. Nobody is coming, Gabriel, Michael, Samuel, none of them. I promise you, I swear. I swear Grace, I will do anything to end your punishment. God, baby, I never knew. I never imagined I would ever see you again," his breath faltered and a small moan escaped through the speaker. He sputtered and disconnected. He sounded broken.

"Monday, February 13th. Third new message," the recording announced.

"Grace. Whatever happens, remember I love you. I will always love you. I think I have a plan. I'm going to try my best to get you to live the rest of your life as Grace. No matter what I have to do. Just…just, if I can do it, just go on and live your life."

I stood up and threw my phone against the wall, it bounced to the floor and the battery flew back at me. "WHAT THE HELL! What the hell else are you going to crap on me with? ENOUGH ALREADY!"

Flinging my door open, I stomped through the hallway and into the bathroom. I ran the water in the shower on the hottest setting and jumped in the scalding water. I scrubbed myself almost raw. *Go on and live my life? What the hell does that mean? Haven't I been stuck doing that crap for two freaking thousand years? Fine! My life! My rules! Last life! Make it count.*

Wrapped in only a towel, I closed myself in my bedroom when I heard loud voices coming in through the front door. Lea was screaming at someone. *Crap, I hope her and Conner aren't fighting.*

I rummaged through my drawers for clean clothes until I heard something slam loudly against my door. I froze. Another something smashed at my door. I watched it vibrate under the pressure.

"Open the door, Grace!"

Shane's voice slid through my veins like acid. He pounded on it again.

Oh really? Really? My rules. My life. Last one. I'm going to make every moment count. I flung my towel on the floor and slid up a pair of black lacy G-string panties. I tugged on the matching bra, because *yes I do have matching sets* (Lea *is* my best friend). I shook my head, making my hair fly all over and yanked open the door. *Holy Dripping Wet Panties! That man should come with a warning label.*

All my time on this hell on earth was worth the look on that boy's face when he saw me. "Ah," was all that came out of that perfect set of lips of his.

I placed my hands on my hips. "So, you're banging and kicking at my door so you can just tell me...ah?"

Dressed in a delicious pair of old faded jeans, scruffed up motorcycle boots and a tight white tee-shirt that showed the shadows and curves of every single one of his muscles, his arms stretched out, leaning against both sides of my door frame. One hand let go of the door and ran itself through his hair, in that sexy way only Shane could.

I watched those blue eyes travel slowly over my legs, sending tingly goose bumps all along my skin. His gaze moved along the length of my inner thighs and gradually rose, then lingered on the tiny V-shaped black lace of my panties. And when they did, I moved my hips slightly and his eyes moved with them. His gaze continued sweeping across my bare stomach and I watched his body stiffen and his knuckles turn white when they followed along the curves of my breasts. When his eyes finally found mine, his breath was heavy and his eyes wide. I could have had an orgasm from the mind fuck he was giving me right there.

I could see a thousand thoughts cross his mind. He leaned in slightly and then stopped himself. "Band meeting tomorrow...at eleven...at the studio," he whispered hoarsely. He said no more words; he just stared into my eyes. He slid his hand through his hair again and held it there. His jaw tensed.

Lea appeared in the hallway shaking Shane from whatever his thoughts were. A sad expression shadowed his face and he turned away, *growling*, and stormed down the hallway towards the front door.

Lea giggled. "Well, it's nice to have my best friend back, where the hell has she been?" she asked smacking me on my bottom. "I told you, matching sets are weapons of mass destruction. I have never seen Shane speechless like that before." She folded her arms and tilted her head at me. "You okay? Can you move, Grace?"

"Ummhmmm. That man just melted the panties right off me with his eyes."

Chapter 11

The dark bitter smell of coffee woke me from another dream of Shane. My body was twisted tightly around my sheets and I could honestly still feel his warm tongue on my inner thigh. That man was going to make me self *cum-bust* right in front of him one day.

I dragged an old button up lumberjack shirt over my shoulders and snuggled into its warmth. Slipping my cold toes in my slippers, I made my way into the kitchen in search of some of that caffeinated mud Lea makes each morning.

I felt his eyes on me before I saw him standing there. *Damn, I didn't think he'd be there. I would have worn next to nothing.* He and Conner were still sweaty and panting from a morning run. His shirt was off and he leaned his body up against the counter and stretched when I walked in. Ignoring him, *okay trying to ignore him*, I reached up for a mug from the cabinets. I felt the material of my shirt ride up to just over my bottom and I heard his low throaty growl when it did. I watched him tear his eyes off my bottom and storm out of the kitchen.

"Catch you later, Conner," he called out when he got to the front door.

I glanced at Conner. "Everything okay?" I asked.

Conner was sitting down at the table with his coffee steaming in front of him. His eyes were glued to my face, serious as all hell. "You slept with Ethan." It wasn't a question. It was a statement.

"You sleep with Lea all the time," I stated back.

"Yeah..."

"And Conner, when you sleep with Lea, do you always have sex?" I asked trying to make my point clear without saying it outright.

"Point taken Grace."

When Conner and Lea left for work, I jumped into the shower and did all that was girly. I left my apartment before I needed to and sat in the small coffee shop on the corner of my block to calm my nerves. I got to the studio at exactly eleven o'clock.

Walking into the studio gave me that feeling that I could only guess some people got when they walked into their places of worship. The euphoric sense that you could find the guidance to your existence, the answer to your prayers, or maybe the path to your soul's freedom, its redemption.

I took a deep breath and stepped in, shutting the door behind me. I left my guitar back at my apartment because I knew there would be no real band practice for me today.

Ethan sat behind his drum kit with his legs stretched out across the top of his bass drum. He twirled a drumstick in one hand. His long platinum blond hair was uncharacteristically loose, and he smiled wide when his eyes met mine.

Brayden sat on one of the couches with his bass laid out across his lap. He ran a hand through his short brown hair and waved hello to me.

"There's our gorgeous girl!" Alex was sitting behind his keyboard and ran out from behind it to grab me in a hug and swing me around like a rag doll.

"Yay! Your casts are off!" I cheered when he let go.

His dark hair flopped in front of his mischievous green eyes. His eyebrows rose up and his cheeks reddened. "Yeah, yesterday. Grace, my love, you look hotter than ever," he laughed.

"Fine. Let's get this shit over," Shane's voice murmured from one of the couches. I looked over at him, but his eyes never turned in my direction. He stood up and walked forward folding his arms across his chest. "Yeah, so Alex is back. We really don't need another guitarist."

There was a second of awkward silence.

"Whoa, what the hell?" Alex asked. "Dude, I'll be only on keyboard now, Grace does guitar, she blows me outta the water anyway." He gave me a wink, "Did you like when I said you *blow me*, that part?"

I just winked back, smiled and gave him an eye roll.

Brayden walked over closer to Alex, "Yeah, this is stupid. Let's just get to practice so we can set up a gig at Boozer's, it's been weeks, dude."

Shane hooked his guitar strap over his shoulders and hung his guitar in front of him. His eyes finally locked onto mine. "Yeah, well we got rules in this band. Nobody can sleep with another band member, so Alex stays on guitar *and* keyboard." His eyes held my stare, waiting for me to break, to shatter, to fall to pieces from his words. *Nope. Isn't going to happen.*

He sauntered over and plugged his guitar into the biggest amp.

Alex's eyebrows pulled together, "Dude, I haven't slept with anyone of you motherfuckers. You're the pretty boy who was in jail for four fucking weeks, *Sir FuckmeBung*."

"I didn't sleep with any one of you guys either," Brayden called out. "Now can we just play?"

Ethan's eyes snapped to mine and a look of horror crossed his face. I shook my head for him not to say anything. It wasn't worth it. Shane wasn't going to believe him. He just wanted to embarrass me and punish me.

I met Shane's stare and smiled at him. "Um, I think Shane is talking about me." The room stilled and all eyes were on me. "Well, now that that is settled. I really did have a blast playing with you guys, and Alex," my eyes swept to Alex who stared open-mouthed at me. "Anytime you want to bring your guitar over to my place, I would love to play with you. I'll probably see you guys at the bar sometime." I turned on my heels and walked out of the studio and down the hall. I didn't look back. There was no way in the world I was going to let Shane Maxton see my expression.

As the door closed, I could hear Alex yelling, "Which lucky son of a bitch got to tap that perfect ass?" Shane's answer was to start playing Bloodhound Gang's *Ballad of Chasey Lain* and just inserted my name in. *If you've never heard the song, Google it and then you'll understand how very disgusted I was with him that I almost vomited in the hallway.*

I made my way up the stairs and out to the front lobby. When I got to the front doors, Ethan was in front of me, out of breath from running, and grabbing at my elbow. "Grace...wait. You can't just walk out like that, please tell me what is going on with Shane."

I continued to walk out of the

front door, but he pulled me to a stop on the sidewalk in front of his building. "Grace, I'm not a child. I don't like playing games. Tell me what's going on."

I shook my head. "Shane caught me leaving your bedroom early in the morning. He automatically thought I slept with you."

"Why didn't you explain to him that nothing happened?"

"Ethan, I tried too. He cut me off every time and I was still drunk, so my verbal sparring skills were nonexistent. I could barely remember to breathe the correct way in front of him, let alone reason with him." I could feel my cheeks redden with my thoughts, "He ended up flinging me over his shoulder and dropped me in front of the Bone Room and asked me if I wanted to fuck him, and I quote, *Because I could really get off on some head right now, since I've been in fucking jail for over a month. I usually don't like my girls still wet from Ethan, but hey, if you're game, but if not, get the fuck out of my hallway.*"

"I knew it, I knew it the first time he met you," Ethan laughed and leaned against the front wall of his building.

I sighed, "What are you talking about?"

"Shane doesn't do jealous, Grace. He has some serious feelings for you," Ethan smiled.

"What the hell color is the sky in your world, Ethan? The man just kicked me out of his band. The only serious feelings he has are extreme horniness and extreme disgust that he didn't get to me first." I walked away.

Ethan was next to me, immediately walking down the street. "The first night he saw you, after that bar fight, he made me search the entire bar for a silver eyed girl so he could get her name, Grace."

"Stop it, Ethan. I know exactly

how Shane felt before we all went to Tucker's parents' house. One of the last things he told me was that he loved me," I said.

Ethan's eyes almost popped out of his head. "Holy shit..."

I held my hands up. "Yeah. But then I walked away with Blake because I was a fool, Ethan. Then he spends a month in jail because everybody assumed the worst in him, even you, one of his best friends. Ethan. You beat the crap out of him! And when he gets out of jail, he finds me sneaking out of your room in the middle of the night, drunk! I'm thinking his feelings might have gone straight to hell since."

Ethan's gaze raised from me to something past my shoulders. I knew by the way the hairs on the back of my neck tingled that it was Shane. But, he just walked past us without saying a word.

Chapter 12

After watching Shane walk away, I said goodbye to Ethan and made my way home. I changed into sweats and spent the rest of the day running in the park. The weather was a mild 60 degrees and the smells of an early spring wafted through the trees. I made a mental note to try to take a trip to Lea's parent's house to pick up my bike, it was definitely moving into riding weather. I ran until my legs almost collapsed and night had fallen.

It was five o'clock when I got back to my apartment and my phone was screaming for attention. There were ten texts and three voice messages from Lea, all telling me I had to come to Boozer's because everybody was going for drinks. *What else is new? That's all these people ever did.*

Pass. Not tonight. There's no way I want to watch Shane throw his tantrums about me and Ethan or mess around with his girls. I showered and still wrapped in my damp towel, flung myself on my mattress and passed out.

Sirens echoed through my skull waking me from a dead sleep. *Oh, what a surprise, it's my cell phone. Again.* In the dark of my room, I hit the screen and saw Lea's face. I swiped it open. "What do you want?" I groaned. "I'm sleeping."

"Get out of bed and come to the bar. Wear something um...slutty." "What? Why? No...I'm sleeping. Leave me alone."

"You need to get your ass over here before Shane goes home with the first skank he catches!" she hissed into the phone. A bubble of jealously surged through my belly making me bolt up. *What the hell?*

Okay. Normal Shane behavior. I really shouldn't be jealous, it's *Shane. Fuckshitfuck.* I'm jealous. "I'll be right there." No use trying to deny it. I can't even fight with myself against the feelings. *I wanted to be the skank he took home.* Centuries of being true and moral, I got my heart broken, then I meet Shane Maxton and I throw all my ethics out the window. *I'm so going to enjoy this. I'm so not ever going to get to see my angel again in heaven, because I'm so going straight to hell.*

Knee high black stiletto heeled boots, tight low rise hip hugging jeans, halter top, wild jet black waves and lipstick the color of deep red wine, I sauntered into the bar.

My stomach plummeted when I saw Shane with a stunning brunette on his lap. *Did he ever pick anyone not stunning, someone just average? Why did they all have to look like super models?* The butterflies in my stomach slammed themselves against my insides cursing profanities at me. Hot bursts of adrenaline spiked across my chest and my fingers trembled. He sat in the middle of the group staring vacantly into a half full beer bottle. One of his hands played with the label of the bottle, peeling it back. The other hand rested on the empty chair next to him, *he wasn't touching the girl on his lap.*

The skank, on the other hand was nuzzling her mouth in his neck. Watching her tongue flick out between her hot pink (Yes, I said *hot freaking pink*, who wears that color but thirteen year olds?) lips, I almost gagged on my own heart as it tried to projectile vomit itself out of my mouth.

I stood there paralyzed, trying to process the messy mudslide of emotions that were screaming through the long dark empty corridors of my insides. *Damn, I hated how this man made me feel, but God, I felt human, alive.*

Conversation was spilling out around the table, yet he sat there unaffected by everything, and everyone, like he didn't belong. Alex sat on the other side of him crooking his finger down the front of one of the waitresses' shirts as she giggled. Brayden, Ethan, Conner, and Lea sat with their backs to me and were talking in some heated conversation, their hands flailing about. Tucker, like the dog he is, was sitting drunkenly ogling

Shane's skank and poking her arm to get her attention.

Then Shane noticed *me*. As if he were trying to memorize each and every contour, his eyes roamed every inch of my body until they locked on my eyes and his lips parted open. His face was tense and pained; he was so fucking perfect it took my breath away. I ignored his stare, because really, it made my freaking heart flutter and my knees weak. And, let's not even think about what I was imagining I could do to him with my tongue or how I wanted to scream at the skank to get off his lap.

"Wow, now that's a beautiful sight right there. Hel...lo, Grace," Tucker called out to me. Everybody turned their heads and smiled.

Except for Shane, who lifted up his beer and drunkenly shouted, "Hey look who it is boys, the Holy fucking Grail of Pussies." He offered me a stupid drunk smirk and downed the rest of his beer. *Uh oh*.

Alex reached over and shoved him on the shoulder, "What the fuck is your problem today, jackhole? Sit down, Grace, don't mind Shane, I think he's on the rag."

Lea pulled over a chair for me and sat me across from Shane, at the very same minute he started shoving his tongue down the girl's throat. I died a little right there, just then. *Died.*

The waitress who was hanging all over Alex stood up and cleared her throat, "Hey Grace, what can I get you tonight?"

Before I could answer, Shane yelled from in between the skanks lips, "Mind Erasers with straws, Mollie. And keep them coming, it's time to play a game." He stood up and the brunette fell to the floor and yelped. He looked down at her and laughed, "Whoops, psf. Better sit in your own seat Marie, this shit is going to get wild." The girl sat down and pouted. *Yes, pouted, the lower lip stuck out and everything.* Hot pink lipstick everywhere. Ugh, even on Shane's face.

I gave her a little wave, "Marie, wow." I looked Shane dead in the eyes smiling. "Shane I'm impressed, usually you don't ever get their first names. She *must* be *special*."

Tucker burst out laughing, "Yeah, for tonight at least. Right, Shane!" He slapped his hands against the table. "Hey Grace, you need someone special for tonight?"

Ethan stood up, walked behind Tucker laughing, and smacked him in the back of his head. "Shut the hell up, are you freaking twelve? Haven't you hit puberty yet, did anyone ever teach you how to speak to women?" he laughed.

Shane's jaw tightened and his eyes narrowed a fraction. "How freaking sweet, Ethan's protecting the Holy Grail."

"Oookay!" Lea cut everybody off. "What drinking game are we

playing?"

Mollie returned with our first round of Mind Eraser's *with straws*. She handed them out and left like her ass was on fire.

Shane scooped up his drink in his hand and held his arms out stretched. He flailed his arms and his drink sloshed over the side of his glass and spilled down the front of Marie's shirt. She didn't even notice. "We're going to play a little game called Answer This. Rules are, you get to ask anyone a question and they either have to answer TRUTHFULLY, or if you're a pussy and don't want to answer, you have to drink your Mind Eraser. Whole damn thing through the straw." He stared straight at me, "And no fucking lies!"

Alex raised his hands, "Oh, me first, and this is to everyone at the table. Okay, answer this...Where is the craziest place you have ever had sex?"

Shane rolled his eyes and sat back down while everyone went down the line giving their answer.

"Bathroom," Brayden said.

"A fast food ball pit in the kid's play area," Alex laughed answering his own question. Everybody moaned. *"What?"* He said red in the face.

Conner and Lea both giggled and said, "Ferris wheel." *How is that even possible?*

When it was Shane's turn, Alex laughed and said, "Please do not say jail cell, because I'll piss myself right here, dude."

"Shut up," Shane laughed. He looked at Marie, "My answer is probably going to change later, but right now fire escape."

"Boozer's bathroom," Marie giggled. *Eww!*

"Car," Tucker said.

"Park," Ethan whispered.

When it was my turn, I leaned

forward, wrapped my lips around the straw, and drank my entire drink. *Holy Mother of All That is Good and Alcoholy! What a head rush. Brain Freeze*! Yum, it was like chocolate coffee.

Shane didn't take his eyes off mine. For a fleeting moment, tightness settled around those ice-cold blue eyes of his and I wondered what his point to playing this game was. Then my knees started to tingle and my teeth went numb. *What the heck was in that drink?*

This went on for three more rounds. People pegged other people in particular or the whole group. I drank two more Mind Erasers, the last one when Alex point blank asked me how many people I had slept with. Shane flipped out when I did and he slammed his hands down on the table and drunkenly yelled, "The point isn't to get fucking smashed, Grace! Be fucking HONEST!"

I just sucked on the straw, with

my eyes locked on his, until it made that slurpy *nothing is left on the bottom* sound and smiled, "Is that what the point is Shane?" I threw my straw at him.

He bolted up out of his seat. "My turn for a question!" he yelled. His ridiculously beautiful face twisted in a scowl, "Answer this, Grace, how was it to fuck Ethan? While you're at it, answer this, while you were fucking Ethan, did you think about that ex-boyfriend of yours that you loved so damn fucking much you couldn't be with me? Remember Grace? The night you told me about him while your hands were wrapped around my dick!" He slammed his palms against the table and his drink spilled across the top it.

Everybody fell silent. Next to me, Lea dropped her head in one of her hands and grabbed one of my hands to hold with the other. My head spun. Thank God, I had a few Mind Eraser's already, because if I were the least bit sober, I would have smacked him.

Again. Harder this time.

I sat up straighter, leaning forward so I could be perfectly clear when I gave my answer. I gave Lea's hand a little squeeze. "I don't know how it is to fuck him Shane, I did not *fuck* Ethan. I have never slept with anyone, actually. I was saving myself for that ex-boyfriend...he was in...um...jail, but when he got out, he didn't want me anymore and left." A sharp wave of embarrassment spiked through my veins. It spread out across my cheeks and down my neck, which I was sure, was leaving crimson streaks through my ivory skin.

Shane dropped back down in his seat, speechless.

Alex looked at me and then looked down into his lap, "Well, good evening there, *Bruce McHardon*, would you like to come out and meet the prettiest little virgin in the world? Grace, please, please, please, may I have your V-card. I will take such good care of it, I promise."

I smiled at him and laughed sarcastically, "Thanks, Alex, but I'm pretty sure I've just been royally fucked over, so I'm good for now. Thanks."

"There's no way you are a virgin! Like, you've never been with a guy before? What do you do?" Marie asked giving me a quick bark of laughter. *Like the dog she was.*

I locked my stare on Shane again, "I've been with guys, just not full blown sex. And what do I do? Well one of my best friends is a vibrator. It goes from *Oh Yeah* to *Who the Hell Needs a Man* in ten seconds flat." I turned my gaze on her, "You should try it, *Marie*. In the long run, it'll be a lot less heartbreaking than Shane can be."

Tucker jumped up, stumbled around the table and drunkenly threw an arm around me, "Grace, you're so beautiful. Please don't give Alex your V-card. I took you to Masa, Grace. We could go there again and get that champagne you love, and then we could get a room at any hotel in the city." One of his hands grasped my knee and I flung it off me enraged. Vomit burned the back of my throat.

"Oh, wow. Hmm...um...I rather stick burning hot pokers in my eyes and eat crap, but thank you so much for the offer Tucker. It was so kind of you, seriously," I said through clenched teeth.

Shane, the jackhat, still sat there, eyes all wide staring at me and brilliantly blue. So damn beautifully blue.

Lea sat next to me with her freaking head in her lap laughing her ass off. She tried to hide it, but I knew by the way her entire body shook that she was hysterical.

Ethan gave me an encouraging smile, "Well, I think it's pretty damn amazing."

Alex grabbed onto one of Ethan's shoulders, "Amazing? Dude,

that's the hottest thing ever. Oh my God, do you remember when she wore those little pink teddy bear pajamas?" He licked his lips looking at me, "Grace, my love, we need to create the most epic experience for you..." *We? Oh, my God, I don't even want to know what he's thinking right now.*

I stood up. I wobbled a bit, *so what.* I rested my hands down on the table so I wouldn't fall over. "Well, thank you everyone. Why the fuck don't ya'll (all of a sudden I was southern) just...just continue the discussion of my virginity (I had a bit of a problem pronouncing it correctly), because in no way would that be, let's say, uncomfortable or embarrassing in any way to me. E...specially in front of Hot Pink Lips there," I said pointing to Marie.

I pushed my chair in and moved backwards. "You guys can all take a vote on who I should hand my V-card to, there's no problem with that, right Shane?" I shoved the table at him a bit, it didn't move much, but I was too drunk to care. "Since I'm not in the fucking band anymore, right? I can fuck any one of these guys. Right? That's not a problem for you, right?"

He looked up at me with glassy eyes. He just stared at me with blank eyes and down turned lips. The expression was heart wrenching.

"Fuckasstard!" I called him.

Marie giggled drunkenly. "What's a fuckasstard, *Virgin*?"

I leveled my eyes to hers. *Holy Mind Erasers, I was so much drunker than five minutes ago when I was sitting down!* Did I say *fuckasstard?* What *is* a fuckasstard? "It's a fucking asshole retard or a fucking ass in a leotard. Shane's both and your lipstick is fucking awesome!" I shoved the table at him one more time for good measure. It didn't move, but I still didn't care.

I walked (stumbled) to the bar and sat myself on a stool (slipping off only twice). "Ry...an," I sang.

Seriously, I sang his name. *Sang it.*

Behind me, I could hear Lea giving Marie a complete verbal smack down. I smiled knowing Marie would never recover from what Lea would embarrass her with.

"Ry...an," I sang again. *Damn I could sing that boy's name.*

Laughing, Ryan came over. "Yes, gorgeous, what would you like?" I leaned over the bar (tipping the stool backwards, yet not falling. Now that's talent). *Wow, Ryan has nice lips.* "Ry. Ry, I need a Shane Eraser. Right. Now. Kay?"

Ryan leaned his elbow on the bar in front of mine and lowered his face so his lips were all I could see. "Grace, do you mean a Mind Eraser?"

I smiled at him. "Yeah, I'm going to need one of those too. Damn Ry. You have really kissable lips. I want to just suck on that lip ring." I slapped my hand over my mouth. "Wow, did I say that out loud? Psf."

Ryan smiled thanks, backed away and started making my drink. Then my ass started ringing and vibrating. It took me a minute to figure out what the hell was going on. Cell phone, back pocket. *Oh right*. I took it out and swiped the screen. It took me a minute.

Text Message 9:13 pm Shane: *I am so fucking sorry*

"Ha! Sure!" I yelled.

Ryan placed the drink in front of me and I drank it so fast I didn't even taste it. I slid the empty glass towards him and tried to smile, but I couldn't feel my face. And honestly, I didn't even freaking know if it was attached to the rest of my body; I was so numb.

Lea was beside me the next minute and wrapped her arms around me. "For what it's worth, Grace. Even if he isn't your angel anymore, that man has serious feelings for you. Put yourself out of your misery and talk to him."

I turned my face to her, "Lea, I don't need anyone to put me out of my misery, that's what the booze is for." I glanced behind us at the table. Shane was still staring blankly at me while everyone seemed to be discussing how, when, where and who my first sexual experience in this body should be. "I'm leaving before the gang bang starts. Besides, no matter how hot he is, that man doesn't deserve me. That man is not for me, that can't be my fate in this life." I spun the stool back around so I wouldn't be facing him.

"Who the hell are you, Grace, to decide that you can tell fate what to do? Has it worked for you yet? And how the hell do you know what your fate is supposed to be? This is how it is now. This, this is what you were given. A chance to live another life as Grace Taylor, don't mess this up for yourself Grace. And that man, right there is so freaking crazy in love with you that he can't even think straight knowing you might have been with someone else. You changed him, Grace, like a God damn lightning bolt to the heart. You can't tell me that you don't feel it, just looking at you two is like everybody is looking at something that's only written about in fairy tales. Take your chance with him, Grace. If it doesn't work, who fucking cares? Move on to the next guy. But don't let this one get away so fast."

Shocked by her words, I stumbled off the stool and turned around. Shane was in my face. My heart slammed and thudded against my chest painfully. He rested both his hands on the bar on either side of me, trapping me. My mouth went dry and my whole body started to tingle.

He moved in closer to me and gently tapped his forehead to mine. My knees turned to jelly and with one hand, he grabbed me around my waist to hold me up. Then he leaned his whole hard body against mine and I sank into him. He took a long deep breath and pulled me against him even closer. Ice-cold blue eyes stared at me for an eternity before he brought his lips to my ear and breathed the words, "Band practice tomorrow at ten. Make sure you bring your guitar this time."

So not what I thought would come out of his mouth. I was hoping for his tongue. Ugh...what the hell is wrong with me?

He let me go and stepped away from me, raking a hand through his hair. He walked backwards, blue eyes still on me. Then he turned around and walked out the door.

"Wow, it's like watching porn when you guys are that close," Lea giggled next to me.

I was still staring at the door. "Lea, I think I lost all the bones in my body, I feel all...fleshy."

"Hmmm...I think you're in heat," was her stupid reply. It made me smile drunkenly anyway, because she was probably right.

Chapter 13

My clock glowed five in the morning, when I felt a cool fingertip run down the length of my arm. When it reached my wrist, it traveled back up caressing my skin gently to my shoulder. More cool fingertips joined and brushed across my chest and neck.

I snapped my eyes open and wrestled myself out of the embrace. I remembered very clearly that I had gone to bed alone, after Lea held my hair back as I vomited everything I had ever ingested in my entire life into our toilet for an hour. Anyone who was in my bed after that was an uninvited guest and was about to get the ass kicking of their life.

I tumbled off the mattress and onto the floor when the lamp I always kept next to my bed flicked on. *By itself.*

Gabriel.

Oh crap, I thought this was all over. "Hello Grace. You're looking...well," he whispered.

I backed away from him until my back hit the wall. "Get out."

In a blur of motion, he was on me, one hand wrapped itself tightly around my waist, the other around the back of my neck and his lips covered mine. "I wanted to give you something," he hummed into my mouth as he kissed me. A rush of sublime pleasure spiked through my body, pure bliss surged through my veins, euphoria seeped through my pores, but the only thing that filled my mind was Shane's beautiful face.

Gabriel pushed my face away with his hands, causing my head to thump hard against the wall. His hands slid down my neck and his ancient blue eyes pierced into mine. "I can give you everything you have ever wanted, Grace. Don't think of him when it's my lips that are on you."

I pushed myself off the wall and leveled my eyes with his, "All I ever wanted was *him*."

"You still love him despite all he's done to you?" He leaned forward, placed his cool lips on my forehead, and chuckled, "Make no mistake, Grace. We will be together."

Then he was gone and I was left sitting alone in my bedroom wondering how Gabriel had gone from trying to kill me, to whatever the hell he was pulling now. After a while, my eyelids were too heavy to hold open any longer and the confusing theories I was debating in my head about Gabriel were too much and I fell back asleep.

At nine o'clock, the alarm clock on my phone went off that Lea so thoughtfully set for me the night before as I hugged the toilet in front of her. I jumped in the shower swearing to myself I'd never drink another Mind Eraser again. I swallowed a handful of aspirin because even the water drops from the shower spray felt painful. I dressed in a simple pair of jeans and purple shirt and slipped on my sneakers.

I had to drink a pot of coffee before I felt halfway human again.

At ten minutes to ten, I grabbed my coat and my guitar and headed out the door. A tiny butterfly flew in slow soaring loops in my belly when I thought about being in the studio again with Shane. *The way that man twisted my body and mind around was so not cool.* What was even worse was the unrelenting desire of me wanting him to. Holy Crappocalypse! I was turning into one of *THOSE GIRLS!* I wanted to punch myself in the face to knock some sense into myself. Ha, if only I could. I shook the thoughts out of my mind.

Outside my front door, a slight breeze moved the trees that lined my street. It smelled of warmth and sunshine and teased my nose with other pleasures of the spring that was yet to come. I smiled to myself as I walked the block noticing a few early sprouting tulips in my neighbor's flowers boxes that hung just below their front windows. Signs of life, new beginnings, and hope. The life of the tulip bulb paralleling mine, waking again to new life after each death sent a shiver through my body. Yet, I smiled knowing that this would be my last one. A strange thought to be happy about when I had a rouge angel trying to kill me. But Gabriel hadn't tried to hurt me that morning, had he? He just kissed me and offered to give me everything I ever wanted. I wondered if killing me would be the end of his plans for taking over the heavens, he couldn't have my soul if it was already there, could he?

I crossed the avenue to Shane's block and wondered if I'd have to spend the rest of my existence on constant guard about Gabriel. I hoped that one day, the Heavens and whoever had some pull up there, would finally figure out that enough was enough with Gabriel and his torture of my soul. If this was my last crack at being a human with a normal life, I didn't want him jumping out at me every so often from behind the curtains to try to make me his...whatever it was he wanted me to be.

I fumbled with the front door to the guy's apartment building almost dropping my guitar case. "Hey, Grace," Alex's voice murmured behind me.

I turned my head and smiled into the extremely hung over face of Alex, "Ha, Alex. You look like I feel." He had deep purple bags under very blood shot eyes.

He held up a fancy cardboard drink holder, "Yeah, I didn't get much sleep last night, but I have coffee. Shane sent me for it this morning when he told us he asked you to come and practice with us today." He leaned his back against the door to hold it open for me, nodding for me to go through. "Black with sweetener, right?"

I stopped walking and turned around laughing, "How'd you know how I liked my coffee?"

Alex's cheeks turned red and the color spread down his neck. For someone who was such a ham and so full of confidence, he sure did blush a lot. "Shane told me." He tilted his head and his green eyes turned serious. "Listen, I got to get this off my mind before we go in there, okay? Mad World isn't just a band that vomits out covers of other people's shit for a crap load of drunk people in a bar. We're a group of composers, writers, artists, and musicians. *You* are a part of that Grace." His smile was genuine. "I don't give a damn who you sleep or don't sleep with, even though I really would love to be your first. I don't care what Shane says, or what the hell was up his ass last night, but you're a huge part of this band now. You were, the minute you walked through the door in the audition and showed us you could play."

I slung my guitar case over my back and threw my arms around him giving him a hug. "Thanks Alex. That means a lot to me."

He barked out a laugh, "Damn girl, don't go rubbing up against me like that, my mind is doing all sorts of freakiness with your ass right now. Get in the studio before I cash in that V-card of yours!" Then he chased me down the stairs and right into the studio.

The door thrust open and slammed itself up against the wall with a bang. Everyone inside moaned and grabbed their heads. Ethan sat behind his drum kit with his forehead on his snare drum and a pair of sunglasses on. "Bro, don't make another sound until I get my coffee."

Brayden was strumming his bass, looked up, and nodded to us as we walked in. He looked like he slept more than anyone did and when he smiled at me, I could have sworn his teeth did that little sparkly cartoon gleam.

Shane sat on one of the couches with his acoustic guitar between his legs and his forehead resting on its neck, he held a small black pick between his lips. My heart stopped at the sight of him and started again double time when his blue eyes locked on mine. His posture became suddenly rigid and he sat motionless as if made of stone. Then came the slump of his muscular arms and shoulders that relaxed with his long deep exhale of breath as if he'd been holding it in waiting for me. The thought sent a cool electric shiver up the middle of my spine that caused my entire body to tremble. His eyes widened when he noticed and then one side of his gorgeous mouth went up to show half a stunning grin.

That's when it really hit me. If I had to stay here without my angel, then a life without having Shane in it was unimaginable, unthinkable, unbelievable, unfair, and just was not going to happen. I was a normal human girl, and now I had no one for my soul to stay faithful to. I can do whatever I wanted. Right then standing in front of that grin of his, being one of Shane's one-night flings was looking almost appetizing to me. Almost.

Ethan's deep voice cut my thoughts short. "Play that new rhythm again Shane, let's all listen to it and improvise. Then we could sit around and think of some lyrics for it."

I unbuckled my case and slid my guitar out. It felt alive in my hands and I couldn't wait for it to sing. With my guitar, I could write my own stories, my own poems, and my own destiny. No one could take away the feelings, the emotions or the truth of my notes. They could hide secrets and provoke images of words that never should be whispered. I could compose the melody of my aching heart and write into it my own happily ever after since no one seemed to think after all my suffering I deserved one. That's okay, I would make my own. My own story where the two distinct beautiful harmonies could merge as one and the sounds of it would...let you see a glimpse of heaven. I tossed my case against the wall with my coat and sat down crossed legged on the floor and tuned up.

"It's got lyrics," Shane murmured as he walked over and sat across from me crossing his legs like mine. Our knees brushed each other's and my body trembled. *Oh my God.*

"What did you say, bro?" Ethan asked.

Shane's eyes met mine; looking at me through those impossibly long dark lashes. Intense. Dangerous. Beautiful. "It has lyrics. I'm just not ready to sing them yet...it's called Until You," he told Ethan but his scorching gaze never left mine. Then out of the silence, a slow addictive melody languidly danced through the strings of his instrument and the world just ceased to exist around me. The notes started as tiny whispers; little echoes of murmurs; of secrets. They rose in volume and intensity and danced themselves along my skin, leaving goose bumps wherever they touched. The melody woke me like I was long dead and it was the first sound to touch my newborn ears.

Shane cocked his head at me, "Come on, girl, play with me," he whispered. His white tee shirt strained against the muscles of his chest and shoulders as his fingers moved along the strings.

A wave of small tremors washed along my hands and the tips of my fingers tingled with anticipation. I wet my lips to try to moisten the desert that sprouted in my mouth. My insides quivered with a slow buildup of something that I couldn't quite grasp at the identity of. *Maybe those elusive butterflies were about to attack.*

I listened closely to the melody Shane twisted into the air. Getting lost in its story, I closed my eyes and let my fingers sway themselves against the strings of my guitar. A stunning smile, more perfect than the sun, passed over his lips encouraging me to play more. I thrust myself into the emotional passion of the riff and I swear I felt something inside me break loose and unravel. Getting lost in the music, my body rocked, each note eased me into forgetting who I was, just leaving my raw soul and my guitar.

My fingers writhed along the strings, slow and steady notes telling of my hunger. His sharp tones answered me back with strength and power. Our harmony quickened together as if we needed a rush to our release, until an explosion of sound tore at our hearts, our souls. You couldn't tell our melodies apart, where his story begun or my story ended. We played as one.

All the anger, all the heartache and sorrow drifted away on each note and passion and intensity seemed to reverberate throughout the room. A raw heated tension twisted from the music and pulsated throughout my body until it murmured in our ears like a soft flapping of a butterfly's wings, unraveling until finally there was silence.

My skin tingled and I was hyper-aware of Shane's eyes on my lips, my eyes, my neck, my hands, all of me. He frantically searched my features caressing me with his eyes, his face paled and he swallowed hard, "I'm so sorry, Grace, I..."

"Please don't," I whispered bringing my gaze to his. "Let's not try to hurt each other anymore with words, there's been enough damage. Let's just play," I pleaded looking away. I know I was being impossible, but we had an audience and the words I wanted to say couldn't be said, *yet*.

His hands lingered over his strings, his focus still on me as the miles of sadness spread themselves out between us. It felt so wrong to be so far away from him and yet so wrong to be so close.

Chapter 14

I stayed at the studio for three hours running through all the Mad World songs with the guys, trying desperately to ignore all the sideways glances Shane was giving me and all the flat out requests from Alex to let him *"go where no penis has gone before."* I left immediately after Alex, who dubbed himself the *Orifice Bandit*, started discussing in detail about blogging the whole experience. *Gah!*

Needing to get coffee drunk, I headed to the nearest Starbucks for some sort of whipped cream infested caffeine. I was in dire need of scoring a sugar rush if I didn't want to go home to bed and crash until tomorrow. And Lea was already complaining that I've been spending too much time trying to crawl back into a coma. I ordered some caramel specialty drink and a scone that looked like it could pack ten pounds onto my bottom just by looking at it. I curled up on one of their ginormous purple couches and devoured it all. Then, and don't judge me, I ordered another coffee, this time chocolate flavored, and um...another giant scone. Hey, everybody deals with their demons their own way, I seem to eat and drink mine.

"Grace?"

Damn, just as I was about to slip into a food coma. I looked up to see Ryan's smiling face. He stood leaning his knee against the arm of the couch holding a coffee, dressed in a pair of black cargo pants and an ancient looking bomber jacket. A faded black baseball cap sat backwards on his head restraining the chunky layers of his blond hair.

"Hey, you doing okay?" He nodded to the empty spot on the couch next to me and asked, "Need some company?"

I gave the couch cushion a little pat, "Sure, Ryan, I'd love some." I gave him a smile when he sat down.

"So, how you been holding up?" he asked fixing a steady gaze on me.

"You must have had one hell of a hangover this morning, huh?"

I felt my cheeks burn. "Yeah, no use denying it, huh? I spent the night hugging the toilet while Lea held my hair back," I laughed.

"Doesn't sound like fun. It got even crazier after you left. I can't see any of those boys getting out of bed this morning," he chuckled. *I was afraid to ask.*

"Ah, they're fine. I just came from practicing with them."

He nodded his head and looked thoughtful for a minute. I studied his mouth as he smiled at me; he had a bottom lip piercing that every now and then he touched with his tongue. It was insanely sexy. "Yeah, I heard you guys are going to play a gig next Saturday, and Friday night we have the notorious Vixen4 playing." He crossed his arms, his dark eyes twinkling. "I can't wait to see you up on stage again. I absolutely love watching you. You're one heck of a musician."

"Thank you," I said. At that moment, my brain chose to remember I told him his lips were kissable the night before and I knew my cheeks had to have turned five shades of red.

Smiling shyly, he pulled himself off the couch, "So, um...I guess I'll see you around."

I tilted my head and nodded, smiling. "Yeah, probably."

"Will you be at the bar tonight?" he asked walking backwards towards the door.

"No. You working tonight?"

"Nope." He lingered by the exit doors and seemed to be deciding something. "Hey, Grace?" He walked back over to the couch and kneeled in front of me. "I don't know if you got anything going on with Shane, I'm doubting it because, well everybody knows how Shane is with girls, I mean look at the stuff he pulled with Marie last night, but well, I was kind of hoping that maybe I could take you out for dinner?"

Everybody knows how Shane is with girls. Oh, that burned; *but it was the truth. And, seriously what the hell did he do with Marie last night?* "Wow. Ryan. Sure, I'd love to go to dinner with you." *Take that, Shane!*

He smiled so wide two adorable dimples popped out on his cheeks, "Are you free tonight?"

"Yeah, I am."

"How about I pick you up around five. What kind of food do you like?"

"Anything but sushi."

****

Lea was sitting by herself in the kitchen with her feet up on the table listening to the small CD player we kept in the kitchen. The newest song from *Pink* filled the room and for some reason she was baking chocolate chip cookies.

I pulled my coat off and threw it over one of the kitchen chairs. "What in the world are you doing? God, it smells like heaven in here." I took a long deep breath and sniffed.

Yanking her feet off the table and dropping them onto the floor, she started jumping up and down. "Oh, my God! Really? Heaven effing smells like my chocolate chip cookies?" she squealed.

"Uh...no. Not really you freak," I laughed. "Why are you baking cookies?" I sat down on one of the chairs and pulled my knees up resting my chin on them.

Lea slumped back onto her chair. "Conner said that I wasn't domesticated. So I'm baking cookies." She shook her head slowly.

A crap load of giggles burst from my mouth. "Lea, it's not like you're not housebroken."

"Grace, he was serious. What am I supposed to do? He is *THE*

ONE!" She plopped her face in her hands and looked up at me with those big brown eyes.

Like I should be giving advice here. "If he is *The One*, then he wasn't complaining about it. Conner is crazy about you for everything you are and everything you aren't."

"You sound like my mother. By the way, I'm visiting them tomorrow and you should come, they haven't seen you since you were in a coma. I have off Monday so I'm staying the night, you don't have to if you don't want to, but it'll be more fun if you stay." She batted her eyes at me.

"Sure," I laughed. "I'll go and even stay the night. I'll pick up my bike. I was just thinking the weather is getting nicer to go riding."

Her eyebrows arched together and she folded her arms across her chest leaning forward. "Hold on a second. Are you drunk again?"

"Um...no why?"

"Because you're smiling." Her eyes widened and she bounced in her seat, "Ohhh...how was band practice. Did you talk to Shane?"

"Practice was great. Shane didn't say anything more than he was sorry and Alex wants to start a blog about me giving my virginity to him. And I have a date tonight."

"Oh, God, which one is it Shane or Alex? Please tell me you are going to pick Shane."

"Nope. Ryan."

"What? Ryan, bartender Ryan? Why can't you go out with Shane?"

"Because, Lea, Shane didn't ask and Ryan did. Shane is too busy with Marie and every other girl who thinks he's a rock star."

"Yeah, but it's Shane..."

"Please don't make it hurt more than it already does. Just help me forget him."

"Yeah, but...what about Shane?"

"I'm immune."

"No, you are not. I'm upset by this new information."

"Well, now. It really blows that I can disappoint you to such a high degree when it comes to the man-whore. Whom, by the way, if you remember correctly tried desperately to humiliate me last night and practically sexed up that Marie girl right on the table in front of me. Why would I want to chase after that?"

"You *have* seen him with his shirt off, right?" she asked cocking her head and lifting a single eyebrow at me.

I rolled my eyes at her so dramatically I thought I might have pulled a muscle. Thinking of Shane was giving me a headache. I threw my hands up into the air in surrender, "Lea. I want to lick him up like a freaking cherry ice pop, let him melt in my mouth, get all sticky and lick my fingers clean. But so does every other girl he meets. And I'm like the last girl in line, a line that freaking wraps around the corner."

Lea winced and grabbed one of my hands. "Gray, I think you're special to him. Look at how he reacted when he thought you slept with Ethan. The way you guys stare at each other, it's just plain pornographic."

I stood up and stretched, wanting desperately to end the conversation. "Look, I'm not going to stand here and lie. You know I want to be with him and maybe I will be. But I made a vow to myself to never be fooled again by a man or a halo wearing asshole with wings. Shane is Shane, he's not going to change for me and I don't know if I'd want him too. If something happens between us, it'll happen. But in the meantime, I thought you'd be happy that I was actually going to go on a regular date, and you didn't have to force me this time. Besides, Ryan is really good looking."

Lea sighed, "Yeah, but he's just not Shane."

"Who's not me?" a low raspy voiced interrupted. His stupid voice made my skin tingle. Lea and I both jumped at the sound of it. Lea's hands flew to her chest and she yelped loudly. "You just scared the crap out of me!"

Conner and Shane stood in the doorway of the kitchen, arms crossed over their chests both donning wrinkled brows. OhmyGod, did he look good. They'd went running, because he stood shirtless with a gleam of sweat that covered his skin. My eyes roamed the contours of the muscles of his chest and the way his tight skin slid down in that hard V-shape that disappeared under the covering of his running pants. *That's just ridiculous, nobody should look that good.*

"Uh," was all I could come up with.

Shane unfolded his arms and walked into the kitchen, tossing his cell phone on the table. He grabbed a water bottle from the refrigerator and leaned his body against the counter. His muscles flexed and stretched as he moved; it made my mouth fill up with way too much saliva. Twisting the cap off, he held the bottle to his lips and gulped the water down. A stream of it dropped down his chin and onto his chest. It was like watching a man's *Axe* cologne commercial. Pinpricks of heat spread across my chest, and I was struggling for air. Dear God, there is just something about this man that makes you want to stick your panties in his pockets and tell him you're half way there...

"Grace has a date tonight," Lea blurted out.

Shane's face twisted in anger and he crunched his empty water bottle with one little clench of his hand. "Letting Alex start his blog?" he asked through clenched teeth.

When I finally found my voice, which seemed to be stuck up my own ass, I wanted to toss myself off a building. "Ah, that would be a no. But, thanks for making me feel like one of your easy skanks. *Again*."

Lea craned her neck in front of my face. "Do you effing see that chest?"

"Shut up," I whispered.

Lea scrambled Conner out of the kitchen, shoving him into the hallway.

Shane lifted his arm and rubbed the back of his neck. The freaking muscles twisting under his skin was absolutely ridiculous. He moved toward me, muscles jumping. *Holy crap, I wasn't about to back down from him.* I jumped up and met him in the middle. I raised my chin to him and jabbed my hands onto my hips. "Think carefully about what you're about to say to me Shane."

One side of his stupid lips curled up and he took another step forward. I felt the edge of the kitchen table as I backed my ass into it. *Damn, I thought*

I was moving forward not backing away from him.

"Don't let him touch you," he whispered as he leaned down and pushed the palms of his hands on the table on either side of me, trapping me between his arms. I stopped breathing.

"Give me a good reason not to," I said.

One hand slid to my waist and moved under my shirt, skimming his fingertips over my skin. He leaned down close, breathing me in. Those damn butterflies flew straight to my groin.

His cell phone rang on the table next to us. A picture of a topless Marie, in the bathroom of Boozer's came to life on the screen. We both stared at the phone for a minute before he pressed ignore and stepped back raking one hand through his hair.

"Wow, Shane. Just wow. How has your dick not have shriveled up and fallen off by now?"

"I didn't sleep with her."

"Ha. Every damn time your lips move, out pops a lie. The problem is, Shane, I don't care if you did. Get out of my way, I have to get ready."

"Don't let him put his hands on you, Grace. Just. Don't."

"Oh sure, good idea, no hands. Yeah, I like the thought of his tongue on me much better." I watched his fists clench and knuckles turn white as I left the room. I slammed the door to the bathroom and ran the water ice cold, ripped off my clothes and stepped in. I loathed that he had that picture of her on the phone, but I loved the fact that he didn't want anyone else to touch me. *Oh, and the fact that I had much bigger boobs than her.* And I know I'm completely acting like I'm thirteen years old, but I've never ever had these feelings before, and well, that fact made it feel a lot better.

Chapter 15

I was blow-drying my hair when Lea slipped into my bedroom. She plopped herself in front of my drawers and opened each one searching for something. I clicked the hair dryer off and opened my closet door.

"Shane's going insane inside," she said looking at me smiling. She pursed her lips and turned her attention to my underwear drawer, "Why can I never find any matching sets?"

"Why?"

"Because when I have my undies and bra match I really feel like I have my crap together and I can do anybody, I mean anything," she giggled and winked. She smiled and did a little cheer when she found a red matching set.

"Focus, Lea. Why is Shane going insane?"

"Maybe because the girl that he's in love with is going on a date with someone else?" She threw the bra and panties at me and I put them on. "Hey, let's have some fun. I double dare you to walk out there like that," she pointed to me, "And let's see if Shane doesn't profess his undying love for you."

"Shut up," I laughed slipping a simple black dress over my head. "Shane Maxton is not in love with me."

Lea walked over to where I stood looking at myself in the mirror and pulled my chin so I could look in her eyes. "Yeah, Grace. I kind of think he is. So just face it, you just caught yourself a Bad Ass, what are you going to do about it?"

"Lea. I'm going out to dinner with Ryan. I'm thinking maybe Shane should shower that skank off from last night before I decide to do anything with him!"

I stormed out of my room and made my way into the living room to grab my coat. Shane was pacing back and forth in front of the couch and

Conner was sitting on one of the chairs. Whatever their conversation was, it stilled as soon as I walked in.

Shane's eyes raked over my legs, my hips, my arms, dragging them slowly over the rest of my body. "Oh God," he whispered as his hands clenched and unclenched at his sides and all I wanted to do was run to him. Those icy cold blue eyes had me paralyzed and I swore I felt my panties melting down my legs. *God, what that man can do to my insides with one of his looks.*

The sound of the doorbell made my mouth dry and I ran to open it so I wouldn't hear it again. Ryan leaned against the doorjamb with a wide smile.

"Man, you look beautiful, Grace," he said pushing off of the door.

A sharp pounding headache burst from behind my eyes and I clamped my teeth down from the pain. Behind me, I could hear Conner and

Shane yelling. The words were all jumbled together like they were stumbling drunkenly to my ears. All I heard was the anguish tone of them. Then Shane pushed through the front door, I leaned back to let him through. As he stepped by, he reached his arm past my waist and thrust a wrapped condom into one of my closed fists. He brushed himself against my hip, leaned in close, glaring at me right in the eyes. Time seemed to slow down at that moment like we were locked eye to eye forever. For an eternity, and I knew what an eternity was. He slowly brought his lips to my ear, "Just pull the fucking trigger on me now, *please*." His warm breath sent shivers along my neck. It made me remember his touch on my skin, his lips on mine. That damn man ruined all other men for me, with those freaking lips that you can forget people in. He could easily erase all my heartache if he wanted to.

I could feel the heat of his body against mine. It felt like an inferno blazed from inside his chest.

"Hey, Shane," Ryan said.

Shane did nothing but shove his hands in his pockets and storm off down the street. Conner was through the door the next second, flying down the stairs after him.

Ryan tugged on his ear and chuckled, "Everything okay?"

My eyes were still on Shane as Conner caught up to him. They walked to the corner of the block together and then disappeared from my sight.

Ryan waited for my reply, puffed out his cheeks with air and blew it out.

I looked at him for the first time since I opened the door. My head shook back and forth and my heart thudded in my chest slow but hard and loud. There were very few things I was sure of at that moment. One, I did not feel like eating anymore. Two, Ryan was not Shane. Three, my palms were sweating from holding onto the door so hard. Four, Ryan was definitely not

Shane.

"Ryan, I'm so sorry. But, I don't think it's a good idea that we go out tonight." I bit my bottom lip when I watched his lips turn down into a frown. "I think there are some things I have to work out with Shane. I'm sorry, but I'm not one of those girls who would lead someone on if I knew I had feelings for someone else."

"Yeah, okay, Grace. If you change your mind though, or if he messes up, give me a call." I didn't watch Ryan walk away. I closed the door and sat down heavily on the floor.

Oh, crap. I was starting to have real feelings for Shane Maxton, and I had no idea what to do about it.

"Gray? Grace? What's wrong?" Lea ran down the hall to me and threw herself on the floor. "What the hell did I miss? I always miss stuff!"

"Nothing. I'm going to change. I'll be out in a minute," I whispered and walked to my room.

Turning the knob on my door, I pushed the door open with my hip and was half way in the room when I felt the drop in temperature. I stepped in further and the door slammed shut by itself behind me. Gabriel leaned against the far wall of my room, arms folded across his chest; his eyes closed.

I threw my coat on the mattress and flung the crunched up condom on the floor. I stalked towards him with my fists shaking. My stomach slammed against the walls of my body and a sharp pain seared through my jaw from clenching my teeth so tightly. "Leave."

Gabriel's eyes blinked open, his stoic expression killing all my thunder. "I miss you."

"You're delusional. Get out." I turned my back to him. *Stupid me.* I was slammed flat on my face across my mattress, all the air knocked out of my lungs. I struggled to move, to lift up my body, but I couldn't, Gabriel's cold steel body was straddled over mine. All my muscles tightened waiting for the blow, the hit, anything.

But, Gabriel just ran his hand gently over my back and through my hair. Vomit burned the back of my throat and tears filled my eyes. The minute I could break free, I was going to kill him. *How do you kill an angel? Put him in sunlight, shove garlic in his face, throw water on him…what?*

He clutched a handful of my hair, tugged my head off the mattress, pulled his face to my ear, and breathed in deeply. In a blur of motion, he flipped my entire body over so I was now laying flat on my back. One of his hands still had my hair as the other one pushed itself up my leg. Both his knees pinned my arms against my body as his lips skimmed over my neck. A pure thick, black darkness seeped through my skin down to my bones when he gently placed his lips to mine. I clamped my mouth shut, but it made no difference, the visions came.

My beloved angel walking away

from me, lounging on his wings in the heavens, and *Shane*. Shane in between the legs of countless women, his eyes burning with lust. Then there was Gabriel, his gentle touch, his warm kisses, his love, "You're my heart, Grace."

I squirmed beneath him and the minute my lips broke free, I turned my head and vomited all over my sheets. "Get off me, Gabriel," I heaved. "The way that you have destroyed my heart, just proves that you don't have one." I spit, shoved and bucked under him loosening his hold until I finally struggled free. When my right hand broke free, I pulled back and punched him in the face. I twisted myself up and kicked him as hard as I could.

He grabbed a hold of my wrist, trying to tug me back to him.

"Stop, Gabriel! Just stop!" I pushed him away. "I get to live this life! I get it! You can't hurt me anymore. I will fight you to the end of this life, Gabriel. And, when it's the end, I get to go to heaven this time. You want to kill me now? I get to *him* faster!"

"Grace. It would be very prudent of you to fear me."

"Oh, go to hell, Gabriel! What are you going to do, flap your wings around and throw your halo at me? Oh, I'm shaking in fear. Really."

His lips pulled up into a snarl, "I can make your last life hell, Love."

"All my lives have been hell, Gabriel, one more ain't going to break me." The slamming open of the front door of my apartment made Gabriel chuckle and then as I blinked my eyes, he disappeared.

Night had fallen and dark shadows danced against the walls of my room. My alarm clock lay upside down, but I could still read the numbers 12:04. Somehow seven hours had passed.

I changed into a small tank top

and boy shorts, threw my sheets into the hamper, and listened at my door to the voices coming from down the hall. Whatever was going on out there had made Gabriel leave.

A light knock on my door rattled the wood against my eavesdropping ears. "Grace, are you awake?" Lea called.

I opened the door and stuck my head out. Lea was in almost the same matching sleepwear as me. Her head nodded towards the kitchen. "I'm gonna need some help tonight." She pulled my arm, dragged me into the living room and held her hands out to show me what was going on. Conner was attempting to do a headstand against the wall and Shane had made a pillow tent on the floor with all the cushions from our couch. The apartment smelt like burnt cookies.

Conner fell on his head and giggled, "There's my beautiful girlfriend. Shane. Shane? Sha...ne? Where the frig is Shane?"

Shane popped his head out of the cushions and waved like an imbecile, "I'm in my fort."

Conner crawled towards the *pillow fort* and looked up at me, "Uh oh, Shane. Look who's here. Shane? Shane?" he whispered. "Dude, ask her to get in the fort with you."

"Okay, that's enough. Come on, Conner, let's go to bed," Lea said pulling him up off the floor. He stumbled drunkenly against the wall giggling and slid against the wall down the hallway with Lea helping him walk. "Grace, Shane really, really, really likes you…," he drunkenly sang.

Lea looked back at me with a small tight smile. "You got Shane?"

I tried to smile back but I don't think it reached my lips, "Yeah, sure." I turned my head back to the pillows as they all crumbled around him.

He looked up at me, stared blankly, and slurred, "God, Grace, you're so fucking exquisite."

I wanted to wrap that moment up in tissue paper and save it forever someplace near my heart, just so I could take it out and look at it when the world was too harsh. The beautiful drunk boy in the pillow fort in my living room telling me I was exquisite. My eyes welled with tears and I needed to take a deep breath of air, yeah that moment was perfect.

I walked over to him and started putting the pillows back on the couch as he sat there and watched me. I opened one of the closets where we keep extra pillows and sheets and fixed the couch for him to sleep on. He staggered to his feet and collapsed on the couch, pulling me down sitting me next to him. He pulled his tee shirt off and threw it on the coffee table. He leaned back against the pillows of the couch and touched his hand to mine.

"How was your date?" he slurred.

I looked down at his fingers softly stroking the skin of my mine and

I entwined his fingers in mine. "I didn't go."

He lay down along the couch and pulled me into his arms laying me against his body. "I know I'm drunk as hell, Grace, but, just stay with me. I need you like I fucking need to breathe."

"Shane..."

Softly he placed his lips on the nape of my neck, just below my ear, inhaled deeply and kissed me. "Shut up and go to sleep, Grace."

Another moment to keep safe...*because this...this felt so perfect.*

Chapter 16

The plan was to leave for Lea's parents at ten o'clock. We were going to drive the Jeep there and leave it, I barely used it and alternate side of the street parking for street cleaning in Manhattan was a pain in the neck.

I slid off the couch around nine that morning and jumped in the shower. I dressed in a simple pair of black yoga pants and a tight pale pink thermal long sleeved shirt. I twisted a tie into my hair and donned a long thick ponytail. I bounced out of my room at the first scent of coffee.

Conner and Shane both sat at the kitchen table holding their head in their hands. Lea leaned up against the counter with a wide grin on her face.

"GOOD MORNING, BOYS!" I yelled at the top of my lungs. Conner cringed and Shane lifted his blood shot eyes at me shaking his head.

"You're pure evil," Shane whispered letting his head collapse back onto his arms.

Conner looked back and forth between Lea and me, "Why the hell are you guys up so early on a Sunday making a racket waking us up?"

Lea placed her hands on her hips shaking her head, "Con, I told you. Grace and I are going to my parents. We'll be back tomorrow. Grace is going to pick up her bike *and* maybe we'll go out dancing tonight." She winked at me, "What do you say, Gray? You up for dancing at one of the beach clubs?"

"Now that sounds like a good idea, I'm going to need to pack a little skirt and some heels then." I poured myself a cup of coffee and stirred in some sweetener.

Shane lifted his head again and leaned back on the kitchen chair. Raising his hands, he folded them behind his head, blood shot blue eyes glaring at me. Cold and calculating. *Uh oh*. He leaned forward with a serious expression on his face, "So how was your date with the bartender last night, finally get laid?"

My coffee cup froze midway to my lips. "Are you serious right now?" Lea gave Conner a sideways glance and both of them started to leave.

I stood up before anyone else could, slamming my cup of coffee down on the table. The dark bitter liquid sloshed over the top and splashed across the table. I slithered up close to him; he didn't make a move to lean away. I was so close to him I could feel the anger radiating off him like heat. I dropped my face to his and met those blue eyes with mine. "He damn near wrecked my ass he was *so big*. Thanks for the condom, one just wasn't enough though. So, yes Shane, I am one well-fucked girl right now!" I moved my face in closer to his and his lips parted. "I didn't know how much I needed to be with him, it's like I needed him like I needed to breathe. Ever felt like that, Shane?"

Shane's jaw tensed and he took a long, deep breath, blowing it back out through clenched teeth. He pulled himself out of his chair, really slow, his eyes never leaving mine. "What did you just say?"

I took a step away from him. I looked over to Lea, "I'm going to pack some more stuff. Let me know when you're ready to leave." I walked around him, his solid body still standing there, muscles all stiff and tight, knuckles white. When I hit the hallway, tears burned my eyes, and I despised myself for letting myself have any feelings for him. I hated being human. I hated this place. I hated being here, stuck here.

"My God, Shane, you are the biggest ass hat in the whole world!" I heard Lea say. "You ran out of the house like a God damn five year old yesterday and she told Ryan she couldn't go out with him! She stayed here the whole night. Alone!" I heard her stomp to the hallway, "And maybe you were too damn drunk to remember, but when I woke up this morning, she was wrapped in your arms on the couch, Shane. She stayed with you the whole night. She's right about you. You don't deserve someone like her."

I slammed the door to my room, tears blurred my vision and an icy cold breeze sent goose bumps across my skin. Gabriel stormed across the room, sharp, steely wings out, stopping an inch from my face. I moved back, banging my body against the door, panic tore my brain. His body crashed into me and his lips slammed onto mine.

Images ripped through my skull, tearing my mind to shreds. Shane at the bar with Conner, in the bathroom with Marie, then another girl, *then another*. My angel laughing down at me then looking away, as if I had never meant anything to him. Gabriel tore his lips off mine, ancient blue eyes locked with mine. His hands raked themselves up my sides, under my shirt, icy claws turning my heart to stone.

I raised my hands to his head

and grasped handfuls of the sharp shards of his hair. I could feel the sharp slices of pain and the spikes cutting through my hands, but it was a distant feeling like it was someone else's body. I pulled his face back towards me and kissed him. Disgust swept through my body, but I could not control my actions; I was a strung up puppet following my master.

His breathing quickened and he kissed me back with sheer lust. Cold hands slid like wet steel against my skin. I swallowed hard as the waves of darkness that were filling me crashed above my head drowning me. A heavy thick shadow blanketed my soul.

A sharp thud against the door stopped the darkness from consuming me. I blinked my eyes open to a cold empty room. "You will happily hand me your soul one day, love, or I'll take everyone and everything you love in this life away. I promise you that, Grace. Give yourself to me and everything we ever wanted will be ours for the taking," the soft whispered words in my ears ran across my skin making it scorch with fiery pinpricks of heat. I raised my hands to my lips and tasted blood. I looked down to my trembling hands. Hundreds of small slices, like paper cuts, covered my palms.

Another sharp thud vibrated against the door. "Grace, please open the door," Shane's husky voice whispered.

Tremors shook my body as I moved to open the door. Shane stood statue-like in the hall, head faced up to the ceiling as if looking, or waiting for divine guidance. I wanted to warn him it never comes, but I couldn't form any words. His eyes fell from the ceiling to my face and he took a step forward. He slowly brought his hands to my chin and touched each side of my face, his breaths came out labored and his voice was hushed and pained, "I don't know how to do this, tell me how to fix us."

Hiding my shaking bleeding hands from him, I leaned my face into his warm hands. "Just be my friend, Shane, start there. Anything else may kill us both."

Chapter 17

I pulled my Jeep to the side and double-parked in front of our apartment. I turned my audio system on and waited for Lea. *So Far Away* by *Avenged Sevenfold* blasted through my speakers. *Perfect song. How do you live without the people you love?*

The Jeep's door opening brought me back from my far away thoughts. Lea yanked the front seat forward and took our bags to the back. Shane and Conner climbed into the backseat silently. Shoving our bags in the small space behind the seats that pretended to be my trunk, Lea then walked back around to the passenger side and climbed in. She pulled the door closed and gave me a small sideways glance. "They wouldn't let us go without them."

As I pulled the Jeep forward, I noticed a small smile tug at the corner of her lips.

"Love this band," Shane murmured from the back seat. I lifted my eyes to the rearview mirror and his stone cold blue eyes shined right back at me. We held onto that stare for a minute until I looked away and turned the volume of the song higher. I didn't want to hear anything else he had to say while he stared at me like that. I focused my thoughts on driving and sang along to the music.

I headed south down Second Avenue and inched through the traffic across the Queens Midtown Tunnel. Lea moaned and complained about how many people lived in the city and Conner continuously kicked at her seat. When we finally emerged from the traffic of the tunnel, we had already been in the Jeep for an hour and I was plotting everyone's death. Tons of cars traveled slowly along with us as we drove through the Queens Midtown Expressway all the way to Woodhaven Blvd. After two hours in stand still traffic, Lea had all the windows open and was singing horribly to *Limp Bizkit's* rendition of *The Who's Behind Blue Eyes*.

Finally, the traffic thinned out and we flew down Cross Bay Blvd over the dark waters of the bay that filled itself with the cold Atlantic Ocean. The March winds outside the Jeep were cool and building in fury. When I pulled up in front of Lea's old Belle Harbor childhood home, a pang of sadness throbbed in my heart when I looked at my old house next door. The memories of Jacob and Lea as children running through the yard down to the beach filled my mind. I killed the ignition and looked up into my rearview mirror; Shane's stare reflected back. I had the strangest feeling his eyes never moved off me, like he had watched me the whole damn ride. My butterflies gave my insides a little kick.

As soon as our feet stepped on the front walk, Lea's mom, Caroline, burst through the front door and ran at us like she hadn't seen us in years. "Anthony! They're finally home!" she called into the doorway of the house. *Oh God, finally home?* She grabbed Lea and me up in her arms and the smell of her vanilla soap wafted to my nose. It did feel like home.

Caroline, let go of Lea, but held me at arm's length and looked me up and down beaming. "You look healthy enough, but you need to put on more weight. You're all skin and bones, dear."

Lea barked out a laughed and patted my shoulders, "Don't worry, Ma, at the rate she's been devouring ice cream and alcohol, she'll pack on the weight within the next week. Her ass is gonna be so big she'll have moons orbiting it."

Caroline rolled her eyes at her daughter, "You need help, dear. Let's go in and say hello to your father." She turned to Shane and Conner and kissed them both on the cheek, "Hello, boys, come on inside. Anthony has a game on and I'll have lunch ready in a minute and we'll see if we can fatten her up a bit today." She grabbed Lea and Conner by the shoulders and shoved them forward.

I remained on the front walk, my future-moon-orbiting-ass and me, with my mouth hanging open. When I stepped forward, Shane caught me and pulled me back. Not fighting him at all *(I mean, come on, who would? His arms were holding me!)* I fell back into him, my back pressed tight up against the front of him, one of his hands held my wrists, restraining me from moving. *Okay, I liked this. I really freaking liked this.* With his other hand, he brushed aside the hair that fell in waves down my neck and brought his mouth to my ear. He sucked his breath in and lowered his voice, "I'm kind of in love with your ass the way it is."

With his body all smashed up against me like that, I could not for the life of me think clearly. "Shane, shut up. I really hate you right now." *And stop making me have sex with you in my head! It's like a porn movie on repeat in here.*

His raspy deep chuckle tickled my neck and shot spikes of heat deep

in my belly. "No, you don't, Gray."
And then? And then the jerk kissed my neck in that awesome panty melting spot right below the ear, with his warm OPEN lips. And I needed a change of panties. ASAFP! Mine were soaking wet.

Now I'm standing in the middle of the block where I've grown up, in front of my almost-family's house with the most delicious man I had ever seen, without wings, who is running his lips against my skin. Usually, this being Shane Manwhore Maxton, I try to practice self-preservation, and not give in. It usually is the only way to survive against Shane Maxton with your heart intact. But this man was affecting my panties in all the right ways. I spun around in his arms easily. It's my lucky day and he's still restraining my wrists, which makes my thighs tremble. "You know, Shane, if you could stop all your insane outbursts against me for five minutes, I would really love to see what that warm tongue of yours could do to the rest of my body."

Those gorgeous blue eyes widened and for a few heartbeats (I heard mine clearly pounding hard against my rib cage) he just stared into my eyes. Then his eyes seemed to darken as my words slid right over him and his hold on me changed. He tightened his grip on my wrists, his whole body stiffened and he pulled me closer to him. He sucked in a slow deep breath and his eyes went to my mouth. God, did I want him to kiss me.

Letting go of one of my wrists, he gently laced his hand through my hair. A hot rush of adrenaline shot through my veins. *Please kiss me. Please kiss me.*

"Are you two coming in? Lunch is almost on the table!" Caroline yelled from the doorway. *Seriously, right now?* Did she not see the ridiculously perfect man just about to kiss me?

Shane let out a low audible moan and his hands fell to my waist and turned me towards the front door. "Ah…yep. We're um…coming, Mrs. R," he said breathlessly. One hand slid to the small of my back and gently pushed me to walk alongside him into the house. His blue eyes looked down at me and he brushed a strand of dark hair that fell across my cheek behind my ear. That damn beautiful smirk that was on his face made me want to climb up his body and lick his lips. *Oh, dear God, I'm in trouble.*

We walked into the house and I just knew my cheeks had to have been flaming bright red because of the questioning look from Lea I was getting. I bit my bottom lip and looked away from her quickly.

"There's the comatose kid! How are you feeling, Gracie?" Lea's father, Anthony asked, opened his arms out wide and grabbed me in a giant hug. "Ah, Jesus, Caroline! You're right, she's all skin and bones." He shoved me in front of one of the plastic covered dining room chairs and pushed my shoulders down until I sat. He kept one hand on my shoulder and the other he held out for Shane to shake. "Hey, and the *rock star* is here too! How you doing, son?"

Shane shook his hand and offered him one of those killer smiles of his, "Hey, Mr. Rossi. Thanks for having me today. I'm doing great. How have you been?"

Anthony Rossi, who has acted as my father for the last ten years, stepped up closer to Shane. "Good, good, son. I'm sure glad that everything was settled and you didn't have anything to do with hurting our Gracie. Lea told me that you were the one to help her when that son of a bitch got his hands on her. We're forever in your debt, Shane. I knew you couldn't have hurt her." He slid in front of the dining room chair at the head of the table and sat down leaning back with his arms folded across his chest. A serious expression crossed his features, "So did anybody get the son of a bitch, yet? Or am I going to have to make some calls…"

"Shut up, dear." Caroline cut him off while placing an enormous platter full of spaghetti and meatballs on the table. She waved her hands at him to settle him down. "Let's have a nice delicious Sunday lunch and not talk about all this horror, please." She fanned her hands over her face dramatically, "You men can talk about all this *Law and Order*, *CSI* crime stuff after eating, Grace has been through enough already. She doesn't want to hear anymore." She walked back into the kitchen only to re-emerge with more food; salad, Italian bread, garlic knots and a huge pitcher of water with slices of fruit floating in it. *Holy crap, she wasn't kidding about fattening me up!*

Lea and Conner sat down next to each other in the two seats across from me, leaving Shane to sit in the chair next to me. My body shook with anticipation. Not only because I was sitting so close to him, but because I knew what Sundays were like at the Rossi house. Crap was about to fly and it was Lea's favorite game and mine.

Every Sunday we had ever spent eating with her parents we secretly played what Lea and I called *Oh Dear*. It's really easy and quite funny if played correctly. You begin the game with two unsuspecting parents that ask the most inappropriate questions to their children. The game starts when one parent player asks another player an inappropriate question while eating dinner. That player has to come up with a funny verbal comeback to the said question without offering up any truthful answers. The winner is the first person to make a parent say *Oh Dear*.

Caroline served everyone a heaping plate of food while Lea and I acted like two thirteen year olds giggling and waiting for the game to start.

Caroline dumped three gigantic mounds of spaghetti on my plate and topped it with four meatballs, three garlic knots and a half of a loaf of Italian bread. I bit my lip to stop myself from laughing. "Gracie, dear. When was the last time you ate any food?" *And the game begins.*

"Um, I had a handful of Tic-tacs on Thursday," I answered. Lea looked down into her food so she wouldn't start laughing already. I slurped up a long strand of spaghetti.

"I can tell, dear. Don't you girls ever cook for yourselves? You do know how to make nutritious foods, don't you?" She leveled her glare at Lea.

Lea looked thoughtful while she chewed on her food. She took her time swallowing and then answered. "Well, we did make some Spam with Oreo Cookie glaze last Wednesday. That was yummy, right guys?"

Shane and Conner looked at her like she just popped her head off.

"I see," Caroline grumbled. "Well does anyone have any good news or surprises to tell us?"

"I won a whole dollar in a scratch off game!" I sang.

"Have you been drinking, dear?" she reprimanded me.

"No more than usual," I smiled.

She gave me a little knowing smirk and put her attention on Lea. "Well, Lea, I just can't understand why you're not married yet," she baited.

"I'm just lucky, I guess. No really, I mean, I love Conner and all but I'm holding out for Johnny Depp," Lea answered batting her eyes.

"And you, Grace? What's your excuse?"

"I'm waiting for the zombie apocalypse, that's the theme of the wedding I want. I figured all the guests could just eat each other and I could really save a few bucks on food, you know?"

"No, no, Caroline. Why should these girls buy the cow when you could get all the milk for free?" Anthony added joining in the game with us.

"Oh my. Well, I just want to know if either of you will be giving me grandchildren anytime soon?"

"I'm allergic," I laughed.

"Conner's family eats their young, so that's a no go for us," she smiled.

"Oh dear," she mumbled.

Chapter 18

After eating, we all sat around the living room too stuffed to move. Shane sat next to me on one of the smaller couches and every so often he'd move and brush the back of his hand against mine sending jolts of electricity up my arm. Then when everyone else was in a heated discussion about who to name the grandchildren after, he slowly slid his pinky along the side of my hand and up to the tip of my elbow. My breath caught. He must have heard it because his eyes instantly locked on mine and one side of that beautiful mouth lifted up in one of his sexy grins.

"Want to take a walk?" he asked in a husky whisper that I could feel softly fall against my neck.

I couldn't help but smile at that beautiful face. "I have a better idea. Want to go for a bike ride?"

Disappointment settled over his face, but he still agreed, "Yeah, sure, but I was kind of hoping I could hold your hand while we walked."

I laughed knowing full well he had no idea what I was really asking him for. "Come on, the garage is out back, and I'll let you hold my hand." I looked over to Lea and smiled, "Shane and I are going for a ride. We won't be too long."

Lea smiled wide, eyes twinkling, "Sure when you guys get back we can get ready and go somewhere on the beach to dance tonight." She gave me a wink. "Have fun."

I grabbed our jackets and we threw them on. Leading him through the backyard I warned, "You might want to zip up; it gets pretty cold by the ocean if we ride fast."

Opening the garage door, I let out a low sigh. One of my most prized treasures sat before me.

"Oh, fuck me. Grace, I thought you said bike! That's a…"

I handed him a helmet from off one of the shelves and placed one on top of my head. My matte black Harley Davidson Super Low 883 sat in the middle of the room, Shane's mouth hanging open wide next to it.

"A Super Low 883?" I laughed. "You still up for a ride, Shane?"

"Crap, Grace! Every single day I spend with you...you have managed to shock me and turn my world upside down..."

I raised my leg, slung it over the bike, and pushed it out of the garage and backyard into the front of the house. Shane walked alongside me stunned.

"Grace, there's no freaking way I'm riding bitch behind you."

I slid myself over the gas tank and patted the seat behind me. Then you drive I said throwing him the keys.

"God, you're so damn beautiful."

He threw his leg over the bike and placed the key in the ignition turning it. The engine roared to life and the vibrations sent shivers through my body. I always felt so powerful with a motorcycle beneath me, between my legs, but now I had Shane behind me and I felt whole, breathless, and insane with want. He expertly kicked it into gear and eased off the clutch. Then he kicked his feet up and I placed my feet on top of his. He wrapped one hand around my waist while the other steered. I leaned back into him and smiled as we cruised down the streets alongside the sandy beaches of the Atlantic Ocean. He wrapped one arm around me and held my hand. I prayed the cops didn't stop us for riding like this.

The salty cold air stung our faces and bit at our ungloved knuckles. The powerful hum and heat of the engine under my legs did nothing but add to the intense desire that burned through me to just spin around and wrap my legs around him. We drove along the side of the crashing waters for a good two hours until he drove up onto the boardwalk and kicked the kickstand down with his foot. Leaning the bike to one side, he climbed off and helped me get down. Wordlessly, he took my hand and pulled me onto the beach, over the sand and right to the cold waves that crashed themselves against the shore. We both shivered from the cold of the air and the ride, but I never felt hotter in my entire life.

He sat down on the sand and pulled me down sitting me beside him. Our hands lingered in each other's and neither of us said anything. We just quietly stared out over the shimmering waters of the Atlantic savoring the warmth that had sparked an inferno in our hands. Butterflies with wings afire danced along my skin.

Shane pulled me closer to him and sat me over his lap with my legs draped over his. The ease of his movements was so fluid, as if he'd pulled millions of girls onto his lap daily, for years. The thought crushed me, and I desperately tried to claw it out of my brain, but I couldn't. The sudden urge to throw myself, and my stupid sabotaging of a perfect moment, into the ice-cold water was suddenly very tempting.

My thoughts wrestled with themselves in my head until he softly cupped my chin in one of his hands and pulled my face to look at him. My heart felt like it was trying to lurch out of my chest and jump right into his hands. He studied my face and a mix of emotions darkened his features, our faces moved closer.

Desperately, I tried to calm my breathing, but he slowly slid his hand from my chin across my jaw, over my neck and into my hair and I'm practically panting. He pulled my head towards him, his lips gently pressed against mine, and then he slowly pulled away. And, I swear my lips ached from the loss of contact with his skin.

He leaned back on his arms and a sexy smile played on his lips, "So what the heck was all that crazy talk with Lea's parents?" *Oh, my God. He wants to talk right now? When we go out later, I am ordering a Sex on the Beach, right in front of him, just so he knows what was on my mind when we were here!*

I moved a bit off his lap and lay down on my side in front of him leaning my head against my hand. "It's just a funny game we play when her mother asks us inappropriate questions, Caroline knows we were just teasing her."

"They've been like parents to you, huh?"

My eyes wandered out across the ocean. "Yea, they took Jacob and me in after my parent's accident and after my release from the hospital."

I looked back at him studying his features, trying to pick out any flaw, or imperfection. Nothing. I would have sworn, once long ago, that angels were only made to look like that.

He watched me watching him. Clearing his throat, he took a deep breath. "So what *did* happen with that ex-boyfriend of yours?"

Our eyes measured each other's for a few moments, lingering on our thoughts before the words could mar our feelings.

I weighed my options in the moment and decided that I wasn't going to run, I wasn't going to fight Shane like I'd always done. I had spent the first weeks of knowing him just judging him for all the girls he's been with. He never did anything to hurt me or lie to me. He saved my life three times and even went to jail for me. I owed this man anything he wanted. And I wanted desperately to give it to him. I had nothing holding me back now.

"I was an idiot," I whispered looking away. "I just loved him so completely that everything and everyone dulled in comparison to him. But it wasn't in his nature to love me the same way. When he had the chance to take me with him, or stay with me, he just left."

He looked at me incredulously. "It's kind of hard to believe that someone would leave you, Grace. Do you still love him?"

The strong shore winds blew at my wild disheveled hair creating a black gossamer veil over my face. It made it easier to deal with Shane watching my heartbreak. "Always and forever, and then an eternity after. A girl will never forget her first perfect innocent kiss."

Shane's blue eyes turned even icier. "The man was a bigger jackoff than I thought."

I smiled at his words, "No, we just weren't supposed to be together. It was a real Romeo and Juliet type of relationship."

Shane sat forward smiling like a Cheshire cat and whispered, *"There is a charm about the forbidden that makes it unspeakably desirable."*

"Mark Twain? Shane, how do you know all those quotes that pop out of your mouth?'

His eyes twinkled and something beautiful and dangerous danced behind them. "How do you know all the people the words belong too?"

"Touché," I smiled.

"*Hear my soul speak. Of the very instant that I saw you, Did my heart fly at your service,*" he whispered.

"Shakespeare. The Tempest." I looked away again wanting to throw myself at him. "*Words have no power to impress the mind without the exquisite horror of their reality.* Poe."

"You know, Grace, you are the only girl that can go toe to toe with me without batting an eye."

I batted my eyes.

He cocked his head and gave me a sideways smile that left me breathless. "Want to head back now? I heard something about taking a little hottie out dancing tonight…" Grabbing my hand, he helped me up and we walked through the sand back to my bike.

"Lucky girl," I laughed as I climbed on the back seat.

"Yea, well, it's pretty much a lost cause. Last time I talked to her, she just wanted me to treat her like one of the guys. It's a damn shame, because I think she's freaking amazing."

"Wow. So what are you going to do about that?"

His ice blue eyes met with mine and then they slowly traveled down to my lips. A low raspy growl, yes I said growl (HOT!) echoed from the back of his throat. He brought his eyes back up to mine, "I'm going to do everything I can fucking think of to change her mind."

His words ripped through my heart and every single butterfly that had ever rented space in that old broken down dusty organ burst out flapping their wings in applause. I gasped from the pressure of it.

Shane smirked and straddled the bike showing his back to me, end of discussion.

I was speechless anyway. I couldn't even think right. Well...mentally he was about eight inches deep in me and I was screaming his name raking my nails down his back.

Chapter 19

For the life of me I couldn't get the water in the shower to run hot enough, and I was barely finished rinsing myself before Lea yanked me out of the shower screaming that I had taken too long and it was her turn. She then continued to yell about the lack of hot water.

We dried and straightened our hair next to each other like we did when we were teenagers. As always, Lea did my makeup and gave me that smoky eyed look that I always thought was too dangerous for me to wear. When she was finished, she gave me a wicked grin, "So, how was your *ride* with Shane?"

I giggled like a little girl. "Very...nice," I beamed.

"That's it? *Nice?*" She pouted. "Do you not understand that I need to live vicariously through you to sleep with Shane? I need him to make you scream so loud that I can feel it, got it? Just throw the *Who-ha* at him!" As she spoke she rummaged through my bag trying to, no doubt, find some sexy underwear, "Grace, did you not bring any…oh, never mind, I bought some…lacy things."

She walked over to her overnight bag and threw me a sexy deep purple pair of bra and undies; tags still on. I had to hand it to her, she was always prepared for an, um…sleepover.

"So, do you like him?"

I slipped the purple set on and shimmied into a small denim skirt. She threw me a deep burgundy low cut shirt I had packed for going out and I caught it when it almost went sailing two feet above my head. "Way more than I should for a one night stand."

"What?" She gawked at me.

"What do you mean *what*?"

"Why would it be only a one night stand?"

I shrugged the shirt on and pulled my hair out of it. "Lea, come on. Shane's history is laid right out there. He's never had a serious girlfriend. I'd be a fool, like every other girl he's ever met to think I'd be different, or that I could change him."

She stood still staring at me, mouth open wide. "Holy heartbreak!

That angel of yours did one hell of a number on you didn't he? Gray, you are probably the only girl in the world that could change Shane. And girl, I think he wants you to."

"A woman shouldn't go into something thinking they could change anyone. Just to accept them."

She jabbed her hands on her hips and I knew I was in trouble. "Look, Gray...a decent guy doesn't just get born and grow up to be Mr. Perfect. They need to be created by a woman. They're like a dumb blank lump of clay and you have to mold them into what you want them to be, while erasing everything their mothers ever taught them and all the horrible internet porn they've watched growing up."

I laughed.

"I am so serious. Do not laugh. Do you realize that men actually think that porn is real? Like a girl is going to scream and thrash around like that for thirty minutes and all you have to do is be the pizza guy! The pizza guy, Grace...and they don't ever eat the pizza first! And let's not even talk about the fact that NO real girls look THAT good! It's like they all come from the planet *No-cellulite-us*."

I laughed harder.

Slipping our feet into our heels, we made our way down the stairs. Caroline whistled a catcall at us, "Those boys of yours are going to drop their jaws when they see the pair of you. Please, one of you, come back with a proposal!"

Laughing we walked out of the house, we planned to meet the guys at a small bar named *Sunsets* right off the beach. Apparently, we were taking way too long to get ready so they left before us. I honestly think it was just to get away from Lea's parents, and I didn't blame them one bit.

When we got into the doorway of the bar, Lea spun me around and fluffed my hair. Then she yanked at the front of my shirt so more of what she called my *large assets* could be *demonstrated*. "Come on, Grace, you got your nasty girl panties on tonight, go inside there and get your badass." Then she smacked me on the ass. Hard. Twice. I think she has issues.

The bar was packed. A small booth held a pink haired DJ and signs for Karaoke plastered the front of it. Lea looked around for Conner and Shane, but I knew from the way my knees trembled and my butterflies slammed against my ribcage that Shane was standing at the bar to the left of us. I turned to face him and his gaze locked onto mine; and all the conversation, noise, and music from the speakers silenced. He was all I saw. He stared at me for a few long moments and then a slow, sexy smile slid across his lips.

His eyes slowly crawled over my body and my heart was pounding hard in my ears.

"Oh, my God, Grace. Shane is completely eye fucking you and I'm creaming in my panties right now. How does that not affect you?"

"Uh…" That and licking my lips was really all I could do or say. Seriously. He was that perfect, and his eyes were *on me*.

"Holy fellatio! You are standing there licking him up with your eyes!

Do you freaking hear the old seventies porn music playing in your head?"

I tore my eyes off Shane and tried to focus them on Lea, "I freaking feel drunk already. Come on, let's go get me some liquid courage to deal with him."

"Yeah, well, don't let your thighs rub to close together, because you look like you're about to have a walking orgasm."

"If only," I laughed as we walked up to the bar next to the guys.

His eyes followed mine as I walked up next to him and laid my hands down flat against the cool wood of the bar. He stepped up close behind me and leaned his hand out on either side of me. Slowly, he moved closer and brought his head down to my right ear. The heat of him tingled every inch of skin on my back, and my bare legs. Every inch of my body, my soul, my mind became painfully aware of him. Even though he was an inch away from me, he wasn't close enough. I leaned into the bar for more support; my knees wobbled. His hot breath scorched my neck and bristled my hair, "What do you want, Grace?"

"My breath back," I whispered.

He nuzzled his face in my hair and an insane tingling feeling shot down my spine and back up again. His raspy chuckle tickled my ear, "You think you're breathless now? Just wait Grace."

I LITERALLY CAN'T WAIT! I didn't want to mess up the moment by screeching that at the top of my lungs so I chose to stay quiet. It was difficult.

"So, for now what would you like?"

I lifted my face to his and turned my body to face him. "Sex on the Beach? A Screaming Orgasm? A Slippery Nipple? A Leg Spreader? A Bend Over Shirley?"

He laughed and pushed his forehead against mine. *Oh, I absolutely adored when he did that.* "What the hell is a Bend Over Shirley?"

"Maybe I'll show you later…"

"You two are making me feel like I need to wear a condom over my head so I can't get pregnant from just listening to the both of you. Shane, it's Raspberry vodka, lemon/lime soda, grenadine syrup and Maraschino Cherries," Lea explained.

He looked at her curiously, eyebrows together, "Huh?"

"Holy sexual tension! Do you even know that we are here with you? We want Margaritas! Let's go Shane, snap out of heat! Conner, man up and dance with me!"

Conner laughed shaking his head, "Why don't you and Grace start and let us men watch? I need a few beers after spending the afternoon with your father telling me what I should name our six children even though I apparently will end up eating them."

"Okay, boys. Enjoy the show then," she winked and pulled me right onto the dance floor. The DJ was playing some song I had never heard of, but it was sexy and had a great beat to it. Lea and I danced to the music and Lea, of course, made a spectacle of herself, putting on a show for the guys just like she said. Thinking, *what the hell*, I danced along with her bumping and grinding. You live once, right? Well, most people do.

When the song was over, we ran back to the bar panting for our Margaritas. The guys just stood there frozen and staring at us. Lea moved me off to the side and giggled, "Looks like they enjoyed the show, huh?"

I sipped on the straw in my drink and watched Shane watch me.

Someone blocked my view of him and I looked up to see a handsome face, bright brown eyes and a dark goatee smiling down at me. "Wow. You guys looked hot dancing out there. Can we buy you two your next drink?"

"Thanks but we are both here with…" Before Lea could even finish, Shane was in front of me pulling me down to the other end of the bar.

He spun on me and backed me up against the bar, "Finish your drink and dance with me." His eyes were intense and I slurped the Margarita dry and smiled. *Head. Rush.*

"Damn, Grace. The way you wrap those beautiful lips around that straw and look at me with those breathtaking eyes, it makes it real hard to focus on anything else." He stepped forward, grabbed me around the waist, and pulled me to the dance floor real slow, hands grasping at my skin.

He slowly slid his hands down to mine, grabbing me by both wrists and slowly placed my hands up over his shoulders and around his neck. He ran his fingertips back down along the bare skin of my arms, circling invisible streaks of heat across my shoulders and continued down over my sides. His hands ran across the bare skin of my waist and gently lay themselves on the small of my back, just under the fabric of my shirt. The pressure of his fingertips became heavier, the warmth and strength of them seeped deep into my skin making a jolt of electricity seer up my spine. The cool tingle spread itself across my back and neck. All thought was lost in my brain. *I just wanted him.*

The songs faded into each other and we danced against each other until Lea pried us apart so I could go to the bathroom with her. A thin layer of sweat covered my body and it hummed like every single one of my pores was alive and breathing.

We pushed through the thick crowds of people and found the bathroom, which had a line that went out the door and down the hallway. We waited on the line all of ten minutes and then busted into the empty men's room and quickly did what we needed to do.

Walking through the crowds again, she hung her arm over my shoulder and whispered in my ear, "Looks like you and Shane are getting along well." She laughed and ran. I tried to give chase but a solid wall moved in front of me. I slammed into it and stepped back, completely losing my bearings from the impact. It was a man. A man made of, what felt like, *steel. Gabriel.*

Gabriel looked down at me, eyes blazing and face twisted in rage. "How about a dance, Grace?"

"No. Get out of my way," I snapped.

He lifted his head back and laughed, his massive shoulders shaking. His head snapped back to mine, "Why not just one little dance? I can't stop thinking of that kiss yesterday."

"She said no. Now get the fuck away from her," Shane replied calmly.

Gabriel looked right into Shane's eyes but spoke to me, "I will have my turn to dance with you, mark my words," he said.

Shane's hands balled up into fists and his knuckles turned bright white. "Turn and leave now, before you won't be able to leave without a fucking medical examiner to haul your dead ass out."

Gabriel gave him a tight smile, "Big words, pretty boy." Then he stalked off and disappeared into the crowd.

Shane grabbed me by the shoulders and looked across my face like he was searching for something. "Are you okay? Did he touch you?"

I shook my head. "No. Thank you." I didn't want to make a big deal out of who Gabriel was and I didn't want Shane to get hurt, so I grabbed his hand and pulled him back to the bar. "Come on, let's just get another drink and forget that psycho."

We made our way to the bar where Lea and Conner were sitting. He told Conner to keep an eye on me and went to the bathroom after ordering me another Margarita.

I sipped my drink and stayed with Lea and Conner, but barely listened to their conversation. They tried to get me involved in the discussion, but I couldn't focus on anything except Gabriel's face and how long Shane had been gone.

Five minutes.

Ten minutes.

Fifteen minutes. Some guy came up to me and started talking about the weather. At least I think that was what he was talking about. He might have mentioned he could cook, but I'm not sure.

Twenty minutes.

Thirty minutes. I jumped off the stool ready to find Gabriel and kick his unholy ass when Shane came up behind me. My new friend who was standing next to me had the audacity to say to Shane, "Excuse me, but this pretty little lady is taken for the rest of the night."

Shane looked at me baring his teeth. I looked at the strange man next to me, baring mine. "What the hell did you just say?" we both asked simultaneously.

The stranger held his chin up to Shane and repeated the offensive remark. I looked at Shane and noticed his hands were scruffed up and his knuckles were bleeding. My heart stopped and then pounded painfully fast.

I turned back my attention to the stranger and laughed.

Shane didn't. His eyes pierced into mine and his throat made a sexy growly sound. I am not kidding. It. Was. *SEXY!*

The stranger moved closer to me, but I started to walk away. Then he grabbed my elbow and spun me around. And I sure as hell spun, but my fists spun with me and I hit him square in the nose with the momentum of my strength and his pull of me. Blood spurted out of his nose, but he made no move to cover it up. He looked at me and his eyes, which I hadn't noticed before, went from an ancient blue to a fiery red. *Oh crap, another one of Gabriel's fallen angels.*

"Touch me again and the next thing you'll feel is six feet of dirt over you." I leaned in closer so Shane wouldn't hear my next threat. "And tell your friend Gabriel the same damn thing. My soul is not up for grabs while I'm here."

I turned to look at Shane and that incredibly sexy smile was plastered over his face.

Crazy fallen angel moved forward again, but Shane just held out his hand, mushed him in the face, and shoved him back hard. The guy went flying into a crowd of dancing bodies and got lost in their movements.

Shane grabbed me by the waist and yanked my body closer to his and I fell right into him. "You have some messed up friends around here."

I slanted my face up to look at him, our lips so close. "None of them are friends."

His eyes went to my lips, and I realized that even with all the time we spent together that day, with his hands all over my skin while we danced, in all the flirting, he hadn't kissed me at all. Well, except for the little peck on the lips at the beach.

I felt my body move forward. His eyes looked back into mine. "Grace, you want to do what you're about to do with me with any of those guys?"

Why does he always want to talk, now? "Ah, that would be a no. And that dumb question you just asked made me not want to do anything I was about to do to you, to you." Holy crap, am I the dumbest woman on the face of the earth? This guy is going to seriously figure out I'm falling for him and run in the other direction faster than my panties can hit the floor!

I walked off the dance floor and back to Lea and Conner, who were huddled against the bar kissing. I reached for my coat and yanked my arms through the sleeves angrily.

"What are you doing?" God, even the tone of his raspy voice just makes you want to rip your own pants off. He should not be legally able to walk around.

"I'm leaving," I answered.

"Why?" He moved forward slowly, holding on to my gaze. Those blue eyes sent shivers down my body. He placed his hands on both sides of me and once AGAIN leaned in and trapped me against the bar. How does he do that I know NOT! Because I was seriously ten feet away from the bar about to leave, and now I wanted to lean back on the damn bar and let him…

I inhaled deeply, which was not a well thought out plan of mine, because his earthy Shane scent hit me like, I don't know, something um, very heavy. I couldn't even think straight with Shane so close to me. "Why Shane?" I gave an unsteady laugh. "Are you serious right now?"

His hand slid down my side and my heart skipped a few beats as he hovered his lips over mine. His other hand reached up and gently skimmed the pad of his thumb over my bottom lip.

"You can't keep doing this to me, Shane," I breathed. "You accuse me of wanting everyone but the only person I want. I'm not one of your groupies Shane. I'm not playing games." My voice trembled. I closed my eyes as he smoothed his lips over my cheek. "You want a night with me, Shane; I will give it to you without a second thought."

Shane's body tensed, his movements stopped. Pulling back, looking at me, he let his arms go limp against his sides. "A night, huh?"

The mental punch to my gut his look gave me left me gasping for air. *Why couldn't he have said to me it could be more? I wanted more than one damn night with him!*

He tipped his head back and laughed. "Come on, let's get out of here." He looked to Conner and Lea and called out to them. "You guys ready?"

They both nodded and grabbed their coats and put them on. Conner and Shane made sure there was enough money left on the bar, but his intense eyes were on me the whole time.

We walked back to the house in silence. The sounds of the ocean lapping against the shore drifted to our eyes and the heavy saltiness of the air burned our noses.

Caroline had the two couches in the living room set with pillows and blankets for the guys to sleep on. She came out of the kitchen when we walked in explaining to us that *premarital sex will send you straight to hell if it happens under her roof without at least a ring and date set.* Lea rolled her eyes and stomped up the stairs to her old bedroom, sighing heavily. I glanced at Shane who sat on the couch smiling and then I walked up the stairs following Lea.

I closed the bedroom door behind us laughing and pointing at Lea, "Oh, you are so going to hell in a hand basket!"

"We should have just gone home after that *all you can eat spaghetti dinner.* I feel like I'm sixteen again."

I crawled out of my clothes and changed into a pale pink tank top with matching boy shorts.

After Lea changed, she pulled down the covers of her bed and we both climbed in. She faced me, leaning her head on her hands. "So, spill. What's going on with you and Shane?"

I let my head fall back on one of the pillows and sighed, "I have no clue. We had a nice time on the bike. We talked at the beach. We flirted. He mauled me on the dance floor. Everything that man did was so freaking erotic it made my head spin." I turned to look at her, "But we didn't kiss, and he accused me of wanting to be with someone I punched in the face on the dance floor."

Lea bolted up. "What? You punched someone in the face?"

"Okay, listen. Don't freak out. Let me try to explain." I sat up and faced her, crossing my legs. "There isn't some crazy guy here, or an intruder who I accidently walked in on like I said to the detectives."

I watched her chest rise and fall faster like she was starting to hyperventilate. I didn't want to tell her everything, but I didn't know what else to do. "Gabriel and the other fallen angels have been behind all the crap that's going on. I think it's mostly Gabriel though."

"Gabriel? Gabriel, the one who helped me save you when you were sixteen when you tried to off yourself?"

I shrugged. "None of this makes any sense, I know. The only thing I know is that when I was in a coma, I was with Gabriel and I saw you and Shane in the hospital room. I saw him call Gabriel like he *knew him*, and that's when Gabriel said that Shane was the angel I had been looking for all these centuries."

Lea's eyes welled with tears, but I continued, feeling a weight lifting off my shoulders I didn't even know I was carrying. "Then Gabriel told me he loved me and offered me…things. I left though. But he caught me again. I don't even know what he did to me, all I know is that I woke up and Jacob untied me because I was chained up. Shane was there and handed me to Michael telling him to do something and that I was worth it, and left me."

"Shane saved you? He was there?"

"Well, yeah. But that was when Shane had Shamsiel's soul in his body. Doesn't matter. I'm here. He's there. Gabriel and the rest of the fallen angels are here and if I choose Gabriel, we can take over the heavens or something crazy like that. And all I want to do is be a normal human being for once, forget about all this crazy angel crap and be with Shane."

"Holy angel crap!"

"Exactly. And tonight when we came out of the bathroom and you ran away from me, Gabriel was right in front of me, and then him and Shane had words. I think Shane went after him, but I never got to ask him. That's when Shane accused me of wanting to be with them."

"I'm so confused right now; I don't even know the words you are saying to me."

"You're confused? Try being me. It's seriously like I have two completely different lives and I have to split myself between them."

"Two different fairytales that don't really belong together?"

"Yeah," I nodded.

"Pick one and go with it. I suggest the one with Shane, because even though Gabriel is beyond *angel hot*, he is creepy as hell. He has always scared the shit out of me, like he was the devil himself."

The devil himself?

I pulled myself out of the bed and stood up.

"Where are you going?" Lea asked yawning.

"Bathroom," I murmured.

She giggled from under the blankets, "Yeah sure, tell Shane I said good night. Oh, and Grace…"

I turned to look at her when I reached the door, "Yeah."

"I think you should tell Shane. Tell him everything. Maybe you can't see it, or you just don't want to trust him, but that man loves you."

"Yeah. Marie too."

I stepped into the hallway and quietly closed the door behind me. The house was dead silent. I tiptoed past Caroline and Anthony's bedroom and past the bathroom. I um…always liked the downstairs bathroom better. Yeah, that's it. I silently slipped down the stairs and heard the soft breaths of sleeping bodies on the couches. *Damn. Oh, well. I might as well really go into the bathroom and wash the makeup off my face.* I wanted to ask him how his knuckles got messed up, and if it had anything to do with Gabriel. There's no way an archangel like Gabriel would let Shane get away with hitting him.

I walked behind one of the couches without a sound. A hot flash burst across my face and chest when I heard his low raspy chuckle. Shane sprang up in front of the couch, grabbed me around the waist and dragged me over the back of the couch and into his arms. I let out a small yelp and he pressed the palm of his hand against my lips.

My eyes focused on his in the dim light that peeked through the blinds of the front bay window. Slowly, he slid his hand away from my lips and down my neck. A sexy smile pulled at his lips.

In one quick move, he flipped me on my back and his hand reached up to brush his warm fingertips along my lips. My breath caught and my lips parted, waiting. *Wanting.* All my thoughts about asking him questions flew out the window.

"Grace Taylor, I am going to kiss you right now and you are not going to run away from me, because you have no excuse now. Then you are going to go back upstairs to bed and all you are going to think about are my fucking lips on yours and nothing else. Not strange men that want to hurt you, or buy you drinks, not Ryan, not Tucker, not even Ethan. I swear to you, Grace, I will not let you think of anything or anyone else until I put my lips back there again."

I pressed my hands against his chest and my fingertips tingled with heat from his skin through his tee shirt. A raw heat swept across my cheeks.

Shane's mouth hovered over mine. His breath husky and ragged. His body pressed against mine and the button of his jeans felt ice cold against my belly where my tank top had ridden up to just below my breasts.

And then his kissed me.

His lips crashed against mine and I was *done. Lost. Gone. His.*

I pulled my knee up and wrapped my leg around his and he groaned deep in his throat.

The sound of him moaning, the sound of his breathing, and the heat of his hands sent me reeling. I wanted more, more than just his touch; it wasn't enough. I clawed at the bottom of his shirt and pulled it up over his head. Our lips broke contact for a second and he growled and slammed his lips against me when the shirt went sailing freely across the room.

His fingers moved in slow circles over me. The searing heat of his touch sent fire through my veins like a pure, unadulterated drug. His lips glided smoothly against mine, the small flickers of his tongue sent me rocking against him. He kissed a hot trace of electricity across my jaw and down my neck. I whimpered when he lifted my shirt and took one of my nipples in his mouth. My body trembled from his lips and he held me tighter.

The couch beneath us could have completely disintegrated and I wouldn't have noticed a damn thing but those lips. I ran my hand along his smooth skin and slipped it between the hard muscles of his stomach and the rough material of his jeans. *Holy Mother of ALL THINGS GIGANTIC!*

"God, Grace," his voice shook. He grabbed at my hand and tugged it reluctantly out of his pants. We looked at each other panting, breathless.

"Go back upstairs, Gray, and go to sleep."

I bit my bottom lip, "I sure as damn hell don't want to, Shane."

"Grace," he whispered as he slid his finger over my swollen lips. "I want to be inside you so damn bad right now. But when I do that, I want to hear you scream my fucking name as you claw your nails down my back. You can't do that here."

"I'm never getting to sleep now," I giggled.

"Baby, I'm going to be taking a cold shower for weeks after this."

"That doesn't really work too well," I said as I stood up and fixed my shirt.

"Remember tonight…for it is the beginning of always," he whispered.

"Dante Alighieri, Shane?"

"Shut up and go to sleep, Grace."

I dragged my humming, tingling body all the way back upstairs, smiling all the way. *That damn man just ruined all other men for me. Once you tasted that man, he made all others go sour in your mouth.* Ah crap, I was in love with him.

Chapter 20

Lea and I woke up to someone in the house blasting Beethoven's Symphony No. 5, and I mean *blasting it*. The walls shook and vibrated along to the music.

I was way beyond exhausted. Sleep had eluded me the entire night. Every time I laid my head against the pillow and closed my eyes, I could feel Shane's lips on me. The Dante quote echoed in my mind looping over and over, mixed with what Lea said about Gabriel being the devil himself. My knees tingled as I dressed and the grin on my face, whenever I remembered Shane's hands on me, was starting to hurt my cheeks.

Lea and I were afraid to walk down the stairs to see what her parents had in store, but the smell of coffee and French toast persuaded us to go.

When I stepped off the last stair, my eyes immediately went to the couch. The butterflies in my belly roared to life and flipped cartwheels. That right there was a sacred couch and it should be dipped in platinum and studded with diamonds. I wondered if they'd let me take it home.

Lea vaulted down the stairs behind me, ran over to the home audio system and slapped it off. Around the dining room table sat Anthony with his head hidden behind *The Wall Street Journal*, and Conner and Shane wide eyed, eating from plates piled with French toast, and all sorts of artery clogging yummy breakfast goodness.

Shane's eyes flashed on me as soon as I stepped through the door and he held my gaze as I grabbed a cup of coffee and sat down across from him. A dangerous smiled played on his lips.

I started to fidget with my coffee cup, when Caroline came in and gave me a harsh glare. "You're not eating breakfast, Gracie? Oh, dear. Really, sweetheart, I've seen more meat on a chicken than you." Then she slammed down a plate with six pieces of French toast slathered in butter and syrup, five links of turkey sausage and a freaking cheesy looking omelet right in front of me.

Shane laughed and I narrowed my eyes at him.

Caroline sat next to me and gave me *THE LOOK*, the one she used to give me as a teenager and thought I was doing something wrong, which was, at least five times a day. "Start eating, dear."

Gah! It's a good thing I love this woman. I ate as much as I possibly could. And, I had a big stupid smile on my face as I did it, because I was planning on having an entire night with Shane to work it off.

After breakfast, Caroline and Anthony forced us all to try their new hot tub with them and their eighty-year-old neighbors. This is not something that I am going to discuss though, because it was honestly wrong and awkward on so many levels that I practically closed my eyes through the entire incident. Let's just say it got worse when other couples were invited and some of them started to become…*frisky*. Lea and I bolted out of the room as soon as a few tops started coming off and one sixty-year-old man held his boxers in the air triumphantly asking how many licks it takes to get to the center of his *tootsie pop*. I shit you not. Shane and Conner were hot on our heels behind us.

We ran through the house laughing and screaming, desperate to be on our way home. Conner and Lea started frantically putting their bags together when Shane stopped me in front of Lea's bedroom door, "Got plans for the rest of the day?"

I looked back at him and my heart just stopped. Then it just started again thudding erratically. What the hell does that mean? I feel like I'm having a heart attack.

"No plans," I whispered. *Test drive your mattress? Let me pretend to be a Skittle and you can taste my rainbow? Fifty Shades me? Please! Oh, holy horror, I'm freaking losing it.*

And I can just about swear to you that he might be able to read my crazy horn-dog mind at that very moment, because he smirks at me like he won a prize at the all you can eat strip club. "Good. I want to spend the rest of the day with you. Want to go for dinner?"

Yummy, Shane. "I'd love to," I say, well actually, I squeaked it, like a mouse. "I, um, was going to ride the bike back and leave the Jeep here. Do you feel up to riding or do you want to take the train back to the city with Lea and Conner?"

He reached his hand up to my face, brushed a loose strand of hair from off my cheek, and tucked it gently behind my ear. I'm a puddle of goo on the floor. "There's no way I'm missing out on a ride between your legs all the way back to Manhattan."

Now, normally, I would run away or say something horribly mean to him, but not now. No way. My angel is gone and this is the last chance I get to live. I am 100% human and those damn butterflies are flapping their wings all over my girly parts. "Um, yeah. I'm ready to go right now."

The ride back was intoxicating. The whole way I feel like my heart is floating free in my chest and hammering itself into my stomach. I have my arms wrapped around his strong waist and every time he stops for a red light, he runs his hands up and down my legs. If this is what living your life to the fullest is, I want to live forever. I don't even care how much it's going to hurt when he's not like this tomorrow, I'm just living each and every single perfect Shane moment.

He takes me along the East River to Long Island City's Water's Edge Restaurant. From their huge open bay windows, the view is breathtaking. The Manhattan skyline twinkled back at us like it was made of diamonds and light.

We were seated at a quiet table lit with tiny tea light candles that floated in a crystal bowl of water. He ordered a bottle of wine and we were completely silent. All I could hear between us was my own heart beating. All I can see were those soulful eyes looking right into mine. His phone started ringing, but he pressed ignore and shut the ringer off.

"I'm glad you cancelled on Ryan," he whispered. His eyes pulled together in a painful expression.

"Yeah, why is that?" I teased.

"I told you before, Grace. I want to kill any man that looks at you."

I swallowed hard, "You remember saying that to me?"

"I remember everything, Grace."

Right there, that moment, I truly think I'm having a heart attack. *I just turned twenty-three, is that a possibility? Does he remember my angel being in his body? Do I ask him? Does he know what's going on with Gabriel?* My mind is racing and careening out of control. Holy crap. I gulp down my entire glass of wine. His phone vibrated spastically on the table; he threw his napkin over it.

"Everything?"

"Yeah, Grace. Especially the part when I asked you to try to find whatever it was you were looking for in me." His words hung heavy and thick around me. They blanketed me with a warmth and urgency. All my questions just floated away from my mind.

"Shane," I breathed. "You are all I can see right now."

I don't remember the rest of the dinner; just the heated tension and the long pulling ache between my thighs. The ride back to my apartment seemed to stoke the fire up higher inside me, and when he pulled the bike to park in front of my apartment, I was engulfed in flames. Before he could get off the bike, I unstrapped my helmet, threw it on the ground and literally slid my entire body around his to face him. He could barely get his helmet off fast enough. His lips devoured mine and the city around us, the rest of the world, just fell away. Cupping my bottom, he stood up, my legs still wrapped around his waist, I whimpered into his mouth. My entire body ached for him. I clutched my thighs tighter around him and grabbed fistfuls of his silky hair. He climbed off the bike carrying me, kissing me, clutching me tight against his very strong, very hard body, while his phone continued to vibrate in his front pocket. *Added bonus for me.*

Shane pulled his head away and stared into my eyes, lips parted, panting. Being the object of the desire in those eyes was the most powerful feeling I had ever had. He licked his perfect lips and growled deep, "Keys. Now."

Giggling, I stuffed a hand quickly in my pocket and pulled out my keys and wiggled them in front of him. "Take me in, Shane. *Please.*"

Holding me up with just one hand, he grabbed the keys with his other and slammed his lips back to mine. He walked up the front steps holding me and jammed my back against the front door. His lips never parted from mine. His missed the keyhole a few times, until he finally opened it and we fell through the doorway. He kicked the door closed behind us, leaned me up against the wall and slid the zipper of my jacket down.

I yanked his jacket off his shoulders and threw in on the floor. My hands clutched his shirt and I pulled him against me continuing our kiss.

"Um. Hey guys!"

We froze. *Ohnononono!*

"Wow. I do hate to stop this beautiful thing that's about to happen, but Conner and Ethan have been trying to call you, Shane, for like an hour already."

Shane tore his eyes from mine to level a glare at Lea, "Get to the point, Lea. Is someone either dead or in jail?" he said out of breath.

Lea took a deep breath and blew it out loudly, "No, worse. Vixen4 just showed up at your apartment and they need a place to crash. And crash your place is exactly what they seem to be doing right now."

Shane's grasp on me tightened. "Damn, I forgot Ethan told them they could stay with us." He looked at me tensed and clenching his jaw. "They're a handful." Sliding his hands down my arms, he reluctantly let me go and raked his hands through his hair. "Grace, I…"

Biting my lip gently I leaned forward, "Will you try your best to come back tonight?"

He cupped his hands around the back of my neck and pulled me in. He caught my bottom lip between his teeth and tugged gently, "God, baby. You are delicious. I'll try my best. If not, nine o'clock practice tomorrow, Vixen4 will be doing studio time after us." He pulled away from me and grabbed his coat from the floor. "I'm going to need to throw a bucket of ice down my pants," he murmured as he slipped out the front door.

Frustrated beyond any relief, I watched him walk away down the block from the window. Lea was next to me laughing, "Is it totally gross that I didn't want to stop you guys because I actually wanted to watch him in action?"

"Ew, Lea."

"Damn. Should have kept that to myself," she quipped. "So where the heck have you guys been?"

"He took me to dinner. Why *did* Shane just leave?"

Lea walked into the kitchen and poured me a glass of wine, I followed with trembling thighs. "Last time Vixen4 were in New York for a show, they got kicked out of the hotel they were staying in, one of the venues they played banned them and all four were arrested. I don't know the whole story, but Conner says they've all been friends since high school and the guys promised to keep an eye on them if they ever played here again."

I sipped my wine and squeezed my thighs tight. How the hell am I going to get through this night when I can still physically feel Shane's hands on me? Please God, let him come back.

He never made it back.

I called him around ten o'clock that night but his phone rang twice then went to voicemail. I didn't leave a message, because I knew how phones worked, he saw that I was calling and clicked ignore. The thought pissed me off, and it made my stomach feel funny, so I just pulled my covers over my head and fell asleep.

I woke up at eight o'clock the next morning tangled in my bed sheets and gasping for air. A terrible feeling churned in the pit of my stomach as nightmares (or maybe they were real) of Gabriel's whispering dark words seeped into my heart. An oppressive gloominess hovered over me and I could do nothing to shake the dread that engulfed me. I showered, dressed, slung my guitar over my shoulder and walked out the door without looking at myself in the mirror. The feeling in the pit of my stomach got worse as I got closer to the studio and not being able to handle the new strange feeling, I decided to stop and get coffee for everyone so I could have a minute to clear my head. Maybe I was just nervous about facing him after what almost happened last night and the night before. And, uh, what I was hoping was going to happen tonight.

No, it couldn't be that. He wanted it just as much as I did, there was no awkwardness about it, it felt like it had to happen or my body would just not work correctly ever again.

Still, my legs trembled as I held onto the brown paper bag of coffee and made my way to Shane's building. The city streets were crowded with people making their way to work, not one person meeting my eyes, just walking around an invisible mass on the sidewalk along with them. Everything felt surreal, a bit too bright and oddly out of sorts.

I opened the lobby door with my index finger, balancing the coffees and my guitar at the same time. I walked silently through the empty lobby, down the steps to the basement and through the silent hallways to the studio. It was dark inside like no one had been there yet. I switched on the light and the room brightened. The clock on the wall read 8:59.

Everybody must still be asleep upstairs. For some reason that thought sent the butterflies in my stomach to roll and thrash against my insides, and not in a good way. They sensed something was wrong.

I took all the coffees out of the bag and placed them on the small table up against the back wall. Pulling the strap of my guitar case over my head and opening it, I took my guitar out and leaned it up against the couch. The clock on the wall read 9:03. These boys were never late.

I walked back through the hallway and up the stairs to the first floor and knocked on the door to Shane's apartment. A very tired looking Ethan opened the door. "Mmmhhhh," he moaned and scratched the top of his head, then cringed like it hurt him to do so.

I was stunned when I looked past him and my stomach completely dropped, I swear, if I looked down I was afraid I'd see my guts splattered all over my feet. Usually the apartment that Shane shared with Ethan and Conner was pristine. You would think that they would live in a shithole because they're three single guys, but no. There were never any couches with the stuffing vomiting to the floor, no half naked schoolgirl posters, empty beer cans or pizza boxes. That was Tucker, Brayden and Alex's apartment; complete with an enormous bowl of condoms on the coffee table, all in different colors.

Shane's apartment looked just like Tucker's on its worst day. Bottles of alcohol were strewn all over, some empty and some that had spilled dark liquid onto the beautiful beige carpet. A lacy neon pink bra rotated slowly on a broken blade of the ceiling fan over the dining room table. A dining room table that now stood lopsided on three legs with a few sleeping bodies that lay underneath. They could very well have been dead bodies; I had no clue yet.

My heart is pumping overtime when I hear Shane's deep raspy voice and I see him walking down the hallway pulling a shirt over his bare chest with a gorgeous dark haired girl walking behind him. She was, um, not wearing much at all, just a pair of red lace panties. *Just panties, NO TOP!* A wave of heat flushed through my entire body and my pulse sped up even faster. I just stood there, at the front door, paralyzed like a damn fool. I wanted to scream at him, to shout, and throw myself on the floor. *How could he?* I wanted to just disappear, just sink into the alcohol stained carpet and never see his flawless face again.

Shane's eyes flickered toward me standing at the door and his expression was tight and unreadable. But, not mine. No, not mine, I could feel my mouth hanging open and the tears stung my eyes as if they were made of fire. And right there, standing there, DYING, I realized I had never truly been introduced to Shane Maxton, had I? This one, standing there, leading a barely dressed girl out of his bedroom, or whatever room they came from, as he dressed to go to band practice with *me*, that's the real Shane. The one who was standing in his living room with a tired and bothered expression across his face staring at me, as if I intruded, that's the real Shane. The one who had me wait for him to come back to my bedroom last night so I could hand him my everything, but was too busy *in* someone else to come. *Oh, Grace…I need you like I need to breathe, blah, blah, blah. Yeah, right! I wanted to throw one of the full bottles of liquor at him that was near my feet and smash some sense into him.*

I tried my best to stare blankly in his direction, pretending I didn't give a shit. But I felt like the walls were closing in on me and I struggled for air.

I had my soul mate taken away from me. I have spent centuries looking for him living the horrible senseless lives of pathetic people. I find my soul mate; lose him again. Get taken by a psychotic Gabriel who wants to make me his, and in my last life of this existence, Shane Maxton breaks my heart before I could even tell him he could have it. Wow. Just wow. Unfreaking believable.

I clench my teeth and squint my eyes so the tears don't finish forming. *Forget him! Who's next?* He shouldn't matter to me. It was just Shane; it was bound to happen, right? *But it did matter, because it was Shane, and he was the only one to make me forget.* "I got coffee for everyone downstairs if practice is still on," I croaked.

Alex climbed out from behind the couch at this point wearing a pair of black boxers with a giant yellow smiley face on the front. "Ah, Grace my love, you always have the most perfect things coming from your lips. Lead me to the coffee."

Alex stumbled past me in his boxers and down the hall to the staircase. Ethan followed him. I smiled, lips trembling, and went to leave with them. Then Shane's hands were grabbing on to me and pulling me back inside to him, digging his fingers desperately into my flesh. His touch seared me and I flinched. The girl strutted past us slowly and bit her lower lip looking from me to Shane. "Let me know if you find my bra, sweetie. I'll round up the girls and we'll meet you in the studio in a bit."

Shane's eyes widened at her and then they met mine. The girl swayed her half-naked ass back down the hallway, giggling. I can't help but watch her walk away. I feel little and insignificant. Heartbroken. But my ass was definitely a lot nicer than hers and I pitied, no, hated Shane for picking the wrong girl. "Damn, Shane, did you choose the wrong girl last night," I whispered.

"Grace, don't. Don't even think any of your stupid shit about me. The only person I wanted to be with last night was you. It's always you."

Slowly, I trailed my eyes away from the sight of her ass and back to Shane. "Sure, Shane. Whatever you say. It's not like I don't know how you are Shane, so please don't mistake me for stupid." I yanked my body away from him and smiled sweetly. "I'm going into the studio to practice.

I'll see you whenever you get there." I walked off down the hallway with tears welling in my eyes, "Remember I brought you boys coffee," I called nonchalantly.

I swiped at my eyes before I stepped into the studio. Ethan and Alex sat hunched over their coffees. Ethan looked up with a curious expression when I walked. "Hey, you okay, Grace?"

"Yep. Fanfreakingawesome!"

Ethan cocked his head. "Your eyes are all red and you seem a bit pissed."

I glared at him. "Nope. Just peachy. Wonderfreakingful."

Alex laughed, "Why do you keep talking like that?"

"NOTHINGISFREAKINGWRONG!"

That shut them both up. I grabbed my coffee and gulped it down. It burned my freaking tongue. How was it possible that it was still burning hot was beyond me. Must be the shit-ass luck of my life.

Shane stormed into the studio with Brayden and a group of four horribly dressed girls. I swear, each one was prettier than the next and I loathed all of them. A whole gang of real life porn stars, *how nice.*

"Oh man, make them go away," Ethan whispered under his breath. He gave a tight glance to Alex who nodded in agreement. "It's going to be a long sleepless week."

The dark haired girl walked herself right up to me and smirked, the other three followed suit, circling me. *Like vultures or sharks about to attack.* From my peripheral view, I watched Ethan get really tight and uncomfortable about how the girls were reacting to me. Alex grabbed his arm and pulled him back as he tried to move forward to help me. "Dude, it's Grace. She'll be fine. Let her piss on her turf."

"Hey there. *Grace.* We're the Vixen4," the dark haired girl sneered, flipping her long brittle hair behind her shoulder. "They call me *Bliss,*" she hissed. They surrounded me closely and I was momentarily floored by how different they looked up close. Old, worn and half-dead, holy crap, Shane slept with the *Crypt Keeper!*

"Oh, is that what they call you? I wonder what they call you when you're not around." I stated sweetly.

Her smile disappeared.

I wanted to vomit thinking that Shane may have had sex with the thing standing in front of me, it burned the back of my throat and I swallowed it down hard. She may have once been pretty, but a hard life oozed from her pores and what looked like track marks scarred her arms. *Stupid, dumb Shane, I will hate you forever for choosing her over me.* Her eyes were dull and bloodshot, ringed with mascara that heavily hung in clumps from her eyelashes.

Bliss stepped even closer to me and grimaced. She outwardly ignored my remark and continued her introductions. "This here is Scratch," she said pointing to a pink haired girl wearing a tutu that matched. "You might want to ask Shane why we call her that, unless you've already seen the scars on his back?" she whispered.

I knew the skank was lying. I can tell you that I have seen every inch of that man's back and committed its perfect contours to my memory, her damn nail marks aren't there. I giggled. "Wow, *Bliss*. The color jealous bitch doesn't suit you, why do you bother wearing it?"

Her mouth opened and closed, and then she laughed sarcastically. "Wow, the little shit has a mouth on her pretty little face. How fucking sweet is that," she laughed again and gave me a snide look. She pointed a bony finger at the two remaining girls. "This is Cream," she said about her blonde haired friend. "And this here is Essex," she jabbed her thumb at the last girl who wore a short military style buzz cut.

Bliss charged at me and stopped an inch in front of my face. I didn't move. I didn't even flinch, not even a tiny bit of eye widening or a gasp. NOTHING! There was no way I was letting this waste of human skin make me feel that I was inferior to her. Because I wasn't. Shane may have thought so, but that doesn't make it true! The minute she opened her mouth to say something, I thought I was truly done for. The stench of alcohol was harsh and bitter, but I held my ground, burning eyes and all.

"She don't look like very much to me, gentlemen," she turned to face Shane and my eyes locked to his. Brayden was holding him back, his eyes were full of hate, and he was looking right at her. I guess he still thought that after screwing her, I'd jump on her sloppy seconds and he didn't want her to mess it up. I laughed. I laughed out loud right in her face, and I watched Shane's anger turn in to what seemed to look like awe. *What the heck?*

"Wow, *Bliss,* how long did it take you to come up with that one? Did it keep you up all night?"

"No Shane kept me up all night," she sneered.

I lifted my gaze to Shane and watched the absolute horror dawn on his face. His beautiful face. He shook his head no and tried to struggle out of Brayden's hold. Ethan jumped up and helped hold him back, but I think it was more for me to see him and send his encouragement. I looked dead in her eyes and smiled another sweet smile. "So, *Bliss*, tell me how much semen do you swallow to actually become that stupid? Why would I care who kept your creepy looking ass up all night? And Shane, well we all know, ***you could slap a wig and stilettos on a fucking three legged chair and Shane would try to fuck it.*** I wouldn't be bragging about getting a piece of Shane, anybody could." I stepped closer to her, bumping into her, like I was a badass street fighter. My adrenaline started shooting fireworks off under my skin and I was about to go all *Bruce Lee* on her ass *Return of the Dragon* style.

"Ah man," Alex murmured. "I love that girl. You guys are so lucky I broke my arms to get her."

I walked right past Bliss thrusting my shoulder into hers, spinning her around like a rag doll. "You guys ready to play?" I asked walking over to my guitar and hauling the old worn out strap over my head. "Or you guys going to bring in the mud and watch Bliss and I go at it for your viewing pleasure."

Alex jumped out of his seat, ran over to me and picked me up twirling me around. He nestled his face near my ear, "You're my favorite girl ever."

Shane pulled him off me and Alex held up his hands laughing. "Relax, bro. She's all of ours, not just yours."

"Get off her, Alex," Shane said as he yanked me out of the studio and into the hallway. He raked his hands through his hair and stood waiting, "Say something to me Grace. Tell me that you know me better than that."

I leaned my back heavily against the wall, my guitar tugging on my shoulders as I strummed a few chords. "Lie to me Shane. Tell me that you didn't leave me and spend the night with her." He stepped back like I slapped him. I shook my head and laughed pulling myself off the wall, "You know what? Don't bother, Shane. We were just friends, so there's no bad crap between us, it's none of my business what and who you do. Let it go, I know we didn't have anything more between us. Let's just do what we do best together, okay?"

He swallowed hard and shook his head slowly, color draining from his face. God, I wanted him to say something to me. *Make it better Shane! Take away this freaking pain, take it away please, I don't want it anymore!* It was physical; I felt it in my gut, like someone had just ripped my insides and pulled them right down to hell. I wanted him to deny everything that I pictured disgustingly in my head. His lips on her, her hands on him, oh God, I really, really wanted him to love me. *Just me.*

But he didn't. And before my body could crumple in on itself, I walked past him, letting him go.

When I went back into the studio, I jammed my chord into the huge amps and I know Ethan caught me wiping the tears from my eyes by the way his body stiffened and the look he gave Shane.

Without waiting for Shane's cue, I started playing Mad World's set and felt pretty damn high when I watched the expressions of Vixen4. I slammed violently on my strings like I was colliding my fists against their faces. My voice exploded against them like slaps across their cheeks, and I tore through riffs with a fury like I wanted to tear through Shane. I wrecked their sorry asses, without even touching them.

Chapter 21

When we played the entire set of all the songs Mad World had ever composed, I walked over to my guitar case and started packing up without saying a word.

"Hey, how about some Janis?" Shane pleaded into the microphone, his voice breaking.

The studio went silent when I lifted my face to him. "I don't really feel like I have any more pieces of my heart to give right now Shane."

I walked out of the studio without looking back. Opening my cell, I pressed Lea's icon and waited for her to answer her work phone.

"Hey, girlie!"

"Hey, Lea. What are you doing after work?" I asked.

"I don't have any plans. What's on your mind?"

"I was thinking about a Boys Hater Club Night, are you in?" I said.

"What happened?" her voice took on a serious tone.

"I walked into Shane's apartment and he was with one of the girls from Vixen4," I explained.

"What do you mean by WITH?" Now she was yelling.

"Exactly? What I saw was Shane pulling a shirt over that chest that you love so much while she trailed behind him without one on herself." I heard Lea gasp on the other end of the phone. "Yeah, she was only wearing a little sliver of panties," I sighed.

"I don't BELIEVE HIM!" She was yelling even louder.

By the time I reached our front door, she had called him every obscene word I'd ever heard, and of course since this is Lea, a bunch I've never heard. We planned to go Boozer's for some dinner, because I knew for a fact that Vixen4 had a show at a club on the West Side and the guys were all going, oh yeah, and I was hoping that Ryan would be there.

Throwing my guitar onto the couch, I raided the refrigerator and ate the first thing I could grab, which was some sort of frozen prepackaged dinner. After cleaning, I changed into sweats, threw on my hoodie and opened my front door to go for a run. Lea wasn't going to be home for at least another three hours and the thought of staying by myself and thinking about Shane was not happening.

Shane was outside, and of course, he was dressed in his running gear. My stomach fluttered. "Yeah, I thought you'd be ready for a run," he said.

"And you thought this because…" I prompted closing and locking the door behind me.

"Because you're pissed off at me and when you get angry you run. It's what helps you think, clears your head."

"You are very arrogant, Shane Maxton, to think that I'd be thinking of you or feel angry with you." I started stretching while I watched his expression closely.

"No, babe. You do think of me, you are angry with me, and Grace, you want me every damn bit as much as I want you."

"Well crap, Shane, now I really need to run."

So I ran and he followed, letting me set my pace. Then he moved along beside me and matched my rhythm. We ran the loops in Central Park for two hours and then we cooled down, walking slowly back to my apartment.

I bounced up my front steps and unlocked the door. I held the door open with my hand and our eyes locked. "Want to come in for some water?"

A sexy smile lit up his face and he followed me in. It took all I had in me not to slap it off. How could he just climb off of one girl and so quickly try to get on another? I mean, I don't think there's anything wrong with it, but it pissed me off because it hurt ME and because I had real feelings for him.

I walked in front of him and grabbed at the bottom of my hoodie and pulled it over my head really slow.

"Ah, Grace," he breathed.

I knew exactly what I was doing. I had on a tiny tank top on underneath that showed off my back. When I shimmied out of my sweats and stood in front of him with just my tiny boy shorts on, I could hear his breath pitch. He was right, I was angry, I did think of him and now I wanted him to know what he missed.

"Come here," Shane whispered as he came up behind me, wrapping his arms around me. He pulled me so close to him that his bare chest was brushing up against my back. *Crap, I missed him taking his shirt off!* He lowered his face into my neck, his breath hot against my damp skin.

I almost lost it completely, all that anger that I wanted to hold on to. The thought of him with Bliss, the way she strutted down the hall and him denying nothing; I turned around to face him. I slid my finger along the lines of his tattoo. "I'd love to hear the story behind this one day," I whispered kissing and gliding my tongue over the inked lines. I looked up at him through my long dark lashes. Shane's lips parted and I could feel his heart pounding against my chest and watched him pant faster with each breath. Knowing that I was the one that was affecting Shane like this made my insides pull.

"God, Grace," he moaned. Shane bent his head down and rested his forehead against mine. His fingers gently ran through my hair grasping handfuls and knotted them into his fists. Holding onto my head firmly he pulled my face to his and hovered his lips over mine. Our eyes locked, it was intense and raw, his breaths hot and sweet over my skin. Then he took the smallest nip of my bottom lip and tugged, pulling back. When he slipped his tongue inside my mouth, I just about came apart in his hands.

"Ahhh no, no. I can't do this," I moaned and pulled away. "I'm done, Shane."

He pulled his face away, his eyes focusing on mine. He stood up straight and ridged, "What's that mean, Grace?"

"I'm. Done. Shane."

The handfuls of my hair he held tightly in his fists pulled tighter. He searched my face and growled, "Grace, what are you done with?"

"You."

His hands flew off me like I was painful to touch. "Don't give up on me, Grace. I'm here with *you* now."

I backed up and moved away from him. I laughed; he was here with me, *NOW!* My brain was torn between asking him to follow me and throwing him out. I wanted him to make me forget what I saw, but I couldn't ask him, and he did nothing to help me erase the thoughts.

"Shane," I shook my head slowly. "You have this special way of making any girl feel…completely insignificant, and I couldn't care less what you say or do, I won't agree to be insignificant, inconsequential or easy replaceable for anyone."

Walking down the hallway I left him standing there watching me. I closed the door quietly to the bathroom, started the shower and slid down to the floor wrapping my arms around my knees. I left the door unlocked, because, God forgive me for being so weak, I wanted Shane to come in. I wanted him to come in after me and tell me I wasn't insignificant and meaningless to him, that I was the one that was special. ***The only one***. And as I sat there, listening to the stream of the water hit the tub and feeling the warm moisture of the air I knew he never would. That special connection I wanted, that intense crazy love that made you completely breathless, that *was* just in fairytales.

I dressed in a pair of tight low-rise jeans and a tiny red shirt that left little to the imagination. The shirt was just a triangular piece of material that was completely open in the back, only held together by a thin black elastic band across my bare skin. It showed off my broken angel wing tattoo and the *Nullum Desiderium, Deus solus me iudicare potest* (No regrets, only God can judge me) scrolled across the middle of my back that was always hidden under the strap of my bra.

I straightened my hair until it was shiny and liquid black reaching to my waist. I added a little bit of makeup, but kept it light.

"Um, wow," Lea said as she opened my bedroom door. "That shirt is crazy! Please tell me you have one in pink for me!"

"In the box on top of your dresser, it was an impulse, late night online purchase, enjoy." I laughed as she bolted out of my room. "I pretty much bought it for Conner," I called.

The squeals that came out of her room were hysterical. She rushed back into my room holding the pink top and a few other matching lacy things I bought when I thought I had someone special to wear them for.

Clutching her new *weapons of mass destruction*, her eyes widened and her smile disappeared when the realization dawned on her. "The pink shirt that was for me, and these beautiful, sexy, lacy things…" she held them out to me. "These were for Shane, weren't they?"

I shrugged. "Believe me, Conner will appreciate them more."

"So that's it. Shane is not an option anymore?"

I sat down on my mattress, hauling my leather boots up my legs. "I know I should just pretend it doesn't hurt and it doesn't matter and just spend time with him. But God, Lea, I can't sit here in front of you and pretend it didn't hurt like hell seeing them. I wanted to be the only one, not just Monday night's girl."

We walked down the hallway and into the living room for our jackets. "How would I act after? I mean, we are in a band together, what if he moved on to the next girl and I flip out on him? I was always an expert at pretending in my other lives, but with Shane, it's so hard. It's so real."

She opened the front door for me and I walked out after her, locking up. "Lea, he was the only one that ever made me forget about Shamsiel."

She hooked her arm in mine as we walked down the street, "Maybe because he was Shamsiel for a while. Does he remember anything? Have you talked to him?"

I shook my head slowly, "When Shane and I are in the same room, we either fight or kiss. Although, yesterday at dinner he said he remembered everything, but I don't know what that means. It kind of got all weird and intense after he said it and we just wanted to get home and get our hands on each other."

We rounded the corner and walked towards Boozer's. "Conner

and I were like that in the beginning too. We couldn't keep our hands off each other, but we were friends first, for a while."

Boozer's had a decent sized crowd, mostly people eating dinner and listening to a recorded CD of Mad World. Shane's raspy voice echoed through the speakers sending shivers along my spine. *I couldn't get away from him, even if I tried, could I?*

When our favorite waitress, Mollie, came over to say hello and we told her about our Boys Hater Club night, she threw her apron on the bar and joined us. From behind the bar, Ryan laughed and shook his head. Another waitress came over and we ordered burgers, fries, milkshakes and chocolate chip cookies with vanilla ice cream.

When our milkshakes were served, we clinked our glasses together laughing. "Hey," Mollie said. "Just think about how great it would be to have a world without men."

"Lots of happy fat women with tons of sex toys?" Lea laughed.

"Oh, stop, Lea. You have a GREAT boyfriend! Conner is good looking and he doesn't even notice any other girls, he's like perfect!" Mollie said. "God I wish I could get Alex to not look at anyone but me!"

I smiled at her, "Oh, you like Alex?"

"I would kill for his attention, but he just peeks down my shirt, or smacks me in the behind, and nothing else!" She lifts up her hands, "What does a girl have to do to get one of those boys to ask her out?"

When our food arrived, Marie slipped into our booth and giggled, "I, uh, heard that this was the Boys Hater Club. I need in."

I almost choked on my burger. "What? From who?"

She pointed a bright pink manicured finger towards Ryan, who laughed and flipped his bar towel over his shoulder winking at me. "So, can I stay?" She eyed me closely and waited. I wondered if we were both hurting from the same guy. I pushed my fries at her and nodded. "The ice cream and cookies are coming next," I smiled.

Marie's eyebrows rose. "How come you're here, though? You seem to have Shane wrapped around your fingers," she said popping a fry into her mouth.

I laughed and sipped at my milkshake. "Yeah, right. Trust me I don't affect Shane in the least," I explained.

"Yeah, well, he wouldn't even give me the time of day because of you," she murmured.

"Wait! What?" Lea snapped.

"That night we were all here drinking. I practically begged him to come into the bathroom with me, he kept telling me about her," she jabbed her fingers at me. "And then you show up, and he kisses me to get you jealous, then leaves!"

"Huh? You didn't fool around with him in the bathroom?" I asked.

"Yeah, I wish," she said.

"But he's got a picture of you in the bathroom topless on his phone!"

She giggled, "They all do."

Holy crap. Why did Gabriel's kiss show me them together?

A heavily tattooed arm reached out in front of me to take my plate and in its place was left a shot glass full of a dark golden liquid. My eyes traveled up the arm and saw Ryan. "Hey, Grace, I thought maybe you girls could use a drink, from one of the nice guys. It's on me," he said as he winked and walked away.

"Well now," Mollie said. "I think Ryan has the hots for Grace!"

I gulped down the shot. "Hey, what do men and diapers have in common?" I looked around to all the shrugs. "They are always on someone's ass and they are always full of shit!"

The four of us laughed and drank milkshakes; *yes, we ordered more*, blasting all things manly. Then Conner and Tucker came in, and Lea said that all the man bashing had to stop immediately.

Conner walked up to our table, with his eyes narrowing and rubbed his chin, "Well, if this isn't a motley crew, I don't know what is." He scanned the table and his eyes widened, "Milkshakes? Oh boy, who is the guy? And what did he do?"

I leveled a stare at Lea, "You tell your boyfriend way too many of our secrets!"

Tucker jumped into the seat next to me and drummed his hands on the table loudly, "Hell...lo, ladies." He slid over closer to me and whispered, "So, what does it feel like to be the most beautiful girl in this room?" *Wow, just the sound of Tucker's voice caused me to have an instant headache.*

"Oh uh, Tucker are you drunk already?" I teased him.

"Nah, I'm not drunk, I'm just intoxicated by you," he murmured.

"Do you own a book of the crapiest pickup lines ever? Where do you hear those lines?" Lea laughed.

He laughed and wrapped an arm around me. I cringed. "Yeah, I guess I just get a bit stupid when Grace is around. I mean look at her, she's beautiful." Then he kissed me on my forehead.

I pulled myself away from him as fast as I could, "Are you on medication for your personality disorder? Don't touch me, Tucker; you make my skin feel crawly."

I zoned out the rest of the conversations, I tuned my ears into the Mad World songs playing, mesmerized by Shane's voice. Everybody's voice buzzed and flew around me, but Shane's lyrics and the melody of his guitar pierced through my soul. And I couldn't help thinking that if he really didn't do anything with Marie because of me, maybe he didn't really do anything with Bliss either.

I excused myself from the laughter and fun of the table and made my way to the bar. I pulled up a stool and slapped a few twenties on the bar. Ryan came over, eyes shining, and bounced on his toes. "Hey, gorgeous, what do you need?" He flicked his lip ring with his tongue, and it gave me a weird feeling in the pit of my stomach because I knew he had to be doing it on purpose. "Need another *Shane Eraser*?"

Heat flushed to my cheeks and I covered my face with my hands, "Oh God, Ryan. I'm pretty pathetic, aren't I?"

He shook his head and nodded to the table, "What's the Boy's Hater Club for? He screwed up didn't he?"

I shrugged, "I don't know if it's me or him who keeps screwing up."

Without me asking for one, he poured me a shot of whiskey and slid it in front of me. "Well, I gotta say, I am one jealous guy right now," he said leaning his elbows on the bar in front of me. "I was hoping he'd mess up big time and I could kiss all your hurt away." That tongue of his flicked out and around his ring, then his top teeth bit into it. *DON'T KEEP LOOKING, GRACE!*

My cheeks burned hotter. I turned my face to stop looking at him and standing at the other end of the bar was Shane.

My heart just stopped. I think it was trying to fling itself out of my body and right into his hands. My chest actually ached and pulled toward him. How can that be normal?

Come on, Grace, you are so much stronger than this! He had sex with Bliss! *What if he didn't?*

I watched the anger flash in Shane's eyes when he saw Ryan hunched over the bar talking to me. His eyes locked back to mine and his face flushed of all its color. Ryan dragged his body back across the bar away from me, leaving me sitting alone.

Shane ran his hand through his hair and slowly shook his head. My chest tightened and a sour thickness filled my throat. He spun on his heels and walked out of the bar.

If I meant nothing to him, if I was just Monday's girl, why would he care if I talked to Ryan? *Because maybe I was wrong about Bliss?*

Chapter 22

I left the bar by myself and practically ran all the way back to my apartment. I told Lea I was leaving and hopping on my bike to search for Shane so I could talk to him. I was only stopping at the apartment so I could change into my riding boots and get my helmet.

I ran down the hallway and tore through my bedroom to find my boots, but when I turned around to leave, Gabriel stood in my doorway.

"I don't have time to play with you right now, Gabriel, get out of my way."

"Running after that little pretty boy of yours? It's so beneath you, Grace," he said, stepping closer.

I said nothing. I couldn't, and I couldn't move either.

"Were you going to try to find him? Tell him that you *love* him? I can show you where he is, Grace. However, I don't have to show you all of Shane's sins now do I, he shows you them himself quite often, it's amusing to watch."

He closed the door behind him, locking it. I was frozen to the spot, my heart hammering; *I just wanted to talk to Shane*.

The air around me grew colder the closer he came, until my body shivered. Gabriel held his hand up and ran his fingertips along my cheek, down my neck and along my collarbone, stopping right above my breasts. Everywhere his fingers touched, an icy darkness pierced my skin. It curled through my flesh and veins and tried to grab hold of my heart. "I like this shirt, Grace, it shows so much of that soft ivory skin of yours."

My lungs felt like they were being squeezed and all the air that was left in them came out in one long painful cough. No more air was let in, and all the ability I had to breathe stopped. My lungs burned and the fire rose instantly into my throat burning my eyes.

Gabriel met his lips with mine and puffed a breath of air through my lips with a kiss. I gasped from it and finally feeling I had control over my body again, fell to my knees.

"Why are you doing this, now?" I wheezed.

"Because, I don't want to exist without you, Grace."

"I don't believe anything that you say, Gabriel. You've lied to me so many times."

He pulled me by the back of my neck to him, pleasure ripping through my spine. "I've kept you safe for centuries. I stayed with you, Grace. ME!"

"Safe, you call that safe? You destroyed me. You ripped my soul of any and all hope. And now you are trying to keep me from Shane? You lied to me when you showed me him and Marie! Why can't I have this life without you in it?"

"Together, Grace, we can be unstoppable."

"Why do you want to be unstoppable, Gabriel?" I crawled closer to him, locking my eyes on his. His grip on the back of my neck tightened. "Archangels aren't supposed to try to take over Heaven.

They're not supposed to do anything against it, they *can't!* You know that it can never happen, right?"

He chuckled. "I was the first archangel to ever fall; the laws of heaven don't apply to me. My lovely Grace, don't you feel the pleasure I can give you when I just touch your skin? Think of that and more." He placed his lips on my neck and pure sublime pleasure rocked through my skin. I could feel it run through my veins like a cold hard drug trying to darken my soul.

"It feels like nothing compared to Shane's touch or Shamsiel's kiss." I pushed away from him and stood up, "All you say are lies, Gabriel. The first archangel to ever fall was..." I stared at him and then all the hairs along my arms and on the back of my neck lifted with icy fear. My heart pounded and I could feel my lips trembling on my next words. *Oh hell no.*

"Abaddon, Accuser, Beelzebub, Devil, Dragon, Father of all lies, Lucifer, Tempter, Carl Sumptom, Blake Bevli. Oh, my dear, I have been called so many things in my time, but Gabriel was the first, and I do like it the best," he laughed.

I backed up against my wall. Well, that just made everything a hell of a lot more screwed up. What the HELL am I supposed to do NOW? "Well, that didn't win you any brownie points with me, Gabriel. It kind of made me vomit a bit in my mouth, honestly. I want to live this life; you could just go back to hell."

"I give you a week."

"You're giving me a week left to live MY LIFE?"

"No, my Grace, I think you'll hold out another week, and then I think you'll beg for me to take your life."

And then he was gone.

The temperature in the room grew warmer and my throat was scorched dry. I couldn't swallow through the burn and I gasped for air choking on the thickness in my own throat. I flung open my door and ran down the hallway into the kitchen. I could hear people in the living room, but I ignored the voices and ripped open the refrigerator, smashing a dozen eggs across the floor, and tore off the cap to a bottle of water. I couldn't gulp it fast enough, my body felt like it was on fire and I couldn't quench the flames. When I finished the bottle, I threw it behind me and opened another one, then another. Tears filled my eyes; the pain just wouldn't go away. Is this what he meant? That I'd suffer for days and I'd break in less than a week? He was the devil, *THE DEVIL!* I'd been friends with the fucking devil for centuries, and he loved me, and OH MY GOD! I could NEVER love him. Eww, he wanted me to have his little red horned babies!

"Grace, are you okay?"

I spun around to the voice. My vision was blurred, like I had been asleep and just woke up and the kitchen became brighter and more colorful. *Holy crap! What the hell is happening to me?*

Lea stood in the doorway to the kitchen; Shane and Conner were behind her. But I couldn't focus on anyone but him. "I'm really thirsty," I croaked.

Shane rushed over to me and placed the back of his hand against my forehead, I fell into his arms. "Grace, you're burning up." He turned his head to Lea, "Get some aspirin and juice." Then I was being lifted into his arms, and I swear I could have died happy right there. The gentle sway of his movements almost lulled me to sleep as I felt him carry me through the hallway. I tried to wrap my arms around his neck, but they were way too heavy. I felt him shift my body as he opened the door to my room, and then his body stiffened.

"God, Grace, you don't have a bed?" He lowered me onto the mattress and brushed a stray hair from off my face. I heard Lea whispering, but her words were too muffled and soft. "Grace, baby. Please open your eyes and take these aspirin." I looked at him though small almond shaped slits, I couldn't get my eyes any wider. *God, he was beautiful, he looked like an angel.* I hoped I didn't say that out loud. I swallowed the pills and closed my eyes again.

"Lea, wait. We can't leave her in these clothes, she's soaking wet from sweating. Find me something she can wear to bed. I'll leave, so you can change her," Shane whispered.

My door clicked closed and my shirt was yanked over my head. "Grace, help me here, you're like a dead weight," Lea said. I tried to open my eyes wider and help her pull the rest of my clothes off, I'm not sure of my success though, because she cursed at me the entire time. "How come you didn't tell me you were sick, I got so scared when you didn't answer the door when I knocked."

"I don't think I'm sick. Gabriel was here," I whispered back.

She let go of the hold she had on me and I collapsed back onto the mattress with a thud. My eyes flew open. Holy crap she dressed me in a tiny pair of boy shorts and a tank top, of course they were made of lace. I squeezed my eyes shut tight cringing on the inside.

Shane was kneeling next to me again and pulled up the covers to my chin. "Get, some sleep, babe." Cool lips touched my forehead.

I opened my eyes halfway and placed a hand on his face. He leaned into my palm. "Don't go, Shane. Stay with me."

A slow smile spread on his lips, "Okay." I felt the mattress move as he got up. My eyesight was foggy, but I watched as Shane strolled across the room, pulled off his shirt and jeans, and threw them into my hamper. I watched the tattoos move against his muscles wearing only a pair of boxers as he walked to switch the light off. The mattress moved next me as he crawled under the covers and wrapped his arms around me pulling me in tight.

His raspy voice whispered softly into my ear, "Are you okay, does anything hurt?"

Sleep was pulling me under and heaviness covered itself around my body. *Just stay with me Shane. The devil says he loves me, and he's coming to get me.* Crap, I hope I didn't say that out loud.

Softly he placed his lips on the nape of my neck, just below my ear, and kissed me. "Shut up and go to sleep, Grace."

I kept waking up in the darkness of my room to someone screaming, only to realize it was my own voice that was screaming.

"Shh," Shane murmured, his hand brushing over my cheek. "You're safe, Grace; I won't let anyone ever hurt you again." His lips pressed a soft sensual kiss over mine. A thousand butterflies caressed their silky wings along my heart, making it drum faster. His words filled me with hope and the longing I felt for him, the pull in my chest, was overwhelming.

His arms wrapped themselves around my body tighter and he gently pulled me closer to him, until my head rested on his smooth chest. Right over the sound of his beating heart, that thundered strong and even under his warm skin. I drifted back to sleep from the music playing through his body.

When I opened my eyes next, a soft glow filtered through the curtains. A soft piano melody wafted through the air from somewhere else in the room; a haunting song that churned the feelings of my soul; *Hallelujah* by *Rufus Wainwright*. My breath caught in my throat when Shane's low raspy voice sung along in quiet whispers close to my ear.

Our bodies were tangled together under my sheets and his warm breath played gently along my skin, sending small shivers through my body. The overwhelming feeling of intimacy, of love and desire, lapped itself like waves along my skin. Every part of my body that touched up against his was like a small fire over my flesh. My legs were wrapped tightly around the hard muscles of one of his thighs, and I feared the slightest shift of my hips would be my undoing.

Shane's hand drew small slow circles along the exposed skin of my lower back, traveling over the sheer material of my shorts until his fingertips met with the bare skin of the back of my legs. My pulse quickened and I gasped for air.

His body shifted, and as his fingers danced delicately down my legs to the back of my knees, he pressed his thighs harder between my legs. I trembled.

He lifted his face over mine and our eyes locked in the soft low light from the window that gingerly fell over our bodies. Those blue eyes searched mine with a hard intensity and an exquisite burn slowly spread down my cheeks, crawling hotly over my neck and across my chest.

Then he slowly rocked his thigh against me and a deep blush stole over the skin of his cheeks. *Oh my God, Shane was blushing.* The simple idea that being with me, wrapped around my body could cause this man to blush…took my breath away.

Not being able to stop myself, I rocked back and forth matching his rhythm. I closed my eyes and groaned inwardly, the butterflies inside dancing along my insides, desperate to take him inside me.

Shane's fingers slid up the back of my thighs again reaching the lacy trim of my panties. He pressed his thigh harder against my core and tightened one hand cupping my bottom, gently running his fingers along the lace trim with another, slipping every once in a while beneath them.

I whimpered from the overwhelming tension building between my legs, making me drive my hips against him.

I dug my teeth into my bottom lip in an effort to hold back a moan, but it came out anyway. Sliding my hands along the tight muscles of his stomach, I could feel his body tremor beneath my own fingertips. My whole body engulfed itself in fire. *I needed him inside me.*

"God Grace," he murmured bringing his lips closer to mine, hovering over them breathing me in, "I never needed someone before the way I need you." Then his lips touched mine, soft and gentle; savoring, nipping and kissing my lips like I was a piece of candy. My heart thudded so damn loud in my chest that I wondered if Shane could hear it, I damn well knew he could feel it slamming itself up against his chest.

"Baby, I need to taste you," he growled. His breath was rough and jagged. He trailed his tongue along my jaw, nipping and sucking at my skin, down my neck and licked hungrily at the top curve of my breasts.

I tore my hands from his skin and yanked down the material of my top that was keeping his lips from tasting more of my skin. My insides turned liquid and I melted into his mouth.

"Hey!" Lea banged on the door. Shane's body tensed alongside me and he groaned pulling himself away. "Pizza's here," she said as she burst into my room. "Let's go, Grace, you need to eat something."

I lifted the sheets over my head and quickly fixed my shirt, "No, go away," I moaned. The ache in between my thighs was maddening, I squeezed my knees together to try to find some sort of relief, but it wasn't enough. And Shane's one hand still cupping my ass didn't help me AT ALL.

"I got one of the pies with *spinach and black olives*," she sang trying to tempt me.

Shane's deep raspy chuckle shook the mattress and he plucked the covers from over my eyes, but both our bodies were still covered. Lea, Conner, Tucker, and the *entire Mad World band* shoved their heads in through my doorway. *DISLIKE!* Shane leaned his face into my neck panting, "I'm locking the damn door next time."

"Next time?" I breathed biting down on my lip hard.

"Yeah, Grace. *Next time*," he whispered pulling back his head to look at me. Blue eyes locked on mine. An intense slow burn swirled in their depths. *Oh my God, why are my friends still* **STANDING AT MY DOOR!** The tension that twisted and tugged between my thighs was driving me insane. *I was just on the edge, the release my body craved, right there, just a little friction more.* One of his hands skated across the front of my panties real slow, taunting me, a sexy mischievous edge to his eyes.

Digging my teeth deeper into my lip, I clutched at his hand and pressed it against me hard, silently begging him with my eyes for more. His eyes dilated into thick black pools and his lips parted in heavy breaths. I rocked myself against the palm of his hand, he lifted my ass with one hand and pressed against me with his other until my insides tensed under his touch, exploded and my entire body quaked with pleasure, "PIZZA, YES, PIZZA!" I shattered and came undone right in the palms of his hands.

Everybody still stood at the door, waiting.

"That was the most exquisite thing I have ever seen," Shane whispered into my ear. "And I'm so damn sorry."

My heart thudded and my scalp tingled as my stomach dropped. "Sorry that happened?"

"No, Grace," he whispered into my hair nuzzling my neck. "I'm sorry I had to stop."

Chapter 23

Lea shoved my audience and Shane out of my bedroom so I could pull myself together. "Gray, you may want to take a shower, you've been in here since Tuesday," she said.

"What do you mean since Tuesday?" I laughed. "What day is it now?" I pulled my arms through the sleeves of my robe and noticed I was wearing something completely different than what I remembered Lea dressing me in on Tuesday night when Gabriel had visited.

"It's Thursday night."

Apparently, I had slept for two full days. Gabriel's influence on my life seemed to be getting worse.

"Maybe you should make an appointment to see a doctor or something tomorrow," she offered as she gently pushed me down the hall and into the bathroom closing the door behind us. "I wanted to take you to the hospital that night, but Shane said after you took the aspirins your fever went down immediately so he just stayed with you." She grinned wickedly.

Turning on the shower as hot as I could, I stepped in and closed the curtain behind me. Lea, of course stayed. "You told me Gabriel was here and that's why you were sick," she said.

I didn't answer her. I just stood under the hot stream of water and scrubbed myself clean.

Lea tore the shower curtain back and crossed her arms watching me, "You better tell me what the hell is going on!" *Was there no privacy in this apartment at ALL!* I closed the curtain back up and rinsed the suds off my skin.

"He shows up and what seems like a five minute conversation between us turns into seven hours of my life missing. The night that I was supposed to go to dinner with Ryan and Shane ran out, remember?" I turned off the water and dried off with a towel that Lea had thrown at me. "When I went into my bedroom and told you I just wanted to change and I'd be out in a minute, he was in my bedroom. It didn't even seem like five minutes passed and then you knocked on the door and it was all of a sudden midnight, I missed out on seven hours."

I wrapped myself in my robe and walked back into my bedroom. Lea followed me. "And Tuesday night?"

"Same thing. He was just *there*, but this time I couldn't breathe or move."

Dressing in a comfy pair of flannel pajama bottoms and a tank top, I held Lea's gaze. She wanted the truth, answers, but I didn't want to scare her. *But I definitely needed to get her ready if I had one more week here, didn't I?*

"Gabriel *says* he's in love with me and he wants me to go with him," I whispered.

"As in go with him and not be HERE ANYMORE?" she started breathing faster, eyes popping out of her head. "What the hell? TELL HIM NO! You're not leaving me Grace!"

Running to her I grabbed her shoulders, "Shh. Lea stop. Of course I keep telling him no. I don't want to be with him, I want to be here. This is my last chance to live a normal human existence and I want it. Please believe me, okay? I know I've drilled it in your head that I wanted something and someone else, but he's gone. Maybe he left to save me, maybe he just didn't love me, I don't know. But I get it now." I twisted my wet hair up into a messy knot and smiled at her.

"What do you get now?" she asked.

"I've spent my entire existence trying to a create this perfect fairytale happily ever after future; bending fate to the way I thought it should be, or living in a past that I was never supposed to have. I've never lived in the present, and cherished the moments I'm in," I explained.

The floorboards creaked near my door. "That sounds like a pretty enlightened view of life," Shane's voice interrupted. He offered me an innocent smile, "Sorry, I didn't mean to cut in, but I wanted to see if you were okay. And, I uh, seem to remember you screaming you uh, wanted pizza."

My cheeks flamed at his words, "Shut up," I whispered smiling. "I'm not enlightened, more like grounded now."

Lea folded her arms over her head, probably trying to keep it from physically exploding. I knew my best friend like she was part of me and I knew she was going insane with worry. She was one of those people who could needle something to death if it bothered her. "Grace is being harassed and WE think that this is the same guy who has been trying to hurt her!" she blurted out. "His name is Gabriel and he just shows up here and threatens her!"

Shane's eyes never left mine, yet they twinkled with mischief and he gave us a little snort. Yes, he *snorted*, like Gabriel was a joke to him. "Well, then I guess that it's a good thing that I'm stuck staying here tonight, huh?" He walked closer to me and shoved his hands in the side pockets of his jeans. "So, Gabriel, huh? Why's he harassing you?"

I watched my big-mouthed best friend sneak out of my room with a self-gratified smug-ass smile on her face. My gosh, that woman would do anything to get Shane and me together! These are the things that I love about her; I'm not going to lie.

I swallowed hard. "He's nobody. Just someone I thought was a friend, but he isn't. It's nothing to worry about," I said simply.

Shane stepped closer. "Well, let's see, Grace. About six weeks ago, someone attacked you in a bar and I got stabbed. Then there was the fire in your apartment someone set on purpose. Oh, yeah, and don't forget the part where some guy stabs you and tears your insides up and you're in a coma for four weeks. And your best friend thinks *Gabriel* has something to do with it, and you think it's nothing?" He touched my cheek with his hand rubbing his thumb along my skin.

My body involuntarily leaned into his touch. *Holy crap, do I have it bad for this guy.*

"I really wish you could believe in me enough to let me know what's really going on so I could protect you," he sighed.

KNEES WEAK! Mayday! Mayday! Girl about to fall even farther in love with Shane! Crap he is so going to hurt me!

"He was my ex's best friend. And he thinks he's in love with me. And well, to make a long story short, he thinks if he can't have me no one else should either."

Muscles and veins strained against the skin of his neck like he was restraining himself and his hands were clenched tightly into white knuckled fists. "That's what this is all about? He *loves you?*" he hissed through clenched teeth.

The way he said it made my skin crawl, like the thought of someone in love with me would be unbelievable. I shrugged as the pain in my chest from his words almost sent me flying across the room. "This has nothing to do with you anyway, so you don't have to bother yourself with it. Anyway, why did you say you're stuck here tonight?"

His brows furrowed and he moved slowly closer to me, pressing his lips together. Lifting his other hand to my face, he cupped my cheeks in his palms. His touch made my muscles weak and I hated it. "I'm not letting anyone hurt you, got it?" He moved closer and slowly brought his lips to mine, "But, I do understand him loving you so much he doesn't want anyone else to have you."

I think I whimpered. I may have melted to the floor at that point too.

His lips slid over mine effortlessly like they were made to kiss me. I brought my hands to his neck; his pulsed thudded wildly under my fingertips.

"Hey! Pizza! Let's go! She's needs to eat, Shane!" Lea yelled next to us.

Still cupping my face, he brought his forehead against mine and laughed, "You know, with Lea around, I can understand why there hasn't been many guys in your life," he teased.

"Shut up," I laughed and playfully smacked him in the arm. "God, though, you're probably right!"

"Come on, you really do need to eat," he said pulling me by the waist into the hallway. He nuzzled his face into my neck as he walked behind me,

"By the way, *everyone* is stuck staying here tonight. Our entire apartment building is having a cleaning service, uh, disinfect what Vixen4 did while they stayed there. Then it will be decorated for Vixen4's after show party tomorrow so they can mess it up again."

The thought of Vixen4 being in his apartment snapped me back to reality and seeing Shane and Bliss together. I needed to remember Shane wasn't a relationship kind of guy. *I just have to live each moment to the fullest, don't think of the stupid mistakes he's made. Don't ruin this, Grace, you don't know how much or how little time you have left.*

Everyone sat in the living room, all in pajamas, eating pizza while *The Exorcist* played on the television. A stack of our favorite horror movies stood on the coffee table next to the pizza boxes, huge bowl of popcorn and sodas. It eerily looked like one of Lea's teenage slumber parties.

I plopped myself on one of the chairs and grabbed a slice of pizza, curling my feet underneath me. Shane sat across the room from me on the other chair, grabbed a handful of popcorn, and popped a few pieces in his mouth.

Alex leaned over the couch and onto the arm of my chair smiling at me. "I can't stop myself from thinking about where I might get to sleep tonight. Any chance that you may need some company later?" he whispered low.

My eyes widened and I laughed at the absurdity of the comment. "No thank you Alex, you slut," I teased rolling my eyes. I tucked my chin in and laughed harder as Alex's stupid smile widened.

"I'll just let you think about it for a while," he laughed back.

I looked up to see Shane watching me. His eyes shifted to Alex and his lips tightened. This, for some reason, made me bite down on my bottom lip and when Shane looked back at me, he noticed. He gave one of his slow sexy smiles.

I couldn't stop my body from responding to his stare and a flush of heat ignited along my cheeks. All across my chest, my skin puckered into tiny goose bumps that traveled down and tightened my nipples against the lace of my bra. *Dear Lord, I thought only crap like that happened in romance novels.* The flexing and twisting of his tan muscles, the hardness under the lines of his tattoos was impossible to tear my gaze away from. This man made me hyper-aware of all my girl parts, and they ached, for the first time ever, *I ached for someone.* Someone real *and sitting right across from me.*

Chapter 24

After *The Exorcist,* we put on *The Shinning* and I went into the kitchen to make some more popcorn. Tucker was grabbing some more bottles of soda out of the refrigerator and hip bumped me as I passed. I almost flew clear across the room as he laughed. I laughed a fake laugh along with him; mentally I was clawing his eyes out of his face. I shoved the popcorn bag into the microwave and pressed the little popcorn button that *NEVER* seemed to pop all the popcorn in the bag. I didn't even know why I used it.

He placed the sodas on the countertop and leaned his long frame against it, "So, have you done anything about that little problem of yours?"

I stopped moving and stared at him, "What problem would that be Tucker?" The popcorn started popping; the sound was honestly more interesting to listen to than Tucker's voice.

"You being a *virgin,*" he whispered trying to talk in a sexy voice. *Pop, pop, pop.*

"See, Tucker that's where me and you have a difference of opinion. I don't see that as a problem. My problem is that I have arrogant assholes who think they are good enough for me to hand it to them in exchange for a stupid dinner of disgusting sushi and expensive champagne."

He moved closer, obviously not hearing anything I had just said. "If you're looking for Mr. Right, Grace, I'm *right* here." *This popcorn was taking way too long.*

"Are your parents siblings?" I asked. I mean, really, *they had to be.*

"You're so adorable when you act all tough like that. Have you given any thought to working for me? I know your medical bills must be crazy with you not working, let me help you out and come work with me as my personal assistant." He wagged his eyebrows like classic Tucker. "We can have lunch breaks together, *alone*, in my office every day." He slithered closer, "I know how to *please* a woman, Grace." *I think I'm hearing the pops popping farther apart now, almost done.*

"Then *please* leave me alone."

"Okay, okay. No naked times during lunch breaks, but seriously come work for me, get to know me better. You won't regret it." *I wanted his head to pop like one of those little kernels, maybe that would stop him from talking.*

"Were you dropped on your head as a baby or did your mother just throw you against a wall?"

"Grace, you're so beautiful I just want to kiss you right now," he stalked closer to me. *Oh crap, I was going to have to knock Tucker out in my kitchen.* I balled my fists tight, both of them.

"That's enough Tucker, leave her alone," Shane's voice cut in behind me. "You just don't know when to quit while you're ahead do you?"

Tucker's eyes widened, "Dude, I'm trying to help her," he jabbed his index finger at me. "She's the most unemployed person I know and I was trying to help her out by offering her a job."

Shane leaned his back on the wall and folded his arms over his chest, "And don't forget offering naked lunch breaks in your office."

Tucker stormed out of the kitchen, "You can't have all the beautiful girls Shane, it's not fair. I'm going out to the bar to hang out with Bliss; you guys are boring the shit out of me!"

Shane looked at me and laughed, "Oh, and to answer your question, I think his mother definitely threw him against the wall. And I fucking love that your hands are balled into fists about to bash his face in." He grabbed the soda that Tucker left and helped me bring the bag of half-popped popcorn and some bowls of chips into the living room.

Before Conner started the third movie, *Silence of the Lambs*, I ran to use the bathroom. As I walked into the hallway, I could feel the temperature drop and the hairs on the back of my neck tingled. I opened the door to Gabriel leaning against the wall; eyes ablaze, "Do you think having a babysitter everywhere you go will stop me?"

I slammed the door in his face. I walked back into the living room and Lea gave me a curious look. "Can you…um…come with me into the bathroom for a minute?"

She arched her brows and nodded her head.

Gabriel wasn't there when we went inside. *Interesting.* I think I may never want to pee alone again. I told Lea, and of course being my best friend, she agreed.

The last thing I remembered was the ending credits to the next movie and Shane laying a soft blanket over me as I curled into a ball on the chair. I had the best dreamless, Gabriel-less sleep of my life.

I woke to the sound of rain pelting against the old glass panes of my living room window at nine in the morning. The room was lit only by the soft glow of the cloudy sky that peeked through the open curtains. Sleeping bodies lay around the room, quietly snoring. Shane was on the chair across from me, his head leaning back, eyes closed. His shirtless chest rose and fell slowly with each sleeping breath. It was hard to look away from him.

Alex was stretched out across the couch hugging a pillow and Brayden was on the floor next to him. I wanted to ask these guys to sleep here every night so Gabriel would leave me alone.

The light in the kitchen was on and I smelled my favorite morning aroma: *coffee*. Ethan was sitting at the table with a giant brown paper bag full of fresh bagels. He was slathering one with butter when I walked in. "Hey you," he smiled looking up at me. "How are you feeling?"

"Like I was never sick," I replied laughing back at him.

"Everything okay between you and Shane now? Doesn't look like you two are trying to kill each other anymore," he asked as he placed a plate in front of me. "I just bought them, they're still warm and you need to eat. I'm starting to see right through you."

I poured myself a mug of coffee and sat at the table with him, completely ignoring the question about Shane. The last thing I needed was for Ethan to make fun of me for being one of those *stupid girls* that fall all over Shane's feet. Choosing a plain bagel, I sliced it open and buttered it. I cut it in half and dunked it in my coffee and then took a bite.

"You dunk your bagel?"

"Yeah, I could dunk just about anything in coffee or milk, don't knock it 'til you try it," I smiled, mouth full of food.

He laughed his deep bellowing laugh, dunked his own bagel in his coffee, and took a bite. "Umm…pretty good," he laughed.

The sharp ring of the doorbell interrupted our conversation, thank God, because I didn't want to hear anything Ethan had to say about Shane.

I heard Shane's voice talking to someone at the front door. I dropped my breakfast and walked out into the hallway to see who was at the door.

Shane stood in the front doorway, eyes brilliantly blue against the cloudy background of the street behind him. Two muscular men were carrying in what looked like a piece of boxed up furniture. "Down the hall last door on the left," Shane was explaining. *Um, that would be my bedroom. Why was he sending strange muscular men into my bedroom with giant boxes? Not that a girl should be complaining about that…*

Noticing me in the doorway to the kitchen, Shane's face lit up with the most amazing smile I'd ever seen on him. *Oh crap, I'm so far gone my knees are weak.* "You have a delivery," he smirked as he strolled over to me.

I could still hear Alex snoring in the living room. "But, I didn't order anything," I explained.

Shane grabbed me by the waist and planted a soft kiss on my temple, "Yeah, but *I* did." He directed me back into the kitchen, hands stills holding onto my hips, "Finish your breakfast." My waist tingled when he took his hands away.

Ethan nodded to Shane when we walked back into the kitchen, "Bagels," he grunted. "We were just going to have a nice little discussion about you," he winked in my direction.

Why was it that it was such a joy in all my friend's lives to be so much in my business?

Shane paused and his eyebrows raised, "Do I even want to know?"

Ethan's smile widened and he sat back folding his arms behind his head, taunting Shane. "Probably not, dude." He smirked at me and asked, "Hey, you're going to the show tonight right?"

"Ugh, I don't really want to," I groaned.

Ethan gave Shane a weird look and Shane just shrugged.

"What the hell is all the banging?" Alex yawned as he walked into the kitchen with Brayden following. "Bagels! Damn I'm staying here tonight too, if we get breakfast every morning!"

"I got the bagels, dilweed," Ethan laughed. "And I bought them for Lea and Grace to thank them for letting us stay here."

Alex gave me a little puppy dog smile, "Oh yeah, thanks Grace. That was the first night this whole week I've slept."

Brayden sighed, "Well, I'm definitely going to stay here until those crazy girls leave, I can't take much more of the partying."

"You guys are always welcome to stay here," I said.

One of the muscular guys who went into my room came into the kitchen, "Excuse me, sir?"

Shane jumped up, walked the gentleman into the hallway, and disappeared for about twenty minutes while we all laughed and finished our breakfast. Within five minutes of watching me, I had all the guys dunking their bagels into their coffees. Ethan leveled a stare at me, "I guess we'll continue our discussion later."

When Shane came in all the guys looked to him waiting. *Okay, what the hell is going on?*

A huge smile broke out across his face, "Okay boys, bring her in!"

I was then carried, *YES CARRIED*, by Ethan, Brayden and Alex (who I swear copped a feel of my boobs) into my bedroom, which was newly furnished with a brand new cherry wood sleigh bed and dresser. I was thrown onto the bed. Did I mention it was king sized? And had new sheets and a pale pink comforter on top.

"Surprise!" the idiots yelled.

My band chipped in and bought me a new bedroom set. *Holy crap, I'm the luckiest girl in the world.*

We spent the rest of my day, the five of us, *my band, my friends, my boys*, jumping on my bed and singing along to Shane and I playing guitar. So far, *best day ever*.

Around three o'clock, Shane disappeared into the kitchen and thirty minutes later the smell of onion and peppers frying wafted through the apartment. Alex, Ethan, Brayden and I, eyed each other and ran for the kitchen. Shane stood in front of the stove pouring a can of dark red kidney beans into a pot and stirred.

"Yeah, bro!" Alex cheered. "Is that your chili I smell?" He ran up behind Shane and looked into the pot. "Woowhoo, Shane's showing off his cooking skills, and we're reaping the benefits!"

Lea came home from work with handfuls of shinny glittery bags from her favorite clothing store. I knew I was going to get in trouble with something in one of those bags, Lea and I always bought each other clothes when we shopped alone. "Holy delicious aroma, Batman! What is that smell?"

It was the best damn chili I'd ever tasted.

Shane sat next to me and stole glances at me the whole time. When he was finished eating, he leaned back against his chair and hooked his ankle around mine under the table. Every now and then, he would lean a little closer to me and touch his hand against mine under the table. My heart swelled every time he did, but I also couldn't help notice that he went out of his way to hide every time he touched me from the others. And I sat there and thought back to all the other times he touched me, it was always like that, he hid it from the rest of the band. Even when we went out with Conner and Lea, he hadn't kissed me on the dance floor, only in the dark living room when everyone was asleep. Even waking up with him yesterday, when everyone was there, all he did was whisper things into my ear; he made it always look so innocent. The only person who had ever witnessed anything was Lea.

After dinner, Brayden and Alex left to help Vixen4 set up for the show. Lea and I took turns showering in the back bathroom and honestly, I don't even want to know how the guys got ready.

As soon as I stepped out of the shower, she was in my face, "Did you sleep with him? What's going on?" she squealed as she jumped up and down wrapped in her towel.

"Almost, but someone interrupted us when the pizza came," I scolded.

"Oh, sorry. Wow, I thought you guys looked a little flushed." She narrowed her eyes at me and pursed her lips, "Wait, so what happened with Bliss? Didn't you say…?"

I ran the towel through my hair and brushed the tangles out. "I didn't ask him." She gave me a disgusted face and I sighed, "Lea, do I really want to know exactly what happened? He had to have slept with her, he's Shane. Yes, I was beyond pissed at him. But then, he does crap like stay with me for three days, holds me all night and buys me a new bedroom set. I'm so confused my damn head is spinning."

We wrapped ourselves in our robes and I let her drag me into my room where my bed was piled with shiny new clothing bags. "What do you think you're going to do?"

"Crap, Lea, I have no idea. Part of me wants to run away from him so it doesn't hurt when he stops the attention. But a bigger part of me is scared that Gabriel is going to do something crazy and I end up really only having a week left, and Lea, I want to spend every last minute with Shane."

"Holy shit, *you're in love with him*," she whispered.

I stared back at her, not blinking and definitely not denying her words.

She cleared her throat and a wickedly devilish smile spread on her lips, "Then you'll definitely need to wear the new outfits I bought us today."

I giggled, "Yeah, why is that?" I asked reaching for the first bag.

"Because, then Shane's not going to even know any other girls exist when he sees you tonight."

The first thing I pulled out of the bag was a sheer tank top and matching panties. *Holy see-through undies!* I, um, tried it own right away and gawked at myself in the mirror. *Did Lea shop at an adult porn store?*

Sheer naughtiness sparked in her eyes when we heard Shane call my name and knock on my door. She nodded her head and whispered, "Open it. Let him take a peek at you in that outfit before he goes to the bar." She pushed me towards the door (like I needed to be pushed, I practically jumped in front of it!) "Believe me, no girl will ever be able to erase the memory of you wearing that!"

Lea wrapped herself in her robe and pretended to busy herself in my closet. I swung the door open and seductively leaned against it. The ultimate badass looked like he was having a heart attack. Shane's eyes glossed over and his lips parted. His gaze looked frantically over my body like he needed to see every part of me all at once. He sucked his breathe in and bit down on his bottom lip. I walked out into the hallway with the tiny sheer tank top on and strutted past him. I knew exactly what I was doing; I had no bra on, and the man bit his bottom lip harder looking at me like his next meal was being served. My fingers brushed along his as I walked past and a burst of prickly heat spread across my shoulders and chest. I didn't yank my hand back and neither did he, we just watched each other. His eyes were so intense my body trembled. "I was just getting dressed, what did you want?" I whispered.

Shane's eyes traveled slowly down my face and my neck, settling on my breasts. He squeezed his eyes shut tight and took a long deep breath.

When he opened them again his eyes were so dilated, I could see no more blue. "I was going to run home to change and meet up with you guys at the bar," his breath was low and husky. "Damn, Grace. I have never seen anyone as beautiful as you. You're beyond exquisite. *You're perfect.*"

I knew damn well that this man probably held a PhD in complimenting women, and had major practice making every girl feel desirable, but God forgive me for being weak, the pleasure of his words surged through my flesh.

I leaned in closer to him and smiled, "Okay, I'll see you there."

"Please don't wear that shirt to the bar," he begged.

I closed the door smiling at him, "See you at the bar, Shane."

I leaned up against the closed door panting. Lea ran over to me giggling, "Holy crap, Grace! You are a PORN STAR!" She jumped up and down, "He is so yours! Oh, my God what are you going to do?"

A loud thump slammed against the door and I knew Shane just

whacked his forehead against the wood. We heard him growl and storm down the hallway yelling for Conner not to let me out of the apartment if he could still see my *goods* when I was done dressing.

Lea giggled and threw herself on my bed, "What are you going to do?"

"I think I'm about to press my self destruct button," I laughed.

Lea smiled, "You know, Grace, I don't care what you think and what you say. I don't think anything happened between him and Bliss and we know he didn't do anything with Marie. I think that man doesn't see anybody but you." She folded her hands on her lap and her eyes softened, "You know, that's the fairy-tale I'd write for you, Grace. *You and Shane.* One hot rock star badass and one beautiful rock star badass with a happily ever after."

I walked past my closet laughing at her romantic thoughts. From the opening of the door a cold breeze washed along my arms and Gabriel's dark voice whispered into my ear, "Oh Grace my love, don't forget my part in the fairy-tale. I'll be the character that slaughters all your friends and captures your heart. *The End*."

Chapter 25

From Lea's goodie bags, I chose a small ripped up denim skirt that hung low on my hips, and a deep purple halter top that tied into a knot behind my neck and along the small of my back keeping my whole back completely bare. Thank God, it was skin tight to hold me in because there was no wearing a bra with a shirt like that. I was terrified to look at myself in the mirror thinking the outfit would be way too slutty, but it looked elegant, especially when my wavy hair cascaded down around me to my waist like a fancy silky black shawl.

"I hate you," Lea teased fixing her long dark blonde hair like mine. I thought she looked even better than me. She wore almost the same outfit as I did, but a darker denim skirt and a crimson red top. She looked stunning.

By the time we finished putting on our make-up, Conner was waiting by the front door with three gigantic umbrellas, lightning brightened the sky through the open door behind him. Venturing out into the rain, I took a deep breath of the moist city air and my butterflies woke up. I loved when it rained in the city, the smell of the grass and trees from Central Park hung thick in the air and the hint of the first wildflowers of spring tickled my nose. We walked to Boozer's silently, all three of us knowing all too well that an entire night with Vixen4 was going to be the longest night of our lives. Thank God I could go home anytime I wanted to, *and hopefully not alone.* But I wasn't stupid, this was the last night Vixen4 was going to be in New York. They were continuing their year-long tour in all the major cities of the U.S. and I knew Bliss was going to try her best to keep Shane and me away from each other all night and all to herself. The thought of his hands on some other girl, especially Bliss, made the vomit rise to my throat.

Outside of Boozer's, a line of people getting soaking wet wrapped around the block while music spilled out of the front doors. Marty the front door bouncer waved us in and patted Lea and I on the ass as we walked past. "Looking good ladies," he called. *Ew.* I swear Conner just laughed.

Brayden and Alex sat at our usual table and Conner walked over to them while Lea and I went right to the bar.

Ryan sauntered over and slid us two cold beers. He leaned over the bar and planted a kiss on my cheek. "You two look amazing," he said.

"Thanks Ry," we both said at the same time. He laughed and walked away to make drinks for the rest of the patrons. Lea and I turned around leaning on the bar and looked out into the crowd.

"Wow, Boozer's hasn't been this packed since the last time you played. Business really slowed down for them while you were in the hospital and Shane was away."

I listened to her talk as I watched a spiked-hair browned eyed guy try to make eye contact with me. He smiled when he finally caught my attention and pushed his way through the crowd to come over to me. "Holy Playgirl Batman! Do you *ever* attract normal looking guys? Damn, if Shane sees this guy talking to you he's going to flip," Lea whispered to me.

"Huh? What are you even thinking right now? Like I'm the type of person to forget about someone I'm in love with and let a guy pick me up in a…" I stared at Lea. "Wait a second. You know something and you're not telling me and holy crap, I just said I loved Shane out loud." I brought my beer to my lips and gulped. *Very un-lady-like, I know.*

She smiled at the oncoming stud and hissed, "I told you, I really *think* Shane is in love with you."

"*Think* or *know*," I tightly smiled back, butterflies wreaking havoc along my insides.

Spiked-haired stud leaned against the bar and smiled down at me with twinkling eyes. He looked at me from head to toe smirking and then said hello to my chest. I'm not lying, he talked right to my chest and didn't look back up. *God where is Shane?*

Almost like he could feel my thoughts of him, Shane walked through the crowd but stilled when he saw me. I smiled at him and his body relaxed.

The man standing next to me lowered his face to my chest; *again,*

I'm not lying, and said, "Hi, I'm Luke."

I glared at him. "Are you actually hoping my boobs are going to talk back to you? Do you think they'll tell you my name?"

Lea laughed so hard she spit her beer across the bar, and it didn't even faze me because it's not the first time *that's* happened.

"I...uh...I," Luke stammered *still staring at my chest*. "Fuck, I'm sorry," he said finally looking into my eyes. "It's just that you're really hot and my friends bet me that I wouldn't be able to stick my tongue down your throat and I, fuck, I shouldn't have said that. Sorry, I'm really drunk and you're really hot."

"Are you related to Tucker Belvi by any chance?" I laughed.

"Huh?" he said eyes on my chest again. "No, never heard of the guy, so can I buy you a drink?"

Then Shane was in between us moving Luke with his index finger away from me. "Move away. Now," he said.

"I was just trying to…" Luke stammered.

"Mine," Shane said. "Move away."

HIS? Oh, I am so yours Shane Maxton.

Luke raised both his hands into the air in surrender, "Sorry, dude. I didn't mean any disrespect; your girl's really hot." Then he stumbled away.

Shane's eyes met mine again. Something lingered behind the blue, something hidden and dangerous and made me want to get in all sorts of trouble. My pulse raced and all I wanted to do was reach out and touch him.

"Shane!" a voice screeched. Bliss shoved her body between us, moved really close to him, and grabbed both his arms. "Babe, I need you right now!" she said pulling him away.

I tore my eyes off his and they locked onto Bliss's bloodshot ones. She held my stare and smirked, then licked her tongue over her lips seductively.

His raspy chuckle wrapped around me, "I'll be right back." Insane thoughts of tackling Bliss to the ground crossed my mind as I watched her drag him into the back hallway. *Oh. My. God.* It's like he just punched me hard in the gut. Why would he just leave with her? Why did he just call me *HIS*, look at me like he wanted to devour me and then *LEAVE TO GO INTO THE BACK ROOM WITH THAT THING?*

Lea snickered, "I'm going to hit that girl so hard she'll have to take off her shoes to shit!"

Mollie and Marie crowded in next to us at the bar. Marie gave me a tight smile, "He's a jerk."

Two blonde girls, who were standing next to us listening to everything that just happened, giggled loudly. The taller one leaned across Mollie and asked me, "Is that Shane from Mad World?"

We all nodded still looking in the direction of the back rooms.

The smaller blonde sighed loudly, "Wow, he's like, a real rock star."

She looked up to the taller blonde who was smiling dreamily

towards the back rooms, "Uh huh, I'll have two of them, please." She craned her neck to look at me, "Was that his girlfriend? How hard do you think it would be for me to get him to take me home?"

"Are you serious right now?" I asked. "You could probably open a damn seafood house with all the crabs he probably has," I hissed.

Lea smiled sweetly at the girls, "Honestly, he has a really tiny penis, believe me I've seen it. It's like, smaller than my pinky. He's my boyfriend's best friend and he stays with us all the time. I've *seen it*." She held up her pinky for the two girls to see.

Marie leaned in, "Well, you know he's gay, right?"

Mollie nodded her head, "Yeah, he's in a serious relationship with his keyboardist Alex." She shrugged her shoulders, "Don't tell them we're saying anything to you, they don't want their fans to know."

The two girls walked away shaking their heads.

"Wow, we are four insane, petty, little liars. Aren't we?" I laughed.

Mollie crossed her arms and huffed, "Girl, I'd just about say anything to keep any of those disgusting barflies away from Alex."

I smiled at Mollie, "Looks like he's checking you out right now," I nodded towards our table to Alex who was eyeing Mollie. "Go on, Mollie. Go *take* his order," I laughed. Lea, Marie and I pulled her to our table, untied her apron, and sat her next to Alex. "You're on a break for a few minutes," I winked at her and sauntered back up to the bar alone.

Ryan held an empty shot glass in front of my face and waved it back and forth in front of my face. "You look like you need a shot. Everything okay?"

"Yes to both questions," I replied.

He poured my favorite whiskey into the glass and I watched the lights of the bar reflect off the surface of the liquid. I slung the drink back and cherished the burn as it slid down my throat. I motioned for Ryan to give me another one, there was no use staying sober tonight, I didn't want to remember anything that happened or was happening with Shane and any girl other than me. I drank my next shot and slammed the glass hard against the bar.

"Damn, what did that shot glass ever do to you?" Shane's voice asked next to me. A loud cursing Bliss was behind him, I swear, frothing at the mouth.

"Ew, Shane," I said pointing at Bliss's weird expression. "Was your dick just in that?"

"Definitely not."

"Don't lie, Shane. Let's go back there and finish what you started," she purred to him as she slid her hands up his chest.

His whole body stiffened at her touch and he yanked her hands off him. "Why don't you stop lying and go get ready for your show. And stop the junk you're shoving up your nose too, you're driving us all crazy."

She pushed at his chest and stormed off cursing at him.

"Wow, what did you do to her that got her so angry with you?" I didn't want to make a scene, but holy crap did I want to start screaming at him.

Shane rolled his eyes at me and shook his head. "It's not what I did Grace; it's what I wouldn't do with her."

I slammed back my third shot wanting him to shut the hell up. "Shane Maxton saying no to a girl, isn't that unheard of? She's pretty *hot* Shane, what gives?" I said as I stood up to face him. My hands clenched into fists at my sides and it took everything in me to stand there and wait for him to break my heart, to my face.

"She's not you," he whispered looking right into my eyes. He slanted his body so close to me I felt heat burn off his body into mine, "Grace, I still have the taste of you on my tongue and the feel of your body in my arms, you're not easy to get off my mind. As a matter of fact, I haven't thought about anything else since I first laid my eyes on you."

I stepped away from him just from the sheer intensity of the look he gave me. It rolled over my entire body like slow waves and I wanted to swim in the waters forever.

He raked his hands through his hair, "No matter what I say Grace, you'll never believe in me, you'll never know the real me." Shane dropped his hands heavily to his sides and walked away backwards from me, giving me a look like I just kicked his puppy clear across the bar. *What the hell just happened? I needed to find if there was anything that happened between him and Bliss before I ran after him.*

In the background, somewhere in the rest of the bar, Vixen4 took the stage and started playing a mix of hard rock and alternative shitty music. Bliss's voice screamed into the microphone and I truly wondered if all the people here in the bar that paid to see them were deaf.

I turned around to the bar again and without saying a word, Ryan placed another shot in front of me. I grabbed the glass and walked over to the table where all my friends sat, all my friends except for Shane. I had no idea where he walked off to.

Slumping into the chair next to Ethan, I placed my drink on the table and stared at it. A thick arm wrapped itself heavily around my shoulders and Ethan's head appeared in front of mine. "You okay? Let me guess, Shane? Are you still pissed at him? I thought you guys were tight again."

I fixed an unblinking stare at him trying desperately not to show any reaction.

"What happened last band practice anyway? What the hell was that about?"

I shrugged. Everyone around me was drinking, laughing and talking. I just wanted to go home, but I knew I wouldn't be alone. Gabriel would be there. "Why are you staring at me like that?"

"Just waiting for you to answer me about Shane. Last time I saw you two together was at band practice and I thought you were going to kick his ass every time he talked to you. Then he's taking care of you when you're sick, and now you look like you're fighting again." He pulled his chair closer to me and nudged me with his elbow. "I thought we were like best buds. Talk."

I cracked up. "You sound like Lea now." I looked in his brown eyes hoping he wouldn't start making fun of me then just sighed and went for it, "I got pissed off because he messed around with Bliss." I held my hand up to him so he wouldn't say anything, "And before you start yelling at me about it, believe me I know I'm an idiot, I've turned into one of his stupid groupies."

Ethan slumped his huge shoulders closer to me, "Grace, you two have some sort of unspoken thing between you. Everybody can see it. You guys do more than write music together, it's like everyone is watching you have this intense sexual experience with each other through your guitars. Put yourselves out of misery and just get together already." He sat back and smirked, "Oh, and sweetheart, I know for a fact Shane never touched Bliss, not even when we were kids. They are like our annoying little troublemaking sisters."

I was rendered speechless. Not like me at all.

"You know, he thought that's why you were pissed off at him at practice. And you know what, I know I said a lot of crap about him to you, but Grace, I've known him my whole life, he's met his match, he's done. He hasn't even noticed any other girls since he saw you that first night. And I think he's tried to, but he just can't, it just always comes back to you."

"Well, she just hauled him into one of the back rooms and he went with her and…"

"Stop, Grace, I was with them. *Nothing* happened. That man hasn't been with anyone since he made me chase after the beautiful girl he saw with the silver eyes. He may have stupidly kissed girls in front of you to get you pissed off, but only because he thought you were with me. Grace, I've talked to him. Trust me."

I gave Ethan a small tight smile; my body was in complete shock. *Shane wasn't with Bliss. Holy crap.*

Holy crap. I was so in love with him I felt lightheaded. I couldn't catch my breath and I sat there panting.

Vixen4 continued their assault on my ears.

Noticing my zoned out demeanor, Lea, Mollie and Marie dragged me onto the dance floor and *made* me dance. Bliss screeched into the microphone about how much love hurt and I couldn't believe it, but I agreed with her.

After a few songs, Ryan jumped over the bar and riled the guys up enough to dance with us. Mollie grabbed Alex, Lea danced with Conner (of course) and Marie jumped in Brayden's arms. Ryan gripped my waist and pulled me up against him. I danced one song with him and feigned needing a drink to get away. When the song ended, Vixen4 said their goodnights, anyway. Bliss screamed a slew of profanities at the audience and they cheered her on.

I asked Lea to go to the bathroom with me and I told her everything Ethan said. Her lips curled up into a smile and shoved me out of the bathroom, "Then what the hell are you still doing in here with me? Go snag your Badass!"

We walked out of the bathroom arm in arm and stopped when we reached the dance floor. The crowds thinned out a bit and most of the people sat at tables drinking and talking. Shane leaned up against the bar, a bottle of tequila next to him. And I'm struggling for air as soon as I see him.

"Oh shit," Lea snapped. I look at her to see what she was cursing about but she was looking straight at Shane. And then I saw *her*. Bliss was standing next to him. She held his hand and sprinkled salt over it then bent down to lick the salt away. His eyes shot straight to mine, a slow seductive smile played on his lips. Bliss tilted her head back, drank her shot, squeezed the lemon over her mouth, and licked her fingers. His eyes were still locked on mine ignoring everything she did.

"Oh, that's it," Lea said. "I'm gonna…"

I placed my hand over her mouth and she looked at me wide eyed. "I got this," I said smiling. "Come on, watch."

I sashayed over to him, never taking my eyes off his. When I got close to them, he nodded at me and Bliss defiantly crossed her arms and widened her stance. "Get lost, Grace, Shane and I want to be alone."

I slithered up closer to him until I could feel his breath hot on my skin. "Well, I was just going to tell you that you're doing your shots all wrong." I reached my arm past his body for a lemon leaning my chest against his. His breath faltered. I reached behind him with my other hand, sliding my chest along his, and poured some tequila into his shot glass leaving it on the edge of the bar.

"Yeah, is that so? Believe me, little girl, I know how to do shots, and I could probably drink your little ass under the table any night!" Bliss snapped.

Bringing my face an inch in front of Shane's, I unbuttoned his jeans and slid the lemon slice between the material of his jeans and his warm skin. A low moan escaped through his lips and my body hummed with desire for him. I bit down on my bottom lip and slowly lifted the bottom of his shirt all the way up to his neck. I clutched the shirt in my fist against his neck and whispered, "You want me to show her, Shane?"

His eyes dilated and one side of his mouth turned up in a provocative grin, "Hell yes, Gray."

Dipping the index finger of my free hand slowly in my mouth to get it wet, I then eased it out and trailed it along his skin from his collarbone, over his chest and down the tight muscles of his stomach. Small tremors shook his body under my touch. Sprinkling the salt along the moist trail, I bent down and licked all the salt away, lightly pressing my tongue along the salty trail starting from the bottom and slowly working my way up. The taste of his skin combined with the salt and knowledge Bliss was watching me, melted my body into a dripping hot mess. Grabbing the shot glass, I swallowed the tequila and bent down to take the lemon wedge from the inside of his jeans. I slammed the glass down and stood up with the lemon between my lips. With his eyes still locked on mine, I gently placed the lemon in between his wide-open mouth and pressed my lips hard against his.

Slowly, I stepped away from him. His breathing was rough and shallow and the lemon was clenched tight between his teeth. My body craved to kiss him.

Shane held his hand out to me with his crooked smile. "Let's get out of here," he whispered in between jagged breaths.

Chapter 26

We ran for our coats and pushed through the crowds to the front door hand in hand.

"You know, Shane," I tightened my hold on his hand. "I just realized you let the Crypt Keeper lick salt off you," I teased.

Shane turned on me in the middle of a swarm of bodies, "Damn straight I did Grace. And it sure as hell was nice to watch you sweat for what was going to happen next."

I leaned up closer to him, the crowd of dancing people moving past us. "Is that what you were going for? You wanted to watch me sweat?"

Shane's gaze fell to my lips, traveled down my neck and over the thin material that barely covered my breasts. His breathing seemed to stop. "Yeah, babe. That's definitely one of the things I'd like to watch you do, among a hell of a lot of other things."

Oh.

Shane's expression changed and he looked past me and growled. I snapped my head around to see what he was getting enraged about and my heart sank. Our friends were gathering their coats and following us out and Bliss stood in the center of them all with a knowing smirk on her face.

It was my turn to growl. And I did, loudly, and pulled him right out the front door with me. Outside the rain and wind whipped through the trees on the street and thunder rocked the pavement.

Immediately, the rain washed over our hair, sliding down our foreheads and dripped off our noses. By the time we reached the corner, our clothes were soaked through, our friends trailing a half a block behind us. *Damn*.

We locked eyes. A low husky rumble tore past his lips and he walked me backwards pushing me against the cold wet brick wall of an apartment building. One of his hands slammed up against the damp bricks of the wall next to my face, the other grabbed my waist, trapping me and he pushed himself hard against me. His breath hot on my skin and huge droplets of rain dripping down our faces. He ran his wet lips along my jaw and trailed his tongue along my neck licking at the raindrops that streamed down it. My body ached, writhing with desire. Hungrily, he pressed his lips to mine and my knees went weak from the kiss and the warmth of his tongue. I threaded my fingers through his wet hair pressing my body harder against him. The sounds of the rain hitting the street and the moans coming from the back of his throat sent sheer electricity through me.

The only reason we pried our bodies apart was the loud voices of our friends walking closer to us.

Not being able to hide in the shadows, we ran ahead.

We reached his apartment building and everyone caught up to us in the lobby and made their way to the two apartments that were open to the party. My stomach dropped.

I leaned against the wall, my wet clothes sticking to it. Taking a deep breath, I sighed loudly, "Can I borrow some dry clothes?"

Without a sound, he stalked toward me. My breath caught in my throat, his eyes looked so intense and they frantically searched my face. "Is that what you want right now, Grace? Dry clothes?" His words unraveled my senses.

"No. Not what I want at all. What do you want?" I whispered.

He leaned in closer, but that low melodic voice of his could be heard crystal clear. "I'll tell you damn well what I want right now, Grace, I want to smother those beautiful nipples of yours in fucking honey and lick and suck them until you beg me you take you."

I gasped at his words...*Uh, yesssss please!*

"Then I want to slowly pull those little lacy boy shorts you wear to the side and taste you so damn bad, I want to bury myself inside you so deep I make you forget what your fucking name is. I want to completely smother and consume you, so all you see is me." *Holy aching trembling knees!* "I want to watch your face when I sink deep inside you, I can just fucking imagine it, the way your hair would spill across the pillow, the way your silky skin would feel under my chest. I want to lose my mind in you." *He's saying the words and I'm like right there, panting underneath him, naked legs wrapped around him.*

"Damn, girl," a voice purred next to us.

I shifted my gaze to the voice that had momentarily broken the spell Shane had over my hormones. Standing beside me was Lea, red-faced and smiling. "Holy crap, Grace! Shane, if she says no, fuck Conner, you can have your way with me!" she laughed.

"I'll meet you guys upstairs!" I snapped at Lea. My body was on fire, and I launched myself down the hallway towards the studio, I didn't even look to see if he was following me, if he didn't, I needed to calm my body down somehow, but God, if he did, I wasn't saying no. I flew down the steps and I heard him follow, "Grace, wait!" *Oh, thank you GOD! Now, please let the studio be empty!*

I slammed open the studio door with open palms, and he was right behind me grabbing his hands around my waist pulling me against him, kicking the door closed behind us. Our clothes were icy cold against our hot wet skin. We tore our coats off and I shivered under the touch of his hands on my hips. My eyes lifted to his and we stared at one another; drops of rain still falling from our hair onto our skin. My heart crashed against my chest and pulsed hot and fast through my body. Reaching up and pulling him down to me, I kissed him and I swear the earth fell out from underneath me. He pulled me in tighter with a deep hungry growl and held his body hard against mine so I could feel every inch of him.

He pressed his body against mine walking me through the darkness of the studio. Every part of my body tingled. With his lips still on mine, hungrily kissing me, we stumbled our way through the dark until my body slammed up against one of the big speakers.

My breath came out in short gasps, "We're on the speaker."

"Uh huh," he chuckled lifting up his arms and clicking the power switch on. The speaker came to life and vibrated underneath my body. *Oh my*

God! It sent shockwaves of pleasure over my skin.

The sweet tequila taste of his tongue flooded my mouth and I moaned. His arms slid over my cold wet skin slowly leaving trails of fire behind. He had to have been able to hear the pounding of my heart as it echoed off the vibrations of the speaker.

"Grace," he whispered pulling his lips from mine. He tugged at my lower lip and leaned his forehead against mine. Cupping the back of my thigh, he slowly lifted my leg and wrapped it around his body. He skimmed his fingertips over my skin as my small skirt rose up over my hips. He stopped his fingers, letting them tease and linger along the lace trim of the backside of my panties. *Oh my God*, my panties were about to catch on fire and I needed him so much.

"Please, Shane. Don't..." I whimpered, gasping for air, rocking my hips against him. *This was the closest I've been to heaven in a long time.*

He slid his thumb under the lace and pulled his face away. His blue eyes searched mine.

"Please...don't stop, Shane," I begged softly. Arching my body towards his, I rocked my hips against him, "Shane if you stop, I swear I will *kill* you."

His raspy laugh melted my insides. "Grace, I'm going to touch you until you scream my name. Then I'm taking you to the party with your scent still on my fingers and your thighs still trembling," he whispered hovering his lips over mine. "I'm going to make you so damn crazy right now that I'll be sure that every single moment you're not with me like this you'll be thinking of what it might be like when I'm deep inside you." He brushed his lips along mine, just barely touching them.

Oh yeah.

Our lips collided. Frenzied, intense, passionate, desperate deep kisses. I raked my hands under his shirt and up his chest. *Skin so smooth and hot.* He moaned into my mouth and his breaths quickened.

His breath slid hot over the wet skin of my neck and across my collarbone. He yanked the material of my shirt away, lowered his mouth over my breasts, and took one of my nipples in his mouth, his heavy lidded eyes still locked on mine. He licked and sucked my nipple, and it felt so damn good, I cried out his name. His tongue was pure ecstasy and his lips had complete power over me, I was his, all of me, for the taking. A hot ache filled between my thighs and I could barely catch my breath.

He bit down softly on one of my nipples and looked up into my eyes. "Say my name again," he whispered.

"*Shane*," I whimpered.

His hands slid all the way under the lace of my undies and his fingers pressed inside me effortlessly. My body just melted over his fingers and he sucked in a husky breath. I cried out and rocked myself against him. He tugged at my nipple with his teeth and slowly slid his fingers deeper inside me, his thumb rubbing small circles against me. My head thudded itself back against the speaker, the vibrations of the bass hummed over every inch of my body making every movement of Shane's erotic as all hell.

He slowly eased his fingers in and out, pushing and pulling inside me and I moaned deep in my throat.

I needed to feel more of him. I skimmed my hand over his body, unbuttoned his jeans, and tore down his zipper. A small moan escaped from his mouth as he brought his lips back up to mine.

I arched my hips away from him and slowly pushed his pants over his hips and heard the change spill out of his pockets when they fell to the floor. I yanked at his boxers until they hung low on his legs and he panted for air.

I slowly grasped my hands around him. He was swollen and throbbing. With his fingers still slowly moving inside me, I rubbed him against the slick tender parts of my flesh that was wet from his touch.

"Oh, God, Grace," he growled. "I want to be inside you so damn bad right now it hurts."

"Don't stop Shane, please," I begged.

"Grace, I'm not *taking* you here, baby. Your first time ain't going to be on a speaker in the studio."

I licked his lips and slid my hand up and down him, "You want to be my first, Shane?"

"No, baby, I'm going to be your last," he breathed.

I completely shattered and fell apart in his hands and I cried out his name over and over. My insides clenched so tight around his fingers I thought I would break them. Waves of unrelenting tremors rocked my entire body from my head to my toes and I never wanted the feeling to stop. He was right, I would not think of anything or anyone until I could completely have him inside me again.

Then, as I tried to even out my breathing, still sliding my hands up and down Shane, the door to the studio slammed open.

"Hey! Shane are you in here?" Bliss's sharp shrill filled the studio. The hum of the speaker echoed an answer, vibrating along the walls. She flicked on the light and I looked down at Shane in my hands. *Um, wow.*

There were just no words. Shane was perfect. Small sublime spasms rippled through my core as I slid him slowly and quietly along my wetness. *So hard.*

Bliss clicked the light switch back off but she stayed in the dark waiting for something, probably to see if he was hiding somewhere. Well he was definitely somewhere. *In my hands, ha Bliss!* Childish, I know.

Shane nuzzled his face in my neck and took long deep breaths, "Grace," he growled into my ear. "Don't. Move." Shane was begging. His voice sounded so desperate it made me ache.

I slowly slid my hands up and down him again and his teeth pressed into my shoulder making my body tremble for more of him. He brought his hands up to my hair and grabbed fistfuls of it, his body rocked with small tremors.

Bliss huffed. Then we heard her heels stomp down the hallway and the door click closed.

Shane pulled his head back, eyes pleading with mine, "Don't move, babe. Please."

But I did. I slid my body down his and took him deep in my mouth until he tickled the back of my throat. His fingers threaded in my hair, his body shivered. I slid my tongue around him and skimmed my mouth slowly up and down him until he tried to pull away. I tightened my grip on his hips and let him explode; hungry for him; *starving*. His knees buckled and I swear I felt faint from the noises he made from coming undone inside my mouth. *Because, seriously, I'd be damned if I was going to let him think of anything or anyone but me until the next time he could be inside me either.*

Chapter 27

I sat next to Lea in Shane's apartment where it looked like someone vomited pink glitter and confetti all over the walls. Above me dangled long iridescent streamers that tickled my hair whenever I stood up. I held an icy cold beer in one hand and I could still taste Shane's kiss on my lips, his hands on my skin.

Thankfully, Shane had dried my clothes and I wasn't dressed in one of his white tank tops and boxer shorts for more than twenty minutes. *Yeah, that got me a lot of stares.*

The entire apartment building was packed; mostly with people we knew from the bar, but there were more than a few people that we had never seen before. Shane tensed up as soon as all the people started arriving; he locked his bedroom door from the outside and stood against the window of the living room, on guard. One of his hands was shoved deep in his pockets while the other held onto a beer that he'd been sipping for the thirty minutes we had been there. Brilliant blue eyes fixed on mine, barely blinking. His dark hair looked wildly disheveled, heat pooled low in my belly, and my pulse quickened knowing that it was my hands that had run through his hair that made it look like that.

"I can't hold it in anymore, I have to use the bathroom," I said leaning on Lea and forcing myself to break eye contact with Shane.

"Yeah, me too," she nodded. "Let's go."

I watched Shane's eyes follow me to the hallway and I could feel them still watching me when I turned my back to him to get into the bathroom. Lea closed the door behind us, locking it, and immediately someone was knocking to get in.

"Give us five minutes! We've having hot lesbian sex in here!" she called out through the door. She whipped her head around and smiled, "*Youbettertellmewhatthefuckhappened betweenyouandShanerightnow!*"

"I was wondering when you would jump on me. Nothing, well we definitely fooled around, but I didn't, he wouldn't, you know…"

"Do you even hear yourself right now?   What does that mean, *Shane wouldn't?*"

I couldn't help the smile that crept across my face, "Said he didn't want my first time to be on a speaker in the studio.   Then, get this, I asked him if he wanted to be my first and he said *no Grace, I'm going to be your last.*"

"On a speaker in the studio? You ASKED him if he wanted to be your first?   Are you in tenth grade again?"

I hung my head in my hands and laughed, "God.   Lea, I'm so not good at this.   I *feel* like I'm fifteen.   This was the first time I've ever let anyone, ever felt anything, ever thought about anyone, other than Shamsiel.   What the hell am I doing wrong?"

"Grace, he said he wanted to be your *last*.   Seems to me you're doing everything right," she offered.

I just hoped I had more than a week left with him.

We emerged from the bathroom to a bunch of strange guys cheering at us.   I had no clue what they were yelling about and then I remembered what Lea had said we were doing when people were knocking on the door. Why are men such idiots?

We crammed our bodies through the crowds of people dancing to someone singing badly on a karaoke machine. As we shoved through the crush of people, I could feel an all too familiar foreboding chill travel down my spine. *Gabriel.* My entire body tightened and I balled my hands into fists. *I am not done here, my time is not up; I won't let it be.* Bitter cold hands met with the skin of my waist, grabbing hold of my flesh, digging their fingers in deep.

My eyes involuntarily blinked and Gabriel was in front me. He held me in a cold, calculating blue stare, locking right onto my eyes and chilling me to my bones. "Grace," his voiced whispered in my ears without his lips moving.

The hallway seemed to shift and move, becoming hypnagogic and dreamlike. Bodies that had shuffled and surged around me before turned shadowy and distant. And the karaoke that had been playing transformed morbidly into harsh discordant carnival music that grated at my insides and made my hands fly to cover my ears.

Gabriel lifted his hand to my face and brushed my jaw with his thumb, "You are as breathtaking as when I first laid my eyes on you." He squeezed his eyes shut tight, and whispered through clenched teeth, "Do not hide from me any longer. They won't be able to save you."

"Leave me alone," I whispered.

"Impossible. I want you too much."

"The feeling is not mutual. Why do we have to go through this over and over? I will not go with you willingly. I do not love you. I do not even like you. I do not believe anything you say. I don't care about anything you say. You are nothing to me!" My voice grew louder and louder until I was screaming.

The hand that had been caressing my face grabbed the back of my neck violently and pulled me towards him. Falling into him, I held my hands out against his chest to push away, but he crushed me to him anyway. He muscled my head to his face as I struggled to break free of his hold. "I will kill them all, my little one. All the ones that take up residence in your heart, until there's no one left for you to want to stay here for," he hissed.

The thousands of veins and capillaries that ran through my body turned, frozen with a deep icy chill, "Then I will do everything I can to destroy you," I whispered.

Gabriel's beautiful angelic lips curled their corners into a devilish smirk, "Yes my heart, you are becoming more like me each day. It just proves how we are so well *matched*." He raked his hands slowly down my neck, dragging them along my shoulders and down my arms.

"Leave me alone."

He laughed, "You're like my little *Job* Grace. Will you stand true to your choice of never being with me when everything is taken from you? Come with me now, Grace, so I don't *have* to hurt you."

"LEAVE ME ALONE, GABRIEL!" I screamed yanking my body away from him and stumbling hard against the wall.

Shane was in front of me instantly and suddenly a tension filled the hallway, something alive and dangerous that you could feel thick against your skin. His eyes caught and held my stare. Terror spiked through my body, if he hurt Shane I would turn into something as evil as Gabriel. Gabriel was right, if he hurt any of my friends I would never rest until I destroyed him, and that made me just as vile as him. My body began to shake with rage.

"Grace," Shane whispered. "Grace, get behind me." He gently shoved me behind him, shielding me from Gabriel.

Lea, Conner and Ethan were next to me before I could take my next breath.

Gabriel's smirk turned more sinister as he glared at me, "How sweet, Grace." He bumped his body against Shane's and whispered into my face, "There are *so many ways* to torture a person, Grace."

"Get the fuck away from her," Shane growled blocking Gabriel's advance at me. Ethan lunged forward towards Shane to help, but Gabriel just turned around and we lost sight of him in a rush of dancing people.

I flung myself at Shane's back wrapping my arms tightly around the front of him so he wouldn't run after Gabriel. I felt his muscles strain and twist against me, "Don't go after him, Shane, just forget him. He's all talk." Tears stung my eyes from the sheer terror of Gabriel's words and my blatant lie. I needed to keep my friends safe, and I had no idea how I would accomplish that. I had no idea about anything anymore.

Shane swung his arm around my head, grabbed me by the shoulder pulling me in front of him, and smiled down at me. He planted a kiss on top of my head and laughed, "Oh, Grace. I've seen you pummel guys a hell of a lot scarier than him. Come on, you need a drink, you're trembling."

He let go of me and handed me to Lea, who was trembling herself. "Are you okay?" she whispered. She asked me nine times before we made it to the kitchen for a drink.

I kept telling Lea I was fine, but all she had to do was take one close look at me and she would know that I was lying.

Once we were in the kitchen, Ethan grabbed a bottle of something from the back corner of one of the cabinets. He twisted the cap off and made us all drink from the bottle. It went around in a circle between the five of us, each taking three giant gulps.

Lea whipped the back of her hand over her lips after the third round, "Holy germ swapping backsplash, Ethan! No cups?"

Ethan leveled a serious stare at her. "Sorry, Lea, but this is one of Vixen4's parties. There is no way any of us should drink anything unless it's from a bottle you have opened yourself."

Lea's eyed bulged and her lips shaped themselves into a small o.

Ethan turned his attention to me, "Who was that? And what did he say to you?"

Shane cut me off before I could come up with a lie, "That *was* her ex's best friend. He's been harassing Grace into going out with him and she doesn't want to have anything to do with him." He scanned my face with furrowed brows, "You don't want anything to do with him, *do you?*"

Butterflies ripped through my stomach and heat splashed across my cheeks, "Shane, I thought I made it perfectly clear in the studio today what I want."

His eyes widened and the corners of his lips lifted into a breathtaking smile, "Damn, Grace. I completely forgot what you said in the studio. You'll have to repeat the conversation to me again sometime, if you want." He handed the bottle to me and brushed his index finger against the back of my hand.

I brought the bottle to my lips and took a drink without breaking my stare with him. "That's not a problem at all. I remember everything I said to you, and everything you said back. I would definitely love to have another discussion on the subject, because I've really been thinking about it and there's so much more I'd like to *add*."

He chuckled, a deep, throaty, sexy sound that tickled every nerve ending in my body, "I'm going to hold you to it."

My cheeks heated more, "Yes, please do. Hold me to it."

"Bam-chicka-waa-waa" Lea slurred. "Watch out Conner, the porn's about to fly!" She slumped against me giggling, "Does anyone think it would be a fuck of a lot safer for Grace if we all went back home? Seriously, ex-boyfriend's friends, Vixen4, I've had enough tonight."

Shane shook his head laughing, "Let's forget about ex-boyfriend's and their douchebag best friends, we're not letting anything happen to her, so why don't we dance or something? This is a party isn't it?"

Lea clapped her hands, "Karaoke?"

"Let's go!" Ethan yelled making a path through the dancing bodies into the living room.

Shane stepped into the living room and pulled the karaoke microphone from some poor girl's hands right before she was about to sing and he handed me the list of songs to look through. "Pick something that means something to you, forget what happened before. Just live and have fun. I promise nothing will happen to you, I won't let *anything* hurt you," his hands settled themselves on the small of my back possessively and my butterflies intensified their wing flapping.

"Oh," Lea said taking one of the lists of songs. "Conner, let's do *You're the One That I Want!*"

Conner laughed and smacked her bottom, "No way, do they have *Paradise by the Dashboard Light*?" They huddled together and scanned the songs with Ethan standing over them.

As I looked through the songs on the laminated pamphlet, I noticed a beautiful, busty, brunette approach Shane next to me. She gave me a small glance and rolled her eyes, and then laughed, setting her sights on Shane. "Hey, Shane. Long time no…see. Why don't we find somewhere a little more private? You know…to catch up."

I felt my face frown. Did she seriously not see me standing here with him?

The girl sashayed past me and stood right in front of me like I didn't exist. She focused her eyes solely on Shane giving him a sultry smile and a wink. "I have a girlfriend who would love to join us."

I sucked in a small, soft breath and dozens of thoughts raced frantically through my mind. *Shane wasn't going anywhere with her and what did I have to offer him? What if Gabriel had his way and I did only have a week left with Shane?* I felt like I could cry because I wanted so much more. My heart was so tired of being broken. I was tired of being broken. Balling up my fist I was about to hit the leech trying to latch onto Shane, but instead, I pushed the numbers to the song I wanted to sing.

Shane looked the girl up and down and shook his head turning his lips downward. "Sweetheart," he said. "You're about two six packs of beer too soon for me. Come back in about thirty minutes after I get myself totally trashed, then maybe you'd be half as beautiful as the woman standing next to me." His eyes locked on mine and something pure and beautiful flickered inside them, making me utterly breathless. "Better yet, don't bother coming back in thirty. I have everything I've ever needed right here."

That, that right there. That's *it*, that *feeling*, that moment of *breathlessness*, that little surge in your chest, the prickle of heat along your skin and the low hot roll of your belly; *that's what being alive is all about.*

I handed Shane the other microphone and switched it on, desperate for him to sing with me. I needed to tell him how I felt that very minute with my voice, my melody. And I needed to hear his voice sing back to me. I needed it more than I needed him to touch me. *I needed him to love me.*

The girl stormed away and the intro guitar rhythm to *Broken by Seether featuring Amy Lee* filled the room and slowly quieted the voices of the crowd.

The beautiful corners of his lips pulled up into a smile when the music reached his ears and his raspy voice sung to me about taking away my pain, and I sung back I'd hold him up high. We were both broken and somehow, somewhere along the way, we found each other.

He silenced the room with the first word he sung, and our voices together pulled the crowd closer. Our voices were raw and savage, filled with an ache that dripped off every note. We were fixed in each other's eyes, all I saw was blue and I knew all he saw was gray. Our smooth powerful voices blanketed the crowd as we slowly danced around in a tight circle focusing just on each other.

Clenching and unclenching his fist around the microphone, his voice melted harmoniously with mine as we exploded in chorus.

Reaching toward me, he hooked his index finger around one of the loops of my skirt, which caused a cool breeze to skim against my bare belly. He slowly, sensuously, pulled me against him. With my body against his, I could feel his pulse race and his heart hammered against his chest as fast as mine did.

When the song ended, screams and hoots erupted and thundered throughout the apartment pulling us from our own little world. Shane held his arms up high and the crowd roared louder. Whooping loudly, he brought the microphone to his lips, "The stunning Grace Taylor of Mad World!" His face flushed with color and he leaned forward and kissed the top of my head.

I tilted my head back laughing, jumped on his coffee table, and raised one arm to point to Shane, "The sexy Shane Maxton of Mad World!"

Everyone in the apartment chanted for more, but I shook my head and tossed the microphone to Lea.

Shane held out a hand to help me down off the table and I took it, jumping into his arms, smiling up into his eyes.

Bringing his lips to my ear and sending electric bolts of heat down my neck he whispered, *"She poured out the liquid music of her voice to quench the thirst of his spirit."*

"Nathaniel Hawthorne, Shane? You kind of amaze me," I sighed.

"Yeah, well you kind of amaze me too."

Lea and Conner's off-key rendition of Meatloaf's song was almost the highlight of the party when they actually acted out all the parts with dramatic facial expressions. I say *almost* because when they were done, Alex and Ethan sang *You're the one that I Want* together, which caused me to laugh so hard I had to, um, throw away my panties in the kitchen garbage. And if you've never laughed so hard you had to do that at least once in your life, well, that's a damn shame. Besides, it wasn't a big thing, there seemed to be a pile of panties in there before mine were tossed on top of them. Oh, and yes, I borrowed a pair of Shane's boxer briefs to wear under my skirt. I'm not daring enough to just go commando, because then all I would be thinking about would be sitting on Shane's lap the whole time.

After changing into his shorts, we all stayed in his room and finished the rest of the bottle we were drinking.

When we all walked out of Shane's room, Bliss and Cream were standing there waiting for us hidden amongst all the sweaty bodies in the hallway. Bliss jumped on Shane. "There you are!" she screamed, pulled his face into hers, and kissed him full on the lips.

I dragged my eyes away from them, an uneasy animalistic feeling pulled somewhere deep inside me.

Shane pushed Bliss's shoulder away and scowled, "What the hell is wrong with you?" The rest of Vixen4 appeared and slithered up to us like cockroaches.

Bliss smiled sweetly at him, "You sounded great singing. We should do some work in the studio together, just you and me."

"No thanks, Mad World is absolutely perfect the way it is right now," he snapped.

Cream giggled, "Shane, you guys aren't much fun anymore."

"Yeah. You guys haven't partied with us too much while we were here, what gives?" Essex cooed.

"Maybe it's their new guitarist," Scratch said. She stared at me and sneered, "What was your name again?"

"I'm sorry, what did you say? I'm not fluent in stupid drunk slut." I looked to Lea innocently, "I don't remember. Lea, did they offer that class in our high school?" The enormous smile on Shane's face after I said that, made me want to climb over all of my friends that stood between us and lick his lips clean of her.

Lea giggled next to me, "Skank 101. No we definitely didn't take that nasty class."

"Bitch," Bliss hissed crossing her arms in front of her chest.

Lea laughed louder, "Oh, one syllable word war. You don't even need a brain to play that game! Okay, my turn! CUNT!"

I shook my head and held up my hands waving them, "No, no no. You can't call her a cunt, she lacks the warmth and depth of one. Slut is much better; it really fits her, *well*, *all* of them better."

Shane's eyes danced with laughter. Ethan, Alex and Conner joined him.

"Fuck off, you stupid bitch!"

Lea huffed next to me, "That's not one syllable. Skank."

"Ass," I added.

"Whore," Lea called.

"Ho!" I yelled.

"Cow," Lea continued.

Bliss's face flamed all different hues of red. *Scary* Crypt Keeper.

Lea gave me a small glance and tilted her head, "Should we move to two syllables or phrases now? It doesn't look like they understand the game."

"Should we talk slower?" I asked.

That's when Bliss lunged at me red-faced, spitting and screaming.

Before anyone could move to stop her, I stepped into her attack and smashed my fist right into her mouth. She flew back a few feet and crumpled to the floor moaning. A shock wave of pure adrenaline surged up my arms and I instantly threw my arms up to block myself from the other members of Vixen4. But none of them made a move for me. They just looked down at Bliss. Shane grabbed me back by the waist and Ethan's giant frame jumped in front of me.

Lea laughed.

Tucker picked that moment to stumble through the sea of people and hip bump me. "Hey, Grace, wanna dance with me?" he slurred.

I ignored him as I watched Vixen4 haul Bliss up off the floor and drag her into the kitchen for ice, or tissues, or another drink; I had no clue.

"What the fuck, Grace?" Tucker ranted as he stumbled over his own feet. "What am I fucking invisible to you now? Whatever. That's cool. I always wanted a fucking superhero power."

Then he passed out, right at my feet.

Chapter 28

Alex and Brayden carried Tucker back to my apartment while the police, who were called by the neighbors from the building next door, ended the party. It was only midnight, but to be honest, I was glad it was over because the only thing I wanted to do was go home with Shane.

Unfortunately, when we got there, Tucker and Alex were sound asleep on the floor in sleeping bags in my bedroom. Apparently, no amount of banging on pots and pans would wake them up.

I threw on a pair of comfortable flannel pajamas and sat in the living room with Ethan, Brayden, Shane and Conner while Lea made hot cocoa for everyone; *her idea*.

Within five minutes, I was called in to help clean up a hot cocoa emergency and aid in the creation of a whole new batch of hot cocoa. She really was horrible in the kitchen. I mean, who messes up hot cocoa? Lea, that's who. Why she thought you could make cocoa from a box of instant pudding is beyond me.

Finally, when everyone had a cup of hot cocoa in their hands, we hung around the living room and watched more horror movies. I sat on the floor with my back against the couch, my shoulder touching Shane's leg. When I leaned my head on his knee I felt his fingers start playing with my hair and goose bumps broke out all along my skin. Staring up at him sitting there in just a pair of pajama bottoms made a strong heat churn deep in my stomach. His strong shoulders, massive lean muscles tensed, just underneath, his flawless skin begged me to touch him.

I shivered and Shane looked down at me catching my eyes with one of his heart stopping gazes that left me dizzy. The way his eyes hungrily devoured every inch of me sitting there, he didn't need to lay a finger on me for me to feel like I had been touched by him.

He leaned his face down next to mine and held out his hand to me with a crooked sexy smile, "Come to bed with me."

Those were the five sexiest words I had ever heard, *in any of my lifetimes*. I wish I could have recorded them and just played them back repeatedly. Seriously.

Holding my hand he lead me through the hallway and through the door to my bedroom. I gave my head a small nod toward our two sleeping friends, Shane just shrugged, and pulled me close to him, "I'm just dying to put my arms around you," he whispered pulling my covers back.

Climbing into my bed, we snuggled our bodies facing each other close together.

He brushed my hair from off my face and his fingertips lingered over my neck. "Tell me more about Gabriel," he murmured.

I shook my head against the pillow. I didn't want to ruin my time lying in bed with Shane by talking about *him*. "I really don't want to talk about him, Shane. I don't want you anywhere near him either. He's a monster."

He leaned his head on his arm and stared deep into my eyes like he was searching for the answers I wouldn't give him there. "I promise Grace, I won't let him hurt you. I'll stay here with you every night if I have too."

"I believe you," I whispered giggling. "And I think you staying here every night might make me feel a little itsy bitty bit better," I teased showing him how little by bringing my index finger to my thumb.

He laughed and I snuggled closer. *Shane and I, can you FREAKING BELIEVE THIS?*

"The way you sang tonight, the way you sang to me, was...you just completely took my breath away, Grace," he whispered. *Um, I love you Shane Maxton. NO. NO, don't say it, Grace.*

"We've sung like that since my audition, haven't we?"

"Yeah, we have." *LOVE. YOU.*

My pulse kicked up a notch just from talking like that with him.

He touched his thumb lightly to my bottom lip and slowly dipped his finger in, "All I thought about was what it was like to be buried between the lips of a woman who could sing like that."

Heart. Racing. I couldn't even string a coherent thought together.

He ran his index finger along my jaw and down my neck, "Why did you choose that song for us to sing?"

Raw heat spiked across my cheeks and tingled the tops of my ears. "I wanted to tell you how I felt. Why I was always so mean to you, Shane."

"Because you feel broken?"

"Completely shattered," I whispered softly.

The pain in his eyes broke my heart. The absolute torn look of his face crushed something deep inside me. He took his hand and brushed away a tear that I hadn't realized escaped and fallen from my welling eyes.

Gently he took hold of my waist, and rolling me over, slid himself on top of me, his knee slipping between my thighs, opening them. My body tumbled easily with his and my legs shifted open and wrapped themselves around his body.

Bringing his hands to my face, he leaned over me, lightly stroking my cheeks with his fingertips. "Then let me in, because I promise you, I will pick up every little broken piece of you, *every single fucking piece, Grace*, and for the rest of my fucking life I will put you back together...I'll make you whole again."

I stopped breathing.

Bringing his lips to my mouth, he traced the outline of them with his. Skimming so softly over them, touching and dragging his so lightly over mine that I could barely feel them, just the warmth of his breath as it mingled with mine. His body shuttered as he parted my lips with his. He laced his hands through my hair and dipped his tongue in against mine. Tiny bursts of tingly pleasure shot across my skin and I moaned into his mouth. Digging my fingers into his back, I tilted my head up to deepen our kiss. We devoured each other's lips, drowning completely, intensely in each other's kisses.

Our lips became desperate, starving, ravenous and wanton. I

gripped my sheets, grasped at his skin, because my world was spinning, kissing him like it was the very last kiss of my life.

Without taking his lips from mine, he leaned up on one arm and with the other tugged at the bottom of my shirt yanking it up. Our lips parted long enough to drag it over my head. Grasping the back of my neck, he pulled me up to his lips again, a low growl rumbled through his throat. My bare skin against his sent a rush of heat to all my nerve endings. A hot rush of fast pumping blood shot through my veins as his hands skimmed over my skin, exploring and playing.

"I can get lost in your lips forever Grace," he murmured against my mouth. "So beautiful. Perfect."

Breathless, I whimpered. Lowering my hands to the waistband of his pajama bottoms, I slid my hands just under the material. I tugged, managing to drag them lower on his hips. There was too much material between us and the ache in between my thighs was maddening.

"Hey!"

We froze.

"Hey, Alex! Get up! Get up! Shane's about to bag Grace!" Tucker's voice tore through the room causing Shane to jump off me. He fumbled for my shirt in the dark, grabbed it and yanked it back over my head.

"Wait! Hold on! I need to get my camera phone!" Alex drunkenly screamed from the floor. "You're not thinking about OUR BLOG, Grace!"

Oh my GOD! *I completely forgot they were there.*

I fought with my shirt until I found my armholes, while the idiots on the floor struggled to get out of their sleeping bags. It would have been hysterically comical if all my damn girl parts WEREN'T ON FIRE!

By the time Tucker reached the light switch and flicked it on, Shane was laying under the covers, arms behind his head relaxing against a pillow. I was sitting up on the other side of the bed sitting cross-legged with my hands folded in my lap. There was, like, a thousand feet between us.

And the distance was physically painful.

Tucker's face was bright red and his nostrils were flaring. "Alex. *I'mnotfuckingkidding* I heard them *kissingandshit!*" he slurred. He jabbed his index finger at Shane and I, "What the fuck were you guys just doing? I know those sounds," he yelled.

Shane and I looked at each other innocently and shrugged. I yawned, "We were sleeping until some drunk asshole sleeping on my floor woke us up with his screaming."

Alex looked from me to Shane and back to me again.

"Fine!" Tucker screamed. "I'm going to take a fucking piss." He stumbled over himself trying to open the door and turned back to face Shane, "Remember you robbing-fucking-backstabber, she was with me first! The fucking minute you toss her for something new, I'm all over that ass."

I watched the skin around Shane's eyes tighten and his jaw clench down. His features turned sharp and ridged and all I wanted to do was lay my hand on his face and take away his anger.

Tucker flicked the light off and we could hear him mumbling and falling down the hallway into the bathroom.

I skated my hand under my covers and along the sheets until I found Shane's and entwined my fingers in his, but his tense muscles did not relax. *Did he really think I would go from him to Tucker? Can we all say, HELL NO!*

"Whoa, Tucker has serious issues. Everybody knows Shane wouldn't sleep with someone in his band, that's against the rules, right bro?" Alex chuckled. "Oh, and hey Grace? You might want to turn your shirt right side out again."

Shane's shoulders relaxed and he laughed back, "Dude, why don't you find another room to sleep in?"

I could hear Alex move and get comfortable in his sleeping bag, "Nuh, uh. But, if you're changing the rules of the band, I'm all for watching."

"You're disgusting," I laughed.

Shane's hands reached for me in the dark and drew me into his arms. "Don't worry, Grace. I'm sure you've heard all those rumors about me and Alex having a torrid affair that we don't want our fans to know about. Well it's true, and he really just wants to watch me, not you."

I laughed loudly and he pulled me closer and nuzzled his face into my neck. "Hey, Alex?"

"Yeah, dude?"

"Desperately want to change the rules," Shane whispered.

"I don't blame you one damn bit. But, Shane, if you hurt her, we'll kill you."

Shane touched his lips to the back of my shoulder right over the tattoo of my broken angel's wing and gently kissed me. "Then I'll be living forever."

"Um, you guys know I'm still right here right? All this bromantic talk is making me think I should leave the room and let the both of you sleep on the bed."

Shane's shoulders shook from his laughter, "Shut up and go to sleep, Grace."

Another six of my favorite words ever.

When Alex's breaths evened out and Tucker stumbled back into the room and continued with his snoring, Shane softly pulled back my hair behind my ear. He leaned up on his elbow behind me and spoke right into my ear, "Grace?"

"Yeah?"

"What *did* you do with Tucker?"

"He just kissed me in his car." I rolled over onto my back and looked directly into his eyes in the dark, ice-cold blue. *Was that what he was upset about before?* "He tried to do more, but I didn't want to. I don't like him like that."

"No more."

It wasn't a question; it was a statement. "No more what?"

"No more kissing anyone but me."

My heart thudded wildly. My butterflies were singing choruses of halleluiah.

I wanted to tell him I didn't have much time left. I wanted to tell him I was so broken that I could never be fixed. I wanted to tell him to run from me and Gabriel and all the evil things I had seen in my life. But I couldn't. I ran from Shane once, I wasn't running away again. My rules now. Even if I had only a few moments left here and I couldn't win against Gabriel, I was going to make every single moment with Shane count. All I wanted was him.

I brushed my lips over his, my heart pounding hard. "No more," I whispered and cuddled into his strong arms. I inhaled deeply, breathing in Shane's scent, and drifted off to sleep.

Chapter 29

The afternoon sun shined through the open curtains splashing light against my eyes. A steady strong heartbeat thudded musically right under my cheek. My body draped across Shane's chest and our legs were tangled together under the covers. My hand lay over the firm muscles that stretched themselves along his stomach, my fingertips reveling in the smoothness and heat of his skin.

A slow sweet burn washed itself gently over my flesh as I slowly ran my hand along the dips and valleys of his skin.

Shane shifted his head, burrowed his face into my hair, and breathed in deeply letting out a slow deep moan. The pounding heartbeat in his chest quickened and a sharp thrill ran up my spine.

His lips brushed along my shoulder as he slid himself over me, moving his body so softly and perfectly so that the hard muscles of his thigh glided teasingly against the V-shape of my pajama bottoms.

Running his lips along my neck and jaw, his hot breaths sent rolls of heat through my insides. Slowly, so very slowly, he trailed his fingertips down my cheeks and neck, hovering his lips just above mine, "I can wake up to this perfection every morning for the rest of my life, Grace."

He placed his palms down on the bed on either side of my face and traced his tongue along my lower lip, then took it gently in between his teeth and nipped at it.

"With a few exceptions," I whispered into his lips.

"Like?"

"A hell of a lot less clothing."

"Grace…" he growled low, shifting to hold himself up on one elbow. He pulled my knee up to wrap my leg around him and slid his hands back down slowly to my outer thighs. He skimmed his fingers beneath my shirt caressing my side and kissed me long, deep and hard. What started out as a slow tender graze of his lips turned into a frenzied desperate kiss. I ran my fingers through his silky dark hair and pulled him in deeper, wanting so much more.

"God it tastes like someone shit in my mouth last night," Tucker moaned from the floor.

Shane and I pulled our lips apart, breathing heavily against each other. "Oh God," he moaned. "Why are they still in here?"

Laughing, and a bit dizzy, I pulled back the covers and sat up, swinging my feet over the edge and dangled them.

Alex's disheveled black hair stuck up adoringly all over his head as he pulled himself off the floor. "If I don't get coffee in me soon, I might kill someone," he croaked. "And Tuck, you taste like that because you're such a fucking asshole."

Tucker bolted up next to him, "Where the fuck am I?" He scanned the room and his eyes widened when he noticed me, then almost popped fully out of their sockets when he noticed Shane. "I slept on the fucking floor in Grace's room? And that douchebag slept in her bed?"

Shane growled and moved to get closer to Tucker but I held my hand out to stop him, "Whoa. Stop. Alex? Shane? Please go make coffee; I need to speak to Tucker alone. Again."

Shane's narrowed eyes snapped to mine and Tucker gave him a smug look. Alex laughed and walked to Shane patting him on the back, "Let's go dude," he said.

Shane walked out of the room with his eyes still narrowed on mine. *Like I was going to jump on Tucker, Psf.*

Tucker slowly got up, massaging his temples, and attempted to sit down on my bed, but I stopped him before he could.

"Oh, hell no." I said. "Do not make yourself comfortable on my bed, Tucker. I wanted to talk to you privately so you could save face in front of your friends, but I'm not going to be nice to you right now. I made myself perfectly clear many times to you that there will be nothing between us, that there is nothing between us. So, I would appreciate it if you stayed out of my bedroom and stop talking your bullshit about us."

"But I thought that maybe…When could I have fucked up so badly?"

"You open your mouth, Tucker, and naturally pops out complete fucked-uppedness. I told you I wasn't interested."

"But you're interested in Shane, right? You'll fuck him Grace and then he'll jump on the next chick like you were nothing, then what?" He sneered.

"And you would be different how?" I asked blatantly.

"I would never fucking hurt you, Grace, not like Shane would."

"Tucker, enough. It's none of your business what or who I sleep with. Hell, Tucker, I'm not even sleeping with anybody. Get off my back and leave me the hell alone. I don't have enough time left to play your stupid games. And if I ever come home and find you sleeping in my bedroom again, I will kick your ass so hard, they'll have to turn you right side out again." I stormed out of the room flustered. I couldn't even believe I said out loud I didn't have enough time left, and I couldn't believe I said it out loud in front of Tucker. But, this was Tucker and he probably hadn't heard anything I just said anyway.

I thundered down the hallway and into the kitchen where everyone was sitting around the table sipping coffee. I grabbed a mug and picked up an empty coffee pot, glaring at everyone around the table. "Who would do such a thing?" Everyone laughed, thinking I was being funny. Obviously, they knew nothing about my caffeine addiction, *jerks*. I made more coffee and complained the whole time.

Tucker sauntered into the kitchen and grabbed a mug, "Oh, Grace," he winked. "Thanks for making coffee for me." Then he hip bumped me again.

Shane shot up out of his seat and our eyes met across the room. "Well, Tucker," I snapped. "I was thinking that the only way you'd ever get me to go anywhere near your crotch is if I made a whole damn pot of coffee and poured it there. So, uh, yeah I'm making this coffee just for you."

Tucker pursed his lips together, "Wow. You have a real mean streak."

"Oh, you have no idea," I said.

"Anywho," Tucker smiled. "Has anyone been in touch today with Vixen4 to see if they got the cleaning service in yet? You guys have a gig tonight and I want to make sure I can take someone home if Shane, Alex and I score some bedbugs tonight." He looked at me and smiled. I should really introduce that freak to Gabriel; they would be awesome evil villains together; Devil Man and Douche Boy. Able to creep a girl out in .5 seconds flat, and kiss them into complete boredom so they want to jump off the tallest building in a single bound...I could just picture Tucker in tights and a cape trying to strut his stuff.

Rolling my eyes, I walked into the living room and flicked on the remote to the television searching through channels. Shane sat on the coffee table in front of me a few minutes later.

"I have to go home and see if everything is okay there, take a shower and stuff for the show. But I really want to talk to you…about last night. And us." His face was pained and serious and it made my heart crash itself against my chest in sharp distressful pangs.

Okay, so that's FREAKING ME OUT!

"Conner is staying here with Lea, so you'll be safe, okay? But I really want to talk to you sometime before the show tonight."

All I could do was nod my head.

Holy crap! This human relationship nonsense was way too emotional and intense for me, how the heck do people keep doing this?

Alex, Brayden, Tucker and Ethan walked in, grabbed their coats and stood in front of Shane waiting for him to move. Shane looked confused, like he wanted to kiss me but not in front of everyone. Then he walked out the front door and just gave me a backwards wave, "Later."

That *burned*.

I looked at the clock on the wall. It was three o'clock in the afternoon and I had another four hours before the show. I walked back into the kitchen with my empty coffee cup and refilled, eyeing Lea.

Conner understood my look and announced he would be spending the rest of the day, until we had to leave, watching television. "Go do your girly primping stuff." He whistled as he walked away.

"Please don't tell me that you were cock blocked by Alex and Tucker last night," she pleaded walking me into her bedroom.

"Well, then I'd be lying." I ran my hands through my tangled hair. "I don't even want to think about last night. All I want to do is take a long hot bath and get ready for tonight's show, and I don't want to have Gabriel show up when I do any of that."

"You know what; you should really tell Shane everything. The truth about Gabriel and about where you come from and find out whose soul is in him now, I don't think he'll freak out as much as you think he would.

Then *he* could be the one to watch you in the bathtub and not me," she laughed. "Come on, let me grab my laptop and I'll sit on the floor in the hallway with the bathroom door open and try to give you some privacy."

I soaked in a scalding hot bath for an hour then stayed in the hallway while Lea took a long bath. We painted our nails and tousled our hair wildly. She laid out an outfit for me on my dresser, a pair of extremely low hip hugging jeans and a low cut shirt that clung to my body like paint so that my nipples could be seen piercing through the material ready to poke men's eyes out. I felt all sorts of hot and desperately wondered if Shane would like to see the silky material thrown onto the floor of his bedroom...We put on our makeup while still wearing our robes, until we had an hour left before we had to leave, then Conner called for Lea to come into the bedroom with him. The guilt I felt when she said no, hit me right in the chest and I waved her off to go spend time with Conner. "Just bash through my door when it's time to leave," I smiled.

Of course, Gabriel was sitting on my bed when I walked in. "Grace."

I stood in the doorway and my anger boiled deep and violent in my veins. "Leave."

Gabriel stood and his perfectly sculptured angelic form moved towards me, "I love watching you when you come fresh from the bath Grace. So soft and pure; *ethereal*."

I hugged my robe tighter around myself, feeling completely naked in front of him.

"Grace. You know I will never stop until I get what I want."

I smiled at him, "Me neither, Gabriel, me neither."

Lea and Conner came smashing through the door screaming. Conner gave Lea a 'told you everything was fine' look and folded his hands across his chest. "Grace, what is wrong with you. We've been knocking on the door for ten minutes and you're not even dressed yet!"

I nodded my head, "Oh, sorry I uh, just took my ear buds out. Lea, can you stay while I get dressed? I'll be right out, Conner, I promise."

Conner shook his head and closed the door behind him.

"WHAT THE HELL IS HAPPENING?" Lea yelled.

I could hear Gabriel's low chuckled thunder in my ears, "She really is quite a precious soul, Grace. I would hate to take her from you."

I swallowed the lump in my throat and suddenly felt the dread of his plans fill me to almost drowning. "I need more time here, Gabriel, please."

"I love to hear you beg, Grace," he whispered back.

Chapter 30

I walked to Boozer's on shaking legs. Gabriel was going to hurt Lea, that I had no doubt in my mind. I had to get far away from here; I couldn't let anything bad happen to her.

I wracked my brain trying to figure out what to do, I was so obsessed and consumed with my thoughts that I hadn't realized we even entered Boozer's until I noticed Shane. He was so painstakingly gorgeous my breath caught. Tilting his head in my direction like he could feel my eyes on him, he stilled. So perfect, like a god among men. *I would remember him like this always.*

When Shane took one look at my expression, he ran to me and grabbed my shoulders, looking wildly into my eyes, "Grace, what's wrong? What happened?"

I looked at him deadpan and my heart deflated, "After the show, I'm going to have to leave for a while, Shane." I opened my mouth to say more but the words wouldn't come. *I love you, Shane. I love Lea. And I wasn't letting Gabriel hurt either of you. I was leaving, running until I found a safe plan.* I was giving myself one more night to sing and play guitar with him.

"Is this about Gabriel? Did something happen? Or is this about me, Grace?"

Ethan walked over to us and lightly drummed his sticks on my shoulders, "Hey, you okay? We have five minutes to get to the stage, why you so late?"

Alex and Brayden pulled us to the stage, Ethan and Shane eyed me frantically.

"I'm fine, I just need a drink," I lied. Not about the drink part though, *that I really needed.*

Ethan jumped to grab our shots that were waiting on one of the speakers. I yanked off my jacket and Shane sucked in a breath when he got a look at my outfit. I should have been all sorts of happy. And I would have been if I didn't have the thought of Gabriel, center stage, in my mind.

Alex plugged my guitar in and Shane pulled me to the side behind the speakers. Ethan watched us carefully from behind his drum kit. I watched Ryan hop onto the stage to introduce us then I noticed how packed Boozer's was. I had never seen it like that before. It made my heart swell and then it made tears well in my eyes. I didn't want to leave any of this. *I loved this life.*

"Babe, you need to tell me right now what's going on."

He called me babe. Damn you, Gabriel!

"Are you in trouble? Is this about Gabriel?" His tone was low and angry. He stalked closer towards me, "What the fuck is going on!" With his tall muscular build, tattoos and face twisted in anger he looked so fierce I cringed.

"Shane, just sing with me, okay? Just play that guitar of yours by my side tonight, the way that only you can." I pleaded.

He tried to say more but he was drowned out by the sounds of the crowd chanting our name. I pulled Shane out in front of the audience and the sound was deafening; it thundered and vibrated the stage under our feet. I pushed Gabriel out of my mind, turned towards Shane and stared into the most beautiful blue eyes I had ever seen since the beginning of time.

I gave him a slow sexy smile and his eyes warmed and his muscles loosened, and I swear I fell in love with him all over again.

Haunting, savage, aching notes danced through his fingers and our first song silenced the crowd immediately. His powerful lamenting soul spread itself through the melody and I matched his sorrow with my rhythm, mingling our harmony into a turbulent ballad.

We tore through all of Mad World's songs. Dark, epic, fast, raw and emotional. We played like it was our last night making music together, and maybe it was. How could I stay, knowing that all the people I love would be hurt? I couldn't.

A magnificent array of sounds and emotions resonated through the bar. It reverberated through our bodies and danced its shadows all over the walls.

Shane's dazzling eyes never disconnected from me. The entire set, he watched me, sang to me, played for me, and listened as I played back. The audience wasn't there. They had disappeared with the sound of his first chords. All I saw was him. All I heard was him. And all I thought was how I never wanted to say to goodbye.

By our third song, we played with our backs touching one another. The intense and electric charges between both of our quivering guitars took over and spiraled into something tangible. I sang, sliding my body around his like I was his skin. We needed to touch each other through every riff, the heat and fire between us was consuming.

As our set finished, the last note succumbing to its silent end, Shane gently tipped my chin up making me look into his eyes. For that brief moment time stopped and it was like seeing heaven. The crowd seemed to hold their breaths in silence, waiting with heavy anticipation for what was yet to come.

He let his guitar swing behind him and cupped my face with his hand. "I love you, Grace Taylor." It barely came out above a whisper from his lips but it echoed through the microphone. And then he kissed me. In front of everyone, *he kissed me.* A slow, deep kiss that sent heat from my lips to every other surface of my skin, and completely and utterly set me on fire.

The crowd roared to life, erupting into an explosion of screams. Ethan's voice boomed into the microphone, "God, Grace, were you the only one who *didn't* know?"

Shane laughed at Ethan, still cupping my face. I was paralyzed; frozen with the fear of Gabriel hurting this man, this man that I love and who just told everyone else he felt the same way for me.

I tore the microphone off my body and tried to smile at him, but I could tell he sensed my panic. "I, um, need a drink." I placed the palm of my hand on his cheek and one tear fell from my eye. "Shane Maxton, I love you more than I ever loved another human being." I leapt off the edge of the stage and walked to the bar where Ryan had a bottle waiting for me. The crowd screamed and hooted, but when I finished my first shot, the silence was deafening.

"I'm not done, Grace," Shane's voice boomed through the speaker's. "Look at me. Really *look at me,* Grace."

I turned my body to face the stage with my next shot in my hand. Lea and Conner were beside me instantly.

Shane's eyes caught and held mine, "I've waited for what feels like two thousand years to tell you how much I love you and to touch your lips again."

The ground seemed to rock beneath my feet and Lea grabbed me to keep me steady. "Listen to him, Gray, listen to him," she whispered as tears streamed down her face.

Shane shifted his guitar in front of his body and a hauntingly ancient ballad unfolded from its strings. Its soft melody tightened my windpipe and I was gasping for air. Shane's expression was so breathtakingly beautiful, tears spilled instantly from my eyes.

Then he sang. Where the notes and melody fell like feathers along my skin, his words tore at the core of my soul and set my world on fire.

> *I didn't know I was lost*
> *Until you found me*
> *I never knew what love was*
> *Until you touched my hand*
>
> *I lost myself long ago*
> *In between your lips*
> *And now here you are*
> *You steal my breath away*
>
> *Until you I never really knew*
> *heaven*
> *Cause until you it was only ever*
> *hell*
> *I didn't know I was so far gone*
> *Until you brought me home*
>
> *I promise you, girl*
> *I know you're shattered*
> *I'll pick up your pieces*
> *And make you whole again*
>
> *Cause until you girl*

I've been shattered too
Since my very first kiss
It's only been you

When the song ended and the last note of his beautiful voice echoed in my heart, he jumped off the stage and ran to me.

My body violently shook with tremors and I sobbed. *Please don't be Gabriel, Shane. Please don't be Gabriel, Shane.*

Shane grabbed my face in his hands crushing me against the bar. Both his hands cupped my face, his thumbs wiping away my tears softly. He pressed his lips gently over mine.

"Please don't be Gabriel, Shane." I squeezed my eyes tight and held onto his arms like they were the only things holding me on this earth.

"No, no, baby. Grace, it's me," he murmured. Tears fell from his eyes. "A feather, Selah. I gave you a feather. That was my gift to you. You asked me when I took you from Gabriel. A feather from an angel's wing."

Whimpering, I threw my arms around his neck and slammed his lips against mine, tasting the salt of our tears. "I love you. I love you. I love you," I sobbed into his mouth.

Lacing his strong fingers through the strands of my hair, he pulled back my face from his and fixed his eyes on mine. The corners of his lips twisted up and that famous sexy smile of his sent pools of heat right to my center. "Say that again, Grace," he begged, nipping my lips.

"I love you, Shane Maxton. Now take me home so I can properly show you how damn much."

The audience chanted for us to kiss again. And we did. Kissing and walking all the way out the front door.

I don't remember the walk back to the apartment. Shane could have sprouted wings and flew me home for all I knew. I do know Lea and Conner were there, because I remember Lea crying big happy tears next to me, maybe he flew us all home. Like I said, no clue. But who cares really? The only important thing, *the only clear thing*, was that I stood in front of

Shane in my bedroom. We stared at each other, long seconds of anticipation, of pure raw heat for one another, of pure true untouched love that coiled tightly in the air between us. It hummed and danced between us like it was alive, *fiercely alive.*

The small lamp on my nightstand cast a warm glow across the room and I noticed then that he had taken one-step closer to me, slowly closing the distance. I wanted to know everything that happened, how, when why? His chest was rising and falling faster, he raked one hand through his gorgeous hair, and all my questions flew out the window. I was completely and forever his and it was so real and thick that it completely sucked all the air out of my lungs. It was so electric and dense that everything felt pure and alive. Me. Him. Air. The bed. Everything. Every single cell that was ever created buzzing between us, sucking us in.

Shane's hands touched my face, touching me like he didn't believe I was real. And I didn't feel real, I felt like a character in some divine ethereal fairytale and there's my prince, my soul mate to save me; no, we save each other.

"Shane," I sighed.

"Grace," he groaned into my mouth as he slowly swept his warm lips over mine. "You, Grace, you're my heaven." There was such a husky tone in his voice that I trembled.

I grasped at his waist, bunching the material of his shirt in my hands and squeezed tight. I nipped at his lips and opened my mouth over his. The growl that rumbled from the back of his throat made my body flame with heat. I slid my hands under his shirt and up his smooth hard chest.

"Gray, I promise I'll be as gentle as I can," he whispered skimming his lips along my jaw to my ear. His hands, his body shuddered against mine.

Pulling my lips from his, I yanked his shirt off, threw it on the floor, and looked deep into his eyes. "Please don't. Don't hold back, Shane. I've waited too damn long; I need every ounce of you right now."

My body slammed against the door. "Thank God, because I have no fucking desire whatsoever to hold back on you," he breathed heavily. And his tongue slipped deep between my lips and he completely devoured me.

Shane lifted my arms and pulled my shirt off, letting it fall, and crashed his lips back against mine pressing my back hard against the cool wood of the door. He ran his fingertips along my skin until he reached the lace cups of my bra and wrenched them down.

He spun me around, pressing the front of my body against the door and unhooked my bra, tearing it from my arms. Slowly his traced his hands over the skin of my shoulders and crushed his body against mine, burying his face in my hair. Wrapping the long dark strands of my hair around his hand, he tugged my hair to one side and delicately smoothed his tongue and lips along my tingling flesh.

I whimpered when his warm wet lips kissed my neck and his hardness pressed into my bottom. Grinding my ass back at him he moaned and turned me back to face him.

Sliding his hands to cup my breasts, he sucked his breath in, brought his head down and took one nipple into his mouth. Holy crap! *My knees, there are butterflies in my knees!* I let my head fall back hard against the door and moaned. With each tug and lick with his mouth, I arched my body into his and he held me down, restraining me with his tight hard muscles. "Your skin's like sugar," he whispered.

I ripped at the button of my jeans and pulled down the zipper, I needed more. I tore his button out next and his pants dropped heavily to my feet. Mine hadn't drop so easily, so he skimmed his hands against the material and guided it all the way down my legs trailing kisses down as his head lowered with them. "So beautiful, Grace."

I could hear myself breathing heavily as I leaned hard against the door, his lips kissing, his tongue licking small circles along my inner thighs. OhmyGodohmyGod. This was, it was...OH MY GOD!

Shane lifted the back of my right knee and slowly ran his mouth over my skin and raised it over his shoulder. I tangled my hands through his hair as he ran his fingers under the front lace of my panties and brushed over me slowly. "You feel like heaven," he said. "God, Grace, I want to slide my tongue over every inch of your skin. I can't help myself when I'm this fucking close to you."

He lifted his head and our eyes locked. Biting down on his lip, he stared at me through those long dark lashes as he slipped his fingers inside me. "So wet," he murmured. Oh God. *I should have done this with him the first damn night I saw him.*

He tore the lace right from my body and his mouth was on me. "Oh," I gasped as I rocked against him. His fingers pumped slowly in and out of me as his tongue licked in circles. His skillful hands along and deep beneath my skin were absolutely exquisite.

My knees started to shake and it felt so damn good I thought I would cry. Okay, so like two tears fell, but they were beautiful happy breathless tears.

"Please, Shane," I whimpered and hauled him up by his hair. His face leveled to mine, he was panting.

He stood up and gazed down at me, bright heavenly blue eyes locked on mine. Gently, he cupped my face in his hands, "You have had my heart with you for thousands of years, and I have been so *empty* until now."

"I'm completely yours, Shane, forever," I whispered. We stilled, savoring the last moment of our innocence, and the beginning of our forever.

He looked at me with eyes that worshipped me…

His breath caught.

My heart pounded fast.

The feel of his smooth skin beneath my fingertips.

Heat radiated from his body in waves.

Never taking his eyes from mine…

He lifted and wrapped my legs around him and slowly eased into me, burying himself deep inside me, making me forever his. He groaned and pressed his forehead to mine. "Ah, Grace," he cried out. He slid back with the most delicious slowness. "I love you so much," he growled with intense burning eyes that took my breath away. An indescribable pleasure tore deep through me and then he slipped all the way out. His arms trembled from holding me up against the door.

Still holding me up, he turned and walked us to the bed throwing us down. Like two frenzied teenagers, we climbed up the bed on top of each other. He held himself over me, braced up on his strong thick arms, looking deep into my eyes. I wrapped my legs around him and pulled him in.

"Fuck, Grace. You feel so good," he whimpered thrusting into me. *That's right*, I made that man *whimper*.

I cried out his name, body trembling. Shudders rocked through him, muscles tense, twisting and dancing over me, through me, deep inside me.

He ravished my body with abandon and I clawed my fingers down his back and screamed his name. Just like he promised I would.

I never knew it could be like this. I never knew. All night he loved me. All night he filled me with pleasure I never knew *existed*. *All night*.

"OhmyGod, Shane. I can't effing move; I think you broke me," I yelped.

Laughing that deep raspy sound I love so much, he wrapped me in his arms and covered us with my comforter. I snuggled my behind into him and our bodies fit perfectly together, like we were each other's missing pieces. His lips pressed against my shoulder and skimmed over the back of my neck. Resting his head against me, I could feel the smile that he had on his face. Gently stroking my hair back he whispered in my ear, "You're mine forever now."

I flipped over to face him. And yeah, the smile on his face was the biggest I'd ever seen, and my heart leapt thinking I had put it there. "How in the world are you here with me?

You left, I watched you leave," I blurted.

His eyes darkened but his smile remained, "What's the point on living in the past? This is where I am right now. Right here in front of you." He nipped tiny butterfly kisses across my face.

I started to freak out. Panic. Attack. "Why won't you tell me? What did you do? What happened?" I lifted my head and leaned on my elbow. "Please tell me, Shane. Please. You had Michael do something, he asked you to make your decision. What did you do?" My heart pounded hard and I seriously started feeling sick.

"I gave it all up," he whispered. "I'm completely human. Mortal. Both of us are."

"What? Why?"

"You were the best part of me, and when they took you away…" He glanced into my eyes and his eyes welled as if tears were threatening. "Truth is, a soul of an angel is only ever capable of one pure true love, and you are mine. It didn't make a difference that you were human. The kiss, the first time my lips were on yours...the hell...I wouldn't take one moment of it back…"

I sucked in my breath hard.

"When I saw you, and you looked so much like you did as Selah, I couldn't think of anything but being with you again. Don't push me away now, Grace. I can't live without you. I want to spend every moment for the rest of my life showing you how much I have loved you. I learned long ago to savor every moment, not to waste a second of it. I once found the other half of my soul and I've spent the last 2000 years in hell, or here just wasting my time until I could be with her again. Did you think that I wouldn't give up everything I could, anything I could to be with you again?"

Tears poured down my cheeks.

"Don't cry, babe. Every damn tear I have seen that fell from those silver eyes broke my heart. This, right here with you is the closest that I'll ever come to heaven. That's all right by me, because you are my heaven, Grace."

I wiped at my tears, "I was going to leave tonight…Gabriel."

"Shh…Grace. Gabriel works on fear and lies."

"He's shown me so many things," I whispered. "I trusted him for so long."

Shane's body tensed, muscles twisting to stone under his skin. He jaw locked tight and spoke through clench teeth, "He shows you things? You mean he…he touches you?"

Oh hell. "Yes."

"He put his fucking lips on you?"

Oh no. "Yes."

"I'm going to fucking kill him."

I let out a long deep breath. "Good. May I help?"

Chapter 31

Electronic beeps and sirens reverberated through the room, piercing the silence of the morning. *Ugh...what is that noise?* My body was comfortably wrapped in a heap of blankets, *burrito style.* I had never felt more relaxed, alive and completely sated before in my entire existence. I groaned loudly as I reached out across the empty bed to find the source of the harsh sounds, *my cell phone.* Without looking, I switched it off.

Why was I alone in bed? Holy CRAP! HE LEFT?

I ripped my eyes open; the room was empty. Looking down at the phone in my hands, I flipped it on to see why it alerted me. A text message.

Shane: 10:18 am Breakfast?

That's when the smell of cinnamon and coffee reached my nose. *Good morning butterflies in my belly, ready for breakfast with Shane?*

I messaged him back. *Grace: 10:18 am Can u b anymore perfect?*

Throwing on a Mad World tee shirt and a pair of old jeans, I opened the door to my bedroom. Taped to the front of my door was a sign written in bold black letters: Devirgination in Progress Do NOT Fucking disturb! *Oh Lea.* I laughed loudly all the way to the bathroom, laughed through freshening up and laughed walking into the kitchen.

Then all the air wrenched out of my lungs and my world, my heart, everything just stopped.

Gabriel was standing in front of the stove, spatula in hand, making me French toast.

Panic. I hyper-fucking-ventilated immediately.

Was last night a dream? No. No, no, no, no. Too real.

Was last night Gabriel? NO! NO! NO! NO! No, Gabriel would have never known the answer to my question. *Right?*

I opened the nearest draw and grabbed the first thing that looked like I could use it as a weapon. *A fucking back scratcher? Really?* I sputtered out a hysterical frantic laugh and Gabriel turned to face me.

"WHERE THE HELL IS SHANE?" I lunged at him shoving my

hands hard against his solid chest. The back scratcher instantly cracked in half and fell to the floor. "What did you do? WHAT DID YOU DO?"

Gabriel's dead eyes glanced slowly to the basement door where our laundry room was and a small sick smile played on his face.

Charging past him, I almost reached the door. But, before I could get to the first step, Gabriel's arms grabbed me like steel vice grip. Screaming, I fought him like a wild animal. All I could think about was Shane down in the basement hurt, all I could feel was a building sickness in my stomach that everything was about to end.

I punched and clawed at his face. I kicked and struggled against him. He counterattacked everything I gave him right back to me, breaking my spirit.

Then, laughing, Gabriel opened the basement door wider and threw me down the stairs. My body slammed violently against the stairway wall and immediately I felt a warm wetness seep down my scalp where my head made contact with cement. My knees buckled automatically and my body tumbled down the hard edges of the stairs as I grasped wildly for the banister. I managed to grip it halfway down, but by that time it was too late, my body felt broken. Blood ran down my face and hands and every muscle under my skin ached and burned like I was on fire. My arms gave up their hold on the railing and I slumped along the wall and slid down the rest of the stairs.

On the cold gritty concrete floor, amongst the tiny pebbles and moisture of the earth below, I lost consciousness. Somewhere deep in the dark recesses of my mind I heard low murmuring voices that frantically increased in volume and frenzy. They muddled together, so that there was no coherence to them, but the emotion radiating from them was clear; fear.

When I could feel the pain of my body again and the voices dimmed, the only sounds that touched my ears was raspy, shallow breathing. My head hammered with pain. I smelled vomit and felt its disgusting stickiness along my chin, down my chest and against my face. I swallowed back more vomit and tasted blood.

Then I opened my eyes.

And I wished I never had. I wished I never came back to Manhattan after my brother died. Never went to the bar that night. And never met him. *Shane*. Shane, who was lying limp and broken in a pool of blood on the cement next to me. His dark hair glistened with deep red streaks and his once brilliant blue eyes stared at me in terror.

Adrenaline surged through my body and I reached for him with shattered arms.

"NO! SHANE!" I flung myself at him and cradled his head. I gripped at his chest, his arms; his neck trying to find a pulse, anything. I could feel myself screaming. I felt the gush of wind rise fiercely through my lungs, but I heard nothing. Nothing, but Gabriel's laugh behind me.

Before I turned from Shane, I watched his eyelids flutter. Sheer terror crashed through me, I needed to get Shane help. I needed to get to a phone. *God, please, please let me save him.*

"Stay with me, Shane," I pleaded over and over. "Please don't leave me." Tears poured openly from my eyes.

Gabriel swung his arms around me, pulling me back, and locked me into his chest. Pure horror spiked and tore against every surface of my skin. "Grace, my love. You *can* still save him," Gabriel murmured into my ear, nipping at it. "Come with me and I will let him live." I struggled against his grip as darkness seeped through my skin, hardening my flesh layer by layer. It ebbed through my veins whispering its beautiful little lies. It called my name, pressed its insidious lips to my soul and offered me a heaven like I'd never known.

I fixed my eyes on Shane, trying to focus on how much and how long I loved him. Shane blinked his eyes at me in what seemed like slow motion. His lips moved slightly and the lightest of whispers caressed my ears, "Don't, Grace, don't listen to him."

A gurgled gasp.

"Time is running out, Grace," Gabriel threatened.

Shane's body trembled and a thin stream of blood fell from the corner of his mouth, spilling to the floor. His expression didn't change, though. And it spoke to me crystal clear. "Your heart belongs to me."

Gabriel raked his lips along my neck and clutched me tighter. "Then, watch him die, Grace." Every nerve ending in my body hummed with Gabriel's desire, and my stomach convulsed against the thought of it.

I whimpered, and then screamed, "I WILL ALWAYS BELONG TO HIM, GABRIEL, NEVER YOU!"

Shane's lips lifted slightly and his body stilled. And then he was gone, taking his last breath, and taking my heart with him. I never fully realized the meaning of the word death until just then and the thought of living this life without him in it wasn't happening…because without him, without him in my life I'm dead inside anyway. I've spent lifetimes looking for him and I wasn't wasting a minute more without him.

"Oh, Grace," Gabriel whispered. "Maybe you will change your heart when I get my hands on Lea?" He released me and I collapsed onto Shane. A broken whimper escaped my lips. *I can't lose him again, I can't.*

Blurry eyed, I pressed my lips to Shane's. "I'll be right there, Shane. I won't stay here without you," I quietly whispered to him.

Chapter 32

With the agony that tore through my body, a strange force of energy surged in my veins. It traveled from somewhere deep in my belly and out over every inch of my skin. Rushing up the stairs, my head was filled with visions of how I would end my life; the best option to me was riding my bike off a bridge.

Gabriel was sitting at my kitchen table eating the damn French toast smiling at me. "Grace," he nodded and stood up to block the kitchen door and my only way out. "Do you really think I am going to let you hurt yourself? No, my love. That body of yours is a little too precious to me."

"You'll never keep me from him, Gabriel. He'll either come back for me or I'll find him." I paced the kitchen trying to find a way out. I was trapped, caged and so *fucking enraged*.

"All that has transpired and you still believe in *him*?" he chuckled.

"Yes, Gabriel. If there is one thing that I have learned in the last two thousand years is to believe in what

Shane and I have. However you try to twist it or mangle it with your jealousy and lust, it will still never affect how my heart and my soul will always be his." I stalked up to him and stood an inch away from his face. "No matter how much you torture me, no matter what you say to me, it will never change the truth. You want to take over heaven, Gabriel? You're going to have to do it without me on your side and I will fight against you every step of the way."

Gabriel laughed. He laughed so hard that he had to sit down again at the table and wipe the tears from his eyes. Disgusted, I stormed past him into the living room, and headed for the front door.

Gabriel's hands grabbed my shoulders back and he spun me around like I was a rag doll. My body shuttered with pain at his touch, and when he wrapped his arms around me, sheer tormenting agony ripped through me in waves. "I told you there are *so many ways* to torture a person. It's one of my most favorite pastimes, my heart. I have a certain skill for it, I've been told."

Wrapping his hands around my throat he lifted me over his head, my feet dangling loosely below me. Behind him, shadows moved together and stepped forward into the room. *Holy hell,* was that a fucking ARMY behind him? My vision blurred and my lungs struggled to pull in air. I kicked my feet out while my windpipe exploded in flames. *I don't care what he does or who he brings, I'm fighting him until I cease to exist.*

I felt myself being thrown from Gabriel's hold and then the blackness came.

And from that darkness I felt *life. I felt hope.*

Then a voice, more like a nuclear explosion, detonated through the darkness. It trembled the ground below my body and thundered through every inch of my soul. It called me by name, snapping my eyes wide open.

Gabriel stood tall, wings outspread near the door, with others like him all fiery eyed and ready to attack.

I froze. What the HELL happened to the hope I just felt? *How the HELL AM I GOING TO FIGHT ALL OF THEM?*

Gabriel laughed lowering his gaze to me and crouched down over me. His eyes were cold and remorseless. I felt the bile rising up from my stomach and the heat splashing colors across my face. But the last thing I was going to do was back down from him. He just took Shane from me and rage was boiling my blood. I want to end him *slowly*.

"You and your merry men there can tear me to shreds, Gabriel, but I *will* go down fighting. You can have my body after it's cold and dead, but *never* my soul." I knew my voice sounded raw and panicked but I held his stare, daring him.

Gabriel grimaced and looked beyond me, eyes flaming brighter.

I twisted my head around to follow his line of sight. On the other side of me was the archangel Michael and two more blue-eyed angels with their arms braced securely around Shane.

I swear to you, I could just about see the butterflies fly out of my mouth. Shane was *STANDING THERE!* My heart stuttered in my chest and pounded so wildly that my lungs began to convulse. He was crouching, ready to attack baring his teeth. Facial features hard as granite and full of rage and vengeance. His muscles strained and twisted against the steel hands that restrained him. "You lay one finger on her, Gabriel, and I WILL FUCKING DESTROY YOU!" He growled. *My avenging angel.*

I tried desperately to catch my breath, but the sobs came. And when the first of my whimpers reached his ears, Shane's eyes locked on mine and for a brief second his eyes softened.

"Oh come now, *Shane.* We both know I've laid more than one finger on her already," his voice grated at my insides like grounded up glass.

Snarling and screaming, Shane's body rocked with tremors and he lunged forward trying violently to charge Gabriel. The two angels holding him back grunted and fought against his pull but lost their grip and stumbled backwards.

Shane slammed Gabriel into the wall with such force it cracked with impact and it crumbled around them. Gabriel's minions circled around them and I jumped up and ran to Shane.

"NO!" I spun around to face Michael. "Michael, *do* something!"

Shane began pummeling Gabriel, pounding him over and over again in the face until his demons threw him off, sending him flying up against the opposite wall. Gabriel stood laughing at Shane and licked his lips. I jumped in front of him and blocked Shane.

"No, Grace! Get behind me!" He yanked me behind him and when his hands touched me, I fell into his arms and wrapped myself around him. Throwing his hands around me, he held me close and kissed my forehead, "I am in fucking complete awe of your strength and your reverence. But you *have* to get behind me babe."

Gabriel charged at us, arms reaching towards us, steel claws grasping. But just as he came close enough to touch me Michael stood between us wings spread the span of the room, and Gabriel stumbled back with fear in his eyes.

Michael faced me and searched my face with his ancient blue irises, looking right into my soul and I felt it being *weighed and measured*.

I stepped forward and held my chin up towards him. "Yes, Michael. Take a good look at my soul and what I have been through because of Gabriel for the last two thousand years or so. Weigh and judge it well, Michael."

The archangels eyed widened and he turned his eyes on Shane, looking at him the same way.

I stepped even closer and leaned in, "The darkest places in hell are reserved for those who maintain their neutrality in times of moral crisis."

Shane jerked his head at me, "Dante Alighieri, Grace?"

One corner of Michael's lips turned up so slight that if you weren't standing as close as I you would have never noticed. "You *are* so much like *Job*, Grace. You never faltered in your search for him, you never lost your faith, never questioned it." His eyes smiled at Shane, "And you. You gave up your heavenly place to be with her. I stand in awe of the both of you."

Turning his face toward Gabriel his lips pulled back. "Gabriel your envy, your lust, your greed and all the trouble you've caused in between are far worse crimes than that of a simple kiss. A simple kiss that may I add was forgiven and sanctioned long ago."

"NO!" Gabriel's voiced boomed. It rocked the ground and made me clasp my hands over my ears and cringe. "I will not let him have her. SHE IS MINE!"

"Enough," a small musical voice sung lovingly into our ears. It jingled lightly like a breeze blowing through wind chimes. The voice touched my heart and a warmth spread throughout my body filling it with the deepest feeling of love that I had ever known. Shane squeezed my hand and I knew he was feeling that same feeling.

I breathed in quickly then exhaled a faltering breath. The power behind the voice overwhelmed me and brought me to my knees and Shane slid down to the floor with me.

The musical voice echoed, reflecting its awe-inspiring sounds throughout the expanse of space around us. Where, for some reason wasn't my apartment any longer. *OH CRAP, am I DEAD?* "It is a pure soul who can hold true the innocence and timelessness of passion in another soul. Each unveiling the greatest pieces of the other, locked together at the heart for eternity," the music sang. And when it ceased, the silence was vociferous and left me empty, yet whole.

Gabriel slithered back, trying to blend himself into the background of the emptiness but Michael would not have it. "Go back where you came from, Gabriel. Your evil cannot darken this tale, it was written from the heavens."

Gabriel blanched. His army of fallen angels slowly faded into the all too familiar furnishings of my living room and the life that I had been living. Gabriel's eyes lingered on me; his voice whispered softly in my thoughts, "I did truly love you, that was never my lie." Then he lowered to his knees, unclenched his fists, and let them fall loosely to the floor. His chest heaved with shallow breaths and his gaze fell away from mine, his body gradually lost color, evaporating into the air. Then Gabriel was gone, and the tightness that I had felt around my heart for so long loosened and I felt I could fully breathe again.

I looked up at Michael and waited to hear our final fate. He smiled down at me then looked to Shane. "Do you still want time here, brother?"

Shane didn't turn to Michael to give him his answer. His blue eyes held onto mine and my heart surged, "No, Michael. I *need* more time here. As long as we possibly can have here, *and then an eternity after that.*"

Oh yeah!

Happy-Epilogue-After

The minute the important tubes and machines were taken away and the only thing left was one IV, I left my lonely hospital bed and climbed gently into Shane's. His battered and bruised face nuzzled against the crook of my neck and we slept in each other's arms like that for days. The doctors and nurses did not complain. They were actually amazed by our closeness, and the sheer miracle of our survival from our horrific *motorcycle accident*.

That's what our fight with Gabriel transformed into. I guess it was a good excuse as any, it's not like anybody would have believed that we both fought with the devil and won. But, I was beyond pissed that my precious motorcycle had been mangled into pieces all over Fifth Avenue. *I mean, seriously?*

I would eventually get another one, and I was happy with that. Material things are easily replaceable, but angels like Shane definitely are not.

"Hey, beautiful," Shane whispered. "What are you thinking about?"

I shifted my banged up body gently to face him. I couldn't help but laugh. Even though he was black and blue from head to toe and mostly purple in the middle, he was still ridiculously gorgeous. And he was *all mine.* I ran my bandaged hand through his dark, silky, hair; *I would never get enough of touching him.* "I just keep thinking about everything that was said and how happy I am lying in this horrible hospital bed with you. Makes me wonder where we go from here. I mean, our lives are open unwritten books, we could do anything together from here, it's just so…"

Shane's crooked smile sent heat across my chest. His eyes danced and his hand slowly lifted to my lips to run his thumb along the bottom of them. "I know where I want to go from here," he murmured. *If he said Boozer's, I was going to pinch him hard on the neck, the only place without a bruise on his body.* I waited with pinched up fingers.

"I want to wake up every day I have left to the warmth of your lips on mine, the sound of your voice singing next to me, the feel of your fingers on my skin and your heart beating music with mine." His eyes shined with love and need. "How about becoming my wife?"

I stared at the man that I had searched forever for and my breath caught in my throat. Tears stung at my eyes. This was the sort of love that people wrote books about. Right in the middle of what I thought was an ordinary life; fate sent me a fairytale, one with a happy ending. A love that makes someone like Shane Maxton doodle silly hearts on a paper with my name in his hospital bed and someone like me to break down all my walls, trust him completely, and say, "Oh, hell, yes!"

Then he brought his lips to mine and he kissed me like it was our very first kiss, and it felt like heaven.

Aha!   See, I promised no cliffhanger!

Thank you all for hanging around to see what happened to Shane and Grace. It was a ton of fun to write the story and get to meet lots of readers who were touched by my words. I hope I did justice to book 2! And *YES*, I am writing Shane's point of view and it should be published soon ☺

Come visit my blog at http://christinezolendz.blogspot.com

Friend me on Facebook or drop an email at ChristineZolendz@aol.com

Or you can visit me on Goodreads. I do have a twitter account, but I always forget to use it!

Thank you to my special Detective in the New York City Police Department who sat down with me to help me formally interview Grace…and help me…um…with the speaker scene and…um…all the other scenes that made me giggle and red faced when I wrote them. (Don't get all excited, I'm married to him, we're allowed to do all that yummy stuff.)

And thank you, Hailey and Emily, for eating lots of mac and cheese and smacking my laptop with your feet every chance you got. Love you both to pieces.